The Last

Seraphim

Book 1

Jake DeBolt

The Last Seraphim

This book is a work of fiction. All of the characters, organization, and events portrayed in this novel are either product of the author's imagination or are used fictitiously.

The Last Seraphim:

Book 1 of The Last Seraphim Trilogy

Written and Published by Jake DeBolt

Edited by Ann DeBolt & Mary Wehunt

Cover Art by Jake DeBolt

First Edition: June 2015

For Jim and Ann DeBolt,

Who raised me, loved me, and support me so well.

& Steph Sho
who has been a
constant source of love
& encouragement this year.
You have been a true &
inspiring example of what
it means to be a woman,
and I feel more blessed
by your presence this year
than anything else. It is
difficult to express just
how much you have meant
to me these last few months,
Hopefully I will be able to
show you how special you
are for many months to come.

Bro love,

Contents

The Last Seraphim

Acknowledgements

I owe a lot of people my thanks for helping this book come to fruition. First and foremost, I thank God for creating me and blessing me with the ability to write and do my best to create something beautiful. Secondly, I thank my parents for raising me and supporting me throughout my life. I thank my siblings for putting up with me and loving me. And I thank my friends for lifting me up. I would like to thank my friends who volunteered to give me feedback and help me edit this book; without y'all, this book wouldn't be nearly as good. There are many more people to thank, but let's go ahead and get on with it.

Prologue

— —~*~— —

'You must eliminate him, or you will lose this war.' King Manthar ignored the voice in his head for the time being and surveyed the field before him. It was getting harder to distinguish between the voice and his own thoughts. Somewhere along the way they became one and the same.

Moving his mount forward, he moved even closer to the city for a better view of the enemy. Manthar's advisors assured him that his was the largest force the world had ever seen. But he knew better than to assume victory; the key to this battle would not be in the numbers. In every battle so far, the key to victory had been one man.

His advisors were currently rousing the soldiers and preparing them for the battle to come. They would be the Generals on the field and direct his forces for him. Manthar watched his men line up in rows and slowly transform the field below him. What used to be green plains were now the stomping grounds of an army in wait.

Manthar watched the opposing army just as closely as his own. Archers lined the city walls, most with their arrows already notched and ready for the first volley.

He watched as arrows flew towards him, eager to take out the enemy's King before the war started. He watched the arrows fly towards him with contempt. Some of the arrows came close to their target, but none was a true threat.

Manthar dismissed them all the same as a minor annoyance. He cared only about the prize that currently resided behind those sixty-foot walls. The city behind those walls had never fallen to any army and for good reason. The walls themselves were impressive, but they were nothing compared to the mountainous formation that protected the other half of the city.

Inside of the city, the castle towers seemed to stretch for miles into the sky. They were a beacon of power and would have towered over any other structure Manthar had ever seen. However, even the tower was dwarfed by the sheer size of the mountain that it was nestled in. A small army could have held this fortress against any number of assailants, or so they thought.

The enemy's cavalry waited inside of the city walls ready to charge at a moment's notice. They were proud and overconfident, just like their General. They really thought that they could win today, but they would see how wrong they were.

King Manthar knew the only way he could possibly lose this battle was if General Moah was left free to wreak havoc on his men. 'Gabriel,' the voice whispered in Manthar's mind. That was the voice's name for Moah. 'General Gabriel,' Manthar mentally amended.

King Manthar was close enough now to see that in between each of the archers were soldiers holding buckets of tar. They were well-practiced in holding the gigantic walls against a siege. Inside the city walls lie millions of people in fear, but they had not fled. They knew that their best chance of survival was to stay in the city. Against any other force they might have been right, but this time they were wrong.

Kicking his steed with his heels, Manthar moved away from the city. Every eye watched him as he rode his stallion along the front lines of his army. He could feel the tension like a taught string. Both sides were as silent as the dead.

Turning in his mount, Manthar took his place in the front of his army and watched as the first volley of arrows was released from atop the city walls. The arrows filled the sky, but not a single one of his men moved from his spot.

Like thunder, the arrows dug into the ground well short of the first line of soldiers. Without prompting, Manthar's archers walked forward and waited right outside of their range.

"Up!" It was the King's privilege to sound the first volley. "To!" His voice carried across the entire field. "Let!" His archers let loose their volley at the same time that the enemy let their second. Casualties were scattered on both sides, but more arrows fell short than hit their marks. The purpose was to keep the defenders on edge. A comfortable archer was a dangerous enemy to face.

And with a yell, Manthar led ten thousand soldiers against the greatest fortress to ever exist. The archers ran with the rest of the men, stopping periodically to release another wave of warning shots at the opposing archers.

The earth shook as a hundred thousand men moved on the city. There were no tricks involved, they would take the city by force. Manthar was the first to reach the city walls. Jumping off of his steed as soon as he reached the walls, he began scaling the wall with his bare hands.

Very few men knew the truth about what he could do, but the opposing soldiers at least knew enough to be scared. A constant rain of arrows barraged him as he approached the wall, but none ever hit their mark.

Every time an arrow would come close to hitting him, Manthar would dodge it with ease. It was one of his most misunderstood powers and one of the most useful in some cases.

He had reached the wall so quickly that he had effectively left his entire army behind and made himself an even bigger target. The arrows continued to miss him no matter how close he came to the top of the wall, but he knew it would not be as easy as that.

Halfway up the wall, Manthar looked up to see multiple tar buckets being dumped on his head. Unconcerned, Manthar swung himself to the side and continued to climb the wall two feet to the right of where he had been before. He never stopped moving as he watched tar and several arrows fly towards the spot that he had just vacated.

He had almost made it to the top of the wall by the time some of the men finally gave up trying to kill him and turned to flee.

Even as he climbed over the edge of the wall, archers shot him point-blank and missed. Those archers were dead before the shock could register on their faces. The archers had never stood a chance as Manthar turned to face several knights who rushed him from all sides.

Before any of the soldiers could engage, Manthar scooped up a sword from a fallen soldier and put his back to the wall for protection. Slipping in and out of stances that he had practiced since childhood, Manthar dodged every swing and methodically picked the soldiers apart. He had an unfair advantage and he used it. They were afraid of him, and they had every right to be.

Manthar rushed them with hurried strikes and kept them off-balance with his onslaught. By the time that he had finished with them, the archers had turned their attention back to his army which had finally caught up behind him.

Ignoring the archers on the wall, Manthar ran towards the next stream of soldiers that were coming up the stairs. The entire city stretched out below him, and in it, an entire army. The city streets wound around scattered houses and worked their way continually upwards toward stone towers.

The city stretched as far as his eye could see, and every single street was filled with soldiers. One soldier, in particular, however, caught Manthar's eye. General Moah sat on his steed and watched Manthar from the paved courtyard directly below him. Surely, they both knew how this would end.

Manthar worked his way down the stairs one soldier at a time. The staircase was full of enemy soldiers that jumped at the opportunity to slay the enemy's King and arrows still randomly flew in from the ramparts, but nothing they did even slowed Manthar as he cut his way to Moah.

So many archers had fruitlessly focused their attention on him that his army had very little resistance in scaling the wall themselves. Manthar saw the panic in their eyes when the remaining archers regrouped with one last attempt to take out the King. As one unit, ten archers aimed at Manthar and released flaming arrows at him and all hell broke loose.

They had obviously intended to catch Manthar by surprise, but he dodged them with just as much ease as before. Manthar redirected the arrows at the soldiers who had been blocking the bottom of the stairs and every single one of them fell. Most of the arrows around him were still on fire as he stepped over the enemies' bodies, and with a raise of his hand, Manthar took control of the flames.

In his less experienced days, he might have had trouble controlling so much fire, but not anymore. He had finally mastered his gift.

The fire danced all around him, wiping out every man and arrow within sight. Steel seared flesh, eyes melted, and men screamed. Using this much of his power threatened to render Manthar unconscious, but he recognized the threat and deflected it to his senses of taste and touch instead: another skill he had learned over time.

He was an unstoppable force, exactly what he was made to be. He was Hell's vengeance on the world, he was King of Aria, Prince of Darkness, Destroyer of Man, and he would kill every single enemy soldier until Gabriel tried to stop him.

Surely enough, Gabriel came eventually. A pile of death had created a barrier around the King by the time the General came to face him. Manthar had expected Gabriel to be exhausted by now, but he didn't look like he had been fighting at all.

Manthar could see tears in the General's eyes when the two men made eye contact through the thin slit in his helmet. For a moment, he was surprised by the tears, but he recovered by telling himself that what he had seen was the sweat running down his face.

"Father," Manthar spoke first when he saw that his father did not plan on speaking.

"You see what happens when a father banishes his own son?" The King's voice was cold and calculating, he was sounding more and more like the voice in his head each day.

"Your entire world burns."

He had thought about what he would say to his father for a long time, but the words were not as satisfying to say as he had thought they would be.

His father's tears were flowing even more freely now, there was no mistaking them for sweat this time. If his face was soft, however, his words were harsh.

"My son died some time ago."

Somewhere deep inside, Manthar heard those words and cringed, but the sensation was fleeting.

"What's stopping you, then?" Manthar was the one who spoke, but his father moved first.

The earth around Manthar shot up like a large stone cage, but Manthar incinerated the rock and broke free immediately. As soon as he got free, the General shot a barrage of rocks at him. One by one Manthar burned them or dodged the projectiles, but he wasn't sure how long he could keep it up.

Slowly, Manthar moved his way closer to his father until he was close enough to engage. With a leap to the side and a sweep of his sword, his blade met his father's just before landing on his father's neck.

The proceeding sword fight was ferocious. They were each too evenly matched with the blade to gain ground against the other, but their abilities were the real weapons.

Manthar intermittently shot fire at his father's face in between swings to throw him off, but his father was just as cunning. With every swing of the sword, the earth moved just enough to throw Manthar off balance.

Either of them would have been unstoppable against anyone else, but not each other. His father had taught Manthar everything he knew. If Manthar guessed correctly, Moah had probably used the exact same trick that Manthar was using.

Both of them had probably dampened their senses of taste and touch just enough to lessen the threat of being rendered unconscious. They might have fought all day before one of them gained the upper hand, but it was their surrounding that eventually determined the victor.

Eventually, Manthar's men overcame the enemy lines and began slaughtering the remaining soldiers. Wave after wave of zealous soldiers charged his father with overwhelming numbers in an attempt to slay the enemy's General. None of them were successful, but it was enough to give Manthar the edge.

Manthar took advantage of Moah's distractions and used his power to summon a nearby flame and aim it at his father. Unable to dodge the blast in time, Moah tried to deflect the flames with his blade and dropped his sword in agony. Moah's hands had been seared by the flames, but he seemed to show no fear as he looked down the blade of Manthar's sword.

Moah's face was like stone, hard and unbreakable no matter the circumstances. Manthar spat on him in disgust and forced him to his knees. His army had almost taken the entire city by this point. There would be no resistance any longer, not with his father on his knees.

Manthar continued to stare into his father's eyes for quite some time, each daring the other to back down. Eventually, Manthar reluctantly pulled his eyes away from his father's, but he would have the last laugh.

In the end, Manthar had been the true winner. His father had finally shown emotion as he had transformed. It was not fear, as Manthar had expected, but sadness that filled his father's eyes at that last moment.

It surprised Manthar that he didn't feel anything as he looked back into his father's eyes. But he supposed that it shouldn't have surprised him. He wasn't the same man that he had once been. He wasn't even really a man anymore, he was a force. He was power personified, and he could not be stopped.

The King felt no emotion as he murdered his father. Moah's head hit the blood-soaked ground with tears still on his face as Manthar stepped over his father's corpse and continued on his rampage.

He continued, that is until he collapsed onto the ground in searing pain. There had been no injury, no attack, and no apparent reason for it, but Manthar found himself nearly immobile with pain.

With effort, Manthar forced himself up to his feet and checked himself for any injuries, but found none. Suspicion slowly took hold of him as Manthar finally turned and saw his father lying on the ground next to him.

War continued to rage around him, but his soldiers were the only ones near them at the moment, and they all steered clear of him now as they rushed towards the enemy.

"What did you do?" Manthar fixed his eyes on his father's corpse and waited for a response that he knew would not come. The battle slowly moved away from Manthar until the only sign that the war was still raging were the sounds of swords clashing in the distance.

For some reason, Manthar couldn't bring himself to turn away from his father's dead body. He watched his father until the pain that had overtaken him began to subside. It was for that reason only that he noticed when his father's body began to move.

The movements were imperceptible at first, but they slowly began to be more obvious as Moah eventually rolled onto his back.

Fear found its way inside of Manthar as he looked his father in the eyes. He wasn't afraid of his father, he told himself that. But he was terrified by the fact that he did not understand what was happening.

'This will require some looking into,' he thought as he watched his father struggle to open his eyes.

Part 1

James

— —~*~— —

James stared up at the ledge that jutted out from the wall about three stories high. He licked his lips in anticipation as he analyzed his climb. His heart started beating faster; this is the kind of thing that he looked forward to. The Valladar Nobles always assumed that their possessions were safe in their tall stone houses.

For most people, the hired guards and stone walls might be enough to intimidate any attempts at theft. Not for James: the extra protection almost made James want to steal their things even more. The Nobles issued a challenge, and he was inclined to accept.

This particular house was one of the largest houses in Valladar. The house's three stories were impressive even in the inner city. Like most Nobles in the upper class, the Drelux family made most of their living through their food supplies. They were some of the biggest providers of seafood in the world, which is a big deal in a world with almost no other food supply.

Trees were nonexistent as of the last few years and the animals that used to live in the wild were rarely spotted anymore. The only real business now came from the Seas.

James did his research on this particular heist, there should be plenty of valuables inside. He couldn't afford to be wrong about that this time, not with the amount of money that he had left. They would need to restock on medicine quickly, and they needed large amounts of money to make that happen.

James currently laid flat against the ground and was effectively hidden from the guards that roamed around the yard. The cover of night and the camouflaged nature of his clothes helped to conceal him from searching eyes. The mud-covered clothes that he wore matched perfectly with the mud that he was lying in. It was quite convenient really.

There were only two guards on duty and their paths never changed. There was roughly a two-minute window in which James would have to scale the wall and climb onto the ledge and into the room on the third floor. Any slower and he would probably be spotted by the guards on their way back. He was lucky that his window was even that long.

It seemed that the guards had become more vigilant since his last heist, but not vigilant enough. They probably didn't have enough incentive to focus very much in the cold of the night. Well, James had plenty of incentive to brave the cold.

James was particularly proud of himself on his last heist; he had stolen enough to buy a month's worth of medicine. But it had been quite some time since then and the upper class was ripe for another hit. As he watched, the guards crossed paths and had their backs turned on one another. A couple more seconds and it would be time to move.

James rolled out of the mud slowly and crept along the yard. As much as his instincts told him to sprint, he knew that movement would catch the unwanted attention of the guards. He would have to settle for the slow crouch across the yard. The best that he could figure, he would have one minute to scale the three stories once he reached the wall.

He slowly approached the spot on the wall that he had chosen earlier and started his ascent. He really couldn't blame the guards for not paying too much atten-tion. No one would have paid attention to this spot be-cause no one would have thought that he could scale this wall. The bricks were well laid and had few if any hand-holds to climb, but there were enough for James to scale.

He had yet to find a wall that he couldn't scale. No matter how small the crevices or how far apart they were, he could always latch on and find his way up. It had always been that way, and he was putting his skill to good use.

James slowly moved up the wall, careful to keep his movements deliberate and steady. His heart started beating faster as he climbed. He wasn't nervous about the climb, but he wasn't a fool either. He refused to draw attention to himself with quick movements or by plummeting to his death. No, as a thief it was his duty to do all things in stealth, even die.

Despite his precautions, he couldn't help but to look out over the city behind him. He had never climbed this high before and couldn't resist a look at the city from this height. He didn't have any time to spare, so his scan was quick, but he saw enough to put a smile on his face.

This is how Nobles must see the city. This was their kingdom and everyone else merely existed to serve them. This was one of his favorite things, to look over the city like he had no cares at all. Not to mention seeing the world like the Nobles saw it helped to fuel the fire of his dislike for the people that put themselves above everyone else.

James tightened his grip on the stone in anger but quickly focused on calming down again. He couldn't afford to lose focus, not while he was hanging this high in the air.

There were not any people around the city at this time of night, but he could easily imagine what the streets looked like during daylight. Common folk moving about like children while the Nobles look down from their window.

'Maybe we are children, but if we are children playing around in the streets, then they are children playing in their castles.'

James focused his attention back on the ledge of the window as he approached the third floor and slowly lifted himself over and through the open window. With one fluid motion, he rolled through the window into the room and proceeded to land on a table. The table immediately shattered and sent James to the ground with a crash.

James' back immediately exploded with pain. Panic shot through him as he imagined wooden pieces sticking through him and punctured organs failing, but as the seconds passed he realized that the pain was subsiding. That must have meant that he had been lucky.

He was so focused on getting inside the window that he hadn't considered what might be waiting for him on the other side. The noise wasn't especially loud, but he was sure that the sound of the table collapsing was plenty loud enough to at least catch the attention of anyone in the house. This would have to be a quick trip.

He sprung up from the floor and ignoring the pain that flared back up through his body, scanned the room quickly. At first he hadn't noticed anyone in the room, but at a closer look he noticed a small form huddled under the blankets of the bed. He must have picked a bedroom to tumble into, and a child's room at that.

James was suddenly a little embarrassed. Not about the thievery, but about making a fool of himself by breaking the child's table. Surely he could have been more careful.

James shook his head and broke his staring match with the blankets that were covering the child. He was trying not to fret over a child's table, but that table was probably worth a fortune. There were not many wooden items left in this world.

He really did need to be more careful, but this was a Noble's home, they can buy as many tables as they want for their kid. It had been mere seconds between James' fall and his frantic search of the room. He was careful to avoid the bed and quickly discovered that there was very little of worth in the room outside of the table that he had already broken.

He would have to search some other part of the house in order to make this break-in worth it, maybe they even had medicine in one of these rooms. That had been part of the reason he had chosen this home, he had heard that they kept a store of medicine somewhere in their house. If he could find that...

James shook his head and forced himself to focus again. He would take what he could get and get out of here. There was no point in being greedy.

He was about to poke his head out of the bedroom door when the child poked her head out of the covers. He caught the motion out of the corner of his eye and turned towards her.

She was a pretty girl, probably around seven or eight years old. She had long blond hair, shaved on one side like every other Noble. It was a sign of wealth to grow out your hair, and a sign of piety to shave the left half of your head.

Everyone was born with an Ashmark on the left side of their head. Hiding your Ashmark was seen as blasphemous, but in reality, only the Nobles had the resources to cut their hair regularly in the first place. James certainly couldn't afford to shave his head, but he wouldn't shave it even if he could.

James knew that the girl must be terrified of him, but she just didn't understand. He was doing this for his sister. How could she know what it was like to live in any other way than how she lived? He wanted to blame her for what he had to do, but he couldn't bring himself to do it. One day she might be a part of the problem, but not yet. Right now she was just a scared little girl.

James slowly unwound the scarf around his neck and took a step towards her. She flinched as if he had threatened her, but she didn't go back under her covers. He took another step, slower this time, and laid the scarf down on the table next to her bed. How many tables did this girl have?

The scarf was one of the best that he had worn. It was a beautiful shade of blue, and well-made probably. It would probably be a little too long on the girl, but it should keep her warm during the cold nights to come.

He slowly stepped back from the table and turned towards the door again. He shouldn't have to worry about the girl; if she planned on calling for help, she would have done so already. James slowly opened the door and heard the girl go back under her covers.

He poked his head out into the hallway and saw a room only a few steps away. That was his best chance to find anything of value before it was too late to escape. He slowly closed the door behind him and moved towards the other door when three men turned the corner right in front of James.

Despite the fact that he was in someone else's home, James really hadn't expected to encounter any other people here. He hadn't even been spotted before tonight except for once, and now he had been caught twice in two minutes. So when the three guards rushed at him, he was delayed in reacting.

All three men had swords and one of them even wore full armor. That guard must have been watching from inside of the home and heard the crash.

Indecision seized him as he tried to figure out what to do. James had no weapon as he hadn't planned on fighting tonight. Before he could really decide on anything, the guards were upon him.

The guards attacked ferociously and it was all he could do to avoid the lightning jabs of the swords. Luckily for James, the hallway wasn't big enough for the three guards to surround him. But it was wide enough for two guards to face him at once, and that was plenty enough for James to deal with.

All three had rushed forward immediately, but the armored guard was stuck behind the other two. Once he realized that he couldn't join in on the fight, he was forced to settle for yelling profanities at James while the other two continued to jab at him.

The armed men handled their swords with skill, but neither landed a hit on James. Their swords were long and curved at the end to make impressive weapons, but they were made for wide swings and a continuous flow of motion rather than quick jabs. Luckily, the hallway didn't have enough room for the guards to swing, so James was left to dodging quick jabs and half-swings by ducking and turning where he could.

Despite the panic that was creeping up into his throat, James was managing to avoid death for the moment. The swords moved like snakes snapping at their prey, but he reacted too quickly for them. The blades were moving too fast to keep track of, but James' instinct somehow kept him one step ahead of the guards.

James was doing better than any of them could have expected, however, he was losing ground quickly. With every thrust, James took a half-step backward and away from his escape route out of the window.

After only seconds, James had been forced towards the end of the hallway. There a door to his left, but nothing else and nowhere to go. The guards' faces, originally triumphant in finding the intruder, had turned sour. They had not expected the fight to last very long against an unarmed thief and were annoyed that he had survived this long.

Maybe they had underestimated him, but they definitely seemed determined now, and the third soldier was eager to prove himself from behind the other two. As James was forced back to the door, the weapons stopped flying for a brief second. They seemed to expect him to take refuge in the room through the door to his left, and that was reason enough not to do it.

James watched them in an attempt to figure out their plan before they executed it. Luckily, he guessed right. After the brief hesitation, the two men lunged with their swords in unison at exactly the same time that James swung open the door to the left of him. Both of the swords stuck in the door and James quickly kicked the door shut again with their swords still in it.

He really hadn't been sure that the swords would be sharp enough to stick in the plastic carbon, but he was glad that he tried it. He didn't kick with enough power to topple the men completely, but both of the guards were put off-balance and James pressed his advantage.

As soon as the door swung back towards the guards, James swept their feet out from under them with a kick and threw himself against the wall to barely avoid a sword thrust from the third guard. Again, it was merely instinct that saved him. He never even saw the sword coming, but he had avoided even a nick from the blade.

The armored guard was just as surprised as James at not making contact with his sword and was off-balance enough for James to rush past him before the guard could regain his bearings.

The armored man tried to grab James as he ran past while the other two guards freed their blades from the door, but James escaped their clutches, rushing back into the girl's room from which he entered. The girl had poked her head out of the blankets again, but as James rushed back into the room, she buried herself back into the bed. James did not blame her for being scared.

He knew that he had mere seconds before he would be forced to face the men again, and they would have room to surround him now. He would not survive another encounter with those men in here.

James rushed for the window immediately and threw himself over the ledge with his feet first. Normally, he would have never attempted this, but desperate times call for extreme measures. He caught the ledge as soon as his head cleared the window and let himself drop a few feet before catching the next handhold. One story at a time, he let himself fall to the ground.

In seconds, he was on the ground running away from the house with three men yelling at him from the window. He could hear the profanities following him out the window as he disappeared into the city. Poor rich girl.

— — —~*~— — —

It was an even darker night by the time that James made it back to his home. He had gone way out of his way to leave several false trails around the city before coming back here, and he was confident that no one could have followed him back. Really there wasn't much point. Nobles never came to the poor sector of the city. They wouldn't dare get their boots muddy if they could help it.

The trek was a solemn one, and he couldn't shake a sense of failure. He had done all that work and hadn't gotten anything out of it. He should have at least grabbed one of the broken pieces of wood from the table, that might have done well in the black-markets. He was running low on money and if he didn't find something soon, they wouldn't have anything to live on at all.

James was almost to his home now. The poor sector was divided into two separate parts. This part of the sector was called the slums. Commoners here lived in buildings made of the plastic carbon, a cheap resource that was used for almost everything. These commoners lived in clusters and packed every inch of the buildings with people. The living here was less than ideal, but compared to where James lived, they had a nice set-up.

As James walked past the building, he watched the huddled masses that lay outside of the doors. Most of them lay on their sides, facing the mud road so that James could see their faces. One particularly young boy stared at James as he walked by. His head was half-shaved to show a quarter-moon Ashmark on his left side.

Most people had the same Ashmark as the boy, what looked like a sliver of the moon. James' Mark was different, and even amongst the poor he had been excluded because of it. It was part of the reason that he preferred to live in seclusion.

Not many people's Ashmarks differed from the moon shape, but James had seen some other Marks besides the moon shape. All of them had been the Marks of other outcasts like him, but none had the exact Mark that he had.

His Mark was especially unique. At least that was what his parents told him. They had acted as if that made him special, but no one else ever thought of it that way. Regardless, if you didn't have a crescent Mark, you were likely to be discriminated against. Better to cover up the Mark by not shaving your head at all. James liked his shaggy hair anyways.

Some others watched him as well, but most of them were not wary of strangers. They didn't have anything left to lose. Those who didn't die from starvation would die from the Sickness or some other disease anyways. They knew that as well as he did, and almost every single one of them had a far-away look in their eyes like they had already given up on their lives.

The Last Seraphim

Even once James had made it to the slums, his walk was still a long one. The city had built a lot of carbon housing for them to the point that they looked like an entire city unto themselves, but there were simply too many people to provide for. James had walked about twenty blocks before he made it out of the slums and into his sector of the city.

They were called mud-people. As stupid as that name was, it made sense. James' boots stuck to the ground with every step. The entire landscape before him was made of mud. The ground was mud, the houses were mud, and the people looked like mud. James had chosen to live in the mud pits because it made the most sense. This was the only way to get privacy. Anyone could build a mud hut and live peacefully, relatively.

The mud pits were on the outskirts of the city and James' hut was on the outskirts of the mud pits. It was a hassle to go anywhere, but it had kept them safe so far. Eventually, James made it to his house and opened the door. He had managed to buy a carbon door for the hut and some of the necessities due to his exploits.

Doors and such were not common in these parts and he had to fight off the occasional thief, as ironic as that was. But not many people knew of the door's existence in the first place, so he usually didn't have to worry. That was the other reason that James preferred living in seclusion.

James softly closed the door behind him and found his sister sitting in their chair. The plastic rocker, as he called it, was one of his more expensive purchases. It was difficult to pay that much money for a chair, but it had been totally worth it when he saw how much she loved it. She pretended not to know how he had afforded it in the first place.

She was asleep, but she had obviously intended to stay up for him. She was still dressed for the day and had apparently dropped the scarf that she was working on. She was quite nice when she was asleep like this. Usually, he was too busy listening to her admonish him to notice how much she had grown in recent years.

James started to change into his sleeping wear when she stirred. He was only half-dressed when she awoke. It took her only a couple of seconds before she gained her bearings and turned her hard gaze on him.

"Where have you been, James? I was worried sick!" She was whispering to avoid attention from anybody that might have been listening, but she still managed to sound like she was yelling at him.

"I was just running some errands, Marie." James put on the best placating voice that he could manage, but she didn't seem to be eased by his words at all. She stood from her chair and squared up right in front of him, putting out her chin as if daring him to lie again. She was much shorter than James; only a little more than five feet with brown hair and blue eyes, yet her stare could intimidate any man.

"I know very well what that means, James." Her voice became calmer than before, but that somehow made her sound even more dangerous. "Do not think me a fool to believe everything you say."

"Marigold," James only used her full name when he needed to pull the older brother card. "Someone needs to provide for us, and your sewing just doesn't make us enough…"

"I know very well that we need money, James." She put an emphasis on his name just as he did to her. "But that does not excuse you for stealing! You could do something honest for a change."

"There is no money to be made doing something honest, Marie! Not for us, anyway! And you know that the medicine for the Sickness is just too expensive. Besides, it's more of an exchange really, an honest exchange even..."

Marie eyed him critically as if his attempt at justifying his actions didn't even deserve a response. "You are a fool if you really believe that, my dear brother." She ruined her look of disapproval with a hint of a smile and James slightly let himself relax from his tensed stance. It looked like she might not stay mad at him for too long this time, he hoped.

She sat back down in her chair and he moved to sit on his bed. Their room consisted of two beds right next to one another and a chair with knitting supplies around it. The effect was so that there were three sitting spots available in the room, an excess amount as far as James was concerned since there were only two of them.

"So what was the exchange this night?" Marie settled in with her knitting supplies and started working on the scarf again with a sense of resignation. She knew that he had to do what he did, she had to know that.

"Well," James had the grace to look ashamed of himself if only it was just an act. "I traded your beautiful blue scarf in return for scaring a little girl. I didn't think to ask her if she thought it was fair, but I think she would agree that it was more than fair." Marie's look was piercing.

"I think I even grew on her a little bit towards the end there."

Marie got up from her chair and punched James in the shoulder just as James was finishing his story with a smile. "What?" James said in mock confusion. "I didn't even steal anything this time! I would have thought you would be happy."

"You scared a poor little girl! That's even worse than stealing." James gave her an incredulous look, "no it isn't!" Both of them briefly forgot to whisper on this last exchange and found themselves forcing whispers.

"And why didn't you get anything from your exchange?" Marie asked with growing worry showing on her face.

"I was just being careful..," James hurried to reassure her. "I just wanted to make sure that I got out of there before the girl raised an alarm, that's all. Just being your regular old careful James," he said with a smile.

If Marie suspected his lie, she didn't say anything about it, but she did look him up and down critically before moving on. "Well, that is another reason that you need to stop your nightly outings. What would have happened if someone did show up to stop you? You wouldn't stand a chance!"

James was slightly uncomfortable, but he had to follow through with the lie. He couldn't let her know how close he had come to dying from his attempt. "That is exactly why I am being careful. I will always come back for you, Marigold." They both smiled at her name this time and James walked over to her and gave her a kiss on her forehead.

"Now get some rest little sister," James said as he threw himself on his bed in preparation for doing exactly as he said. "How about an exchange?" Marie replied with a sly grin as she began to get ready for bed herself.

"What exchange could this be?" James asked as he turned his head away from his pillow. "A fair one, I hope." He smiled at his response and forced himself to open his eyes again. He had already been well on his way to snoring soundly.

"I will get some rest," Marie stated as she got into her bed, "but you must promise me something." James tensed up again when he saw that she had suddenly reverted back to her disapproving look.

"Promise me that you won't steal from the Nobles anymore. We can figure something else out, James. I know we can."

Marie was looking at him with so much concern that he felt compelled to listen to her, but he had lived this way for so long already. He wasn't sure why, but he knew what he had to say.

"Okay, Marigold; I will."

She smiled at him and turned over in her bed to go to sleep as James continued to lay there with his eyes open. He wasn't sure if he meant it or not, but he wanted to mean it. If stealing meant that she would be unhappy, then maybe he should look for other ways to make money. She was his responsibility, and he would take care of her no matter what.

"You promised." She must have suspected his thoughts on the matter. "Just remember that, James. You promised."

James stayed up for a long time before finally falling asleep. He would listen to his sister, but he had to do something first. He couldn't leave her survival up to chance, not when he could make sure that she lived. He had made his decision and he was at peace with it, but it would be harder than anything that he had ever done before.

The castle held the only store of medicine in the city, and there was enough to live off of for a lifetime. As dangerous as it was, he needed to get into that storage. If he succeeded, Marie wouldn't have to worry about him anymore. He could just sit around with her all day until they were old and gray, completely safe from harm.

Already working through the details in his head, James rolled over on his side and shut his eyes. For someone who was about to risk his life, sleep came quickly and easily.

Arianna

— —~*~— —

Arianna walked down the corridor with a plate of food in her hands. A woman in an apron followed behind her with a frustrated grimace aimed at her back. Gratilda always looked that way when Arianna insisted on carrying her brother's meals to his chambers. She said it 'wasn't proper' or something like that.

Arianna would have thought that the servants would be used to it by now, but they always followed her to his room. They acted as if they expected her to randomly change her mind in the middle of one of her deliveries. A dumb expectation if you asked her, but she supposed that they were just trying to do their duties.

She and Aaron used to be so close, but he had grown distant over this past year. They used to share every meal together, and now she hardly saw him do anything but follow around their dad or lock himself in his room. One of these days, he would let her in to eat together, she knew it would just be a matter of time.

She continued to walk down the stone hall and finally reached the closed doors of her brother's chambers.

The trip was a lengthy one that spanned from the kitchens on the second floor to Aaron's chambers on the tenth. That distance would have been daunting to most people, but not to the Princess. She had made the trip once every day this week, all in an attempt to spend time with her older brother.

Arianna reached Aaron's door and waited patiently as she squared up with the tray in her hands. In the past she might have tried to knock on the door while she balanced the tray on her hip or set the tray down before knocking, but she had learned that these attempts were much slower than her servants.

Gratilda and all of the other servants always beat her to the door and always knocked for her, whether she wanted them to or not. So she resigned herself to standing and waiting as Gratilda rushed forward and knocked on her brother's door.

Ten seconds later and there was no response.

"Again please, Gratilda." Gratilda was a pretty girl, but she was always so serious. She had obviously been expecting the order and moved quickly to knock on Aaron's door once more. This was a daily ritual that had eventually merely become a part of their lives. Arianna was preparing to ask Gratilda to knock once more when one of the doors swung inward.

"Ahh," Aaron was smiling politely at her on the other side of the doorway. "Why isn't it two of my favorite ladies." His face never altered from his polite smile; it was a smile that never reached his eyes, but it was the best that he seemed to have to offer. She couldn't help but get the feeling that she was annoying him whenever she showed up like this.

"Indeed, and we are here bearing gifts," Arianna replied in an overly jovial manner as she handed him his lunch. She had resolved to bring as much joy as possible to her older brother. She knew that being around their father so much recently, he needed all the light-heartedness that he could get.

Gratilda didn't respond to Aaron but merely blushed as she looked down at her feet. Arianna was half-convinced that Gratilda came with her solely to be able to see the Prince. She never spoke a word about him, but she could do little more than blush whenever he spoke to them.

She supposed that her brother was an attractive man in his own right. He was nearly six feet tall with wide shoulders and had long blond hair marking his Noble blood.

For some reason, he ignored social propriety by not shaving the left side of his head, but most people ignored the blatant blasphemy due to the fact that he was the Prince. He hadn't always grown his hair out like that, but ever since their mother's death he had ignored their priests and covered his Ashmark.

She understood his frustration, but she could never cover her Mark like that. Even if it was different from everyone else's, she was kind of proud of that. Her Ashmark was somewhat of a mystery in that no one could quite tell what it was.

People knew that there were many types of marks, but some were so rare that no one ever saw them twice. And it seemed that her's was that kind of Mark. Sometimes it looked like a star to her, but other times it just looked like a shapeless blob. Either way, she was proud of it.

Glancing to her side, Arianna could see that Gratilda was still blushing at Aaron. So what if he was good looking? It was no cause to make a person go catatonic around him. It was just silliness on Gratilda's part as far as Arianna was concerned.

Besides, she didn't think that Aaron was ready for a relationship, not anymore. Tragedy often altered people in dramatic ways, but it seemed that Aaron was affected more than most. He didn't look any different than a year ago, but internally he was completely different.

"I appreciate it, Ari." Aaron took the tray of food gently from his sister, "I do not know what I would do without you." They were empty words, meant to be flattering, but his voice was strained and his eyes were hard. He even went to the trouble of using her nickname. She would take false appreciation over the occasional tired silence that existed between them at times. She could tell that it was exhausting for him to be around her, or anyone else for that matter.

"Well, will you be letting me in then?" It was an empty question really, she could see the answer in his eyes already. Apologetically, Aaron shook his head. "Not today, Ari." He had said the same thing every other day as well.

Reluctantly, Ari took a step back from his door as if to signal that he didn't have to keep speaking with her. Gratilda did the same, though obviously reluctant to be leaving his presence so quickly.

Aaron set the tray down behind him on one of his tables and moved to close his door. "Thank you," Aaron visibly relaxed his shoulders as the two girls stepped back and slowly shut the door with another one of his polite smiles.

Gratilda exhaled loudly as soon as Aaron had shut the door and looked slightly embarrassed as she turned to walk back towards the kitchens. She was obviously nervous about the fact that Ari might have noticed she was attracted to Ari's brother. Ari would not be surprised if Gratilda didn't accompany her to any of his meals for a while after being so obvious.

Ari smiled to herself. She didn't have a problem with Gratilda liking her brother though she was mildly confused by it herself. She would be quite amused at seeing what would happen if they tried dating. She pictured Aaron and Gratilda with a nice picnic on the floor of his chamber or on a quiet stroll around his balcony. 'They could have been happy,' she thought, 'once upon a time.'

Ari chuckled to herself at the thought and walked the other direction from Gratilda. She didn't really have a destination in mind, but she definitely didn't want to awkwardly walk in the same direction as Gratilda after her abrupt departure earlier.

Ari couldn't help but break into a little fit of laughter at the image of those two on a date. Would Gratilda ever have said a word in their entire relationship if that had happened? She could only imagine the girl's stern face as he fed her a strawberry while holding that recidivous polite smile of his.

Her laughing stopped as soon as she turned the corner. Her teacher, Sister Fiona, was at the other end of the hall and walking towards Ari with a stare that could freeze a grown man, but not Ari. Ari turned and ran back down the hallway that she had just crossed as fast as she could manage.

Technically, Ari was supposed to be in class right now. It wasn't really that she had anything better to do, she just never really understood the point of her lessons. She already knew everything that she needed to know. A queen need not learn history or warfare, strategy or equations. She would do very little as queen except being a good wife to the King.

She might not even be a queen. She might be eternally stuck as a Princess, fated to stay in the castle for as long as she lived. As boring as that sounded to Ari, it proved her point very well. She didn't need to go to class, but Sister Fiona refused to acknowledge it. As often as Ari skipped her lessons, Sister Fiona searched for her.

The teacher showed some determination, Ari could give her that. The sister searched every day, but Ari had become particularly good at hiding and had avoided a good majority of her classes in the past year.

Ari reached the end of the stone hall right after Sister Fiona turned the corner after her. The sister hadn't given into a full-out sprint yet, but she looked to be increasing speed as she closed in on her prey.

Ari turned the next corner and rushed past Gratilda, who hadn't gotten very far into her return to the kitchens. Ari smiled as she passed the servant girl, but she had no time to be distracted by her flustered maid. By the time that she reached the spiraling stairway, Sister Fiona was halfway down the hall and gaining on her.

Ari had very few choices left. She ran down the stairs to the ninth floor and saw that she had the hall to herself if only for a second. Ari glanced back towards the stairway, knowing that she would see the sister appear any moment and shut her eyes.

Ari was out of breath and the adrenaline was making it hard for Ari to focus, but she had practiced this many times. She just hoped that she could pull this off under pressure.

She needed to concentrate on pulling it off, but she knew that it would work. She only needed a second of silence as she thought about what she wanted to accomplish. Three seconds later and she knew that she had done it.

As she opened her eyes and looked down at herself and saw that she had successfully transformed her body. She no longer looked like Princess Arianna. Her usual golden hair had turned into a commoner's dark brown. Her eyes were no longer green, but a muddy color and too dark to tell clearly. Most importantly, her usual high cheek bones and small nose were replaced with a round face and a nose that was slightly too big for her face. She had never managed it so quickly before.

She was still somewhat attractive in her opinion, but clearly a commoner. No one would mistake her for the Princess, no one but the King or Dis maybe. They were the only two that knew her secret and they were sure to keep it that way.

Ari walked towards the stairs after double checking that the transformation was complete. Arianna was nearly knocked over by Sister Fiona who had abandoned her calm trot for a reckless sprint as she turned into the hall.

Sister took Ari in with a quick look and seemed to be flustered as she obviously struggled with her desire to keep running or ask why a commoner was on the ninth floor of the castle. She took neither approach as she took Ari by the shoulders.

"Girl, have you seen the Princess?" Sister Fiona was obviously trying not to sound frantic, but the effect was one that probably would have frightened any actual commoner. Ari would have laughed, and almost did. But a commoner would have answered as quickly as possible as to not offend the Noblewoman.

"No, my Lady!" Ari was able to squeal as she bowed her head. Ari fervently hoped that Fiona could not see her barely concealed smile. Most commoners would have mistaken the sister for a Noble, so Ari figured that Lady would be the appropriate title.

Sister Fiona gave Ari a hard look before letting her go and turning to run down to the next floor of the castle. Ari rarely had to use her special skill, but it was an exhilarating experience. Ari would have to make a note to herself not to use that same disguise on the sister again, she would surely be suspicious of seeing the same commoner multiple times in the castle.

Ari was nervous about changing back into her own skin, but she couldn't risk being questioned by someone to capture a Princess. She checked the hallway again quickly and closed her eyes to transform back into her normal body.

The ability had come unexpectedly at an early age and had seemed to baffle both of her parents at first. Ari had no idea what she had done, and her parents would have never believed it possible if they hadn't witnessed it first-hand. No one knew where it came from, but it had proven very useful over the years.

Her father knew that it would be trouble as she grew up, and he surely suspected that she used it to avoid her responsibilities, but he was too busy to confront her himself. He had to send his bodyguard instead, Dismus, to keep her in line. King Aandal and Dismus were the only two people in the world that knew about her little power now, and it was up to Dismus to make sure that she did not abuse it.

Her mother had encouraged the use of her power. Maybe she knew that Ari wouldn't be able to help herself, or maybe she thought that it would be healthy to escape once and a while. Either way, her mother would often en-courage her to experiment with it and control it. Those days had passed, along with her mother.

Ari opened her eyes and checked herself to make sure that she was back to normal, and then made her way up to the eleventh floor where her chambers lie.

— —~*~— —

Ari sat on a stool in her room and stared at her painting. Caught in a moment of indecision about her next stroke, she put her paintbrush down and sat back for a second to look at her work. She hadn't been painting very long in life, she really only took it up in the past year or so. Painting used to be her mother's favorite hobby and Ari used to love to watch her work.

Now Ari had begun to master the craft in just under a year. She knew that she had a long way to go to become a true master painter, but she had learned quickly so far. Painting had brought her peace very frequently in the past year, and it seemed to help her process her life.

This particular painting was special to her. She was not done with it yet, but it would soon be her best work to date. Her mother was depicted in various shades of blue and green, smiling down at her daughter with her shining blue eyes and golden hair. Ari painted herself with yellows and greens to show the warmth and safety of her mother's arms. She was proud of the work, but she was still struggling to accurately depict her mother's eyes. She couldn't seem to catch the warmth or care that she remembered from her mother's gaze.

She knew that she could do it, though. Slow and steady, she thought. "One stroke at a time," that's what her mother always said.

She was very nearly about to attempt a few strokes of color in her mother's eyes when there were a few knocks on the door. If this was Sister Fiona again then she would most likely have to give in and let her give the lesson for the day. There were few places to hide in her chambers, unfortunately, and she couldn't hide the painting fast enough to convince her that she wasn't there.

Ari never stopped looking at her painting as she yelled, "come in!" Her face was a mask of concentration when the door opened and Dismus walked into the room. Ari watched him from the corner of her eye but otherwise didn't acknowledge him. She would let him start the conversation whenever he finished his quick scan of the room.

He always checked a room as soon as he walked in. If Ari didn't know any better, she might have thought that he was paranoid. But she knew as well as he that very few people were dumb enough to try sneaking up on him.

He was an older man, maybe middle-aged, but he was the greatest warrior that she had ever seen. He also ignored the religious obligation to shave his head, though his hair was dark and cut short. But that was expected of foreigners; they just didn't know any better. His vigilance was for her sake, not his, and so she waited for him to finish.

After a few moments of sweeping the room, Dismus walked over to Ari and stood behind her as he gazed at the canvas. After a few moments of silence, Dismus spoke almost reverently.

"You are both so very beautiful," He said it like the statement was merely an undeniable fact and not his own opinion. "I wish that you two had more time together."

Ari never looked away from the painting. She couldn't think of a response to his statement, so she just sat on her stool in silence. He must have sensed that she was uncomfortable with the topic and quickly changed it.

"You are becoming very good with that brush, Ari," he said as he put his hand on her shoulder. "Almost as good as she was."

"I have a long way to go before I reach her level," she said matter-of-factly. "She hardly thought at all when she painted; she would just hum and brush with her paints as if it was like breathing to her."

"I would not know, my Princess, but I have seen her paintings in the castle, and your painting might be the most beautiful of all of them." Dismus continued to stand behind her as she stared at the painting. He seemed to be waiting for some sort of response from her, but she was suddenly not in the mood for talking.

She liked Dis, she really did. But she could not pull herself out of her melancholy when she thought too much about her mother. Her mother had been dead for almost a year now, and she missed her just as much as she did on the first day.

Everything had changed and yet, nothing had changed. Life went on just as it always had, but without her mother. The kingdom kept spinning its wheels, but without a queen. Father was still the King, but without a wife, and he refused to remarry. Aaron was still the Prince, but he went into hiding. Herself, she was still the Princess, but now she was the woman of the castle. And it was her job to make things better. Somehow, someway, she would make things better.

Dismus spoke again, clearly sensing her mood. "I just wanted to check on you. You weren't at class again." It wasn't an accusation, just a statement of fact. "I'm glad you are... well." It sounded like he was going to use a different word but decided to settle. He walked out of the room leisurely but with a grace that spoke of his self-assurance. It was clear by the way that he held himself that he was dangerous and that he was aware of it.

Ari watched him go but didn't move until he shut the door behind him. It was only then that she allowed herself to look back at the painting and focus on the picture. She imagined that her mother was still here, holding Ari like she used to.

She didn't move a muscle or even make a sound, but the tears started streaming down her face as she stared into her mother's face. It felt good to cry. It seemed as if all of her emotions were captured in her tears and by shedding them she was purging herself of all of her sorrow. She did not usually cry, but she welcomed it.

At least for a moment, there was nothing else except for her tears. There were no worries, no future, no class to stress about. There was only Ari and the puddle that she was quickly forming on her floor. Still crying, she raised her brush again and slowly formed strokes on her mother's eyes.

Maybe she couldn't make them perfect, but she would keep trying until they were as beautiful as she could possibly manage. The tears subsided as she worked on the painting and peace began to replace turmoil. She would have to try harder with Aaron tomorrow; maybe he would let her in if she made a dessert.

James

— —~*~— —

James moved silently in the night but his heart wouldn't stop racing inside of his chest. He was taking a risk tonight by targeting the King himself, but he was desperate. He had nothing to show for his break-in from last night and they were quickly running out of money for medicine. Really, the King was the perfect target for him if he didn't think about the deadly consequences or the very improbable success rate.

James watched from across the rooftop of a home that stood directly across from the gate to the castle. This would be harder than any of his heists combined. He needed to sneak to the outer gates that were two stories high and scale them. Once passed the outer gates, he would have to cross roughly a hundred yards of the flat yard and proceed to scale at least another six stories worth of smooth stone to reach an open balcony. He had to do all of this without being spotted by any of the numerous guards that roamed the yard.

He wasn't even sure about where his target was. Surely they had to have many things of value in the castle, but there was only one store of medicine and he had no idea where they kept it. His best guess was that it would be high up in the tower somewhere where it would be better protected, but there were way too many stories for that to be particularly helpful. Either way, he would have to do everything he could to make this worth it.

James watched for an opening before he made his move to the outer gate. There were sentries all along the top of the wall, but they were spread out enough that he might be able to make it undetected if he moved quietly enough. He had watched the soldiers long enough now to know that they hardly ever looked down at the wall, so he should be able to make it if he just made it to the wall before they spotted him.

James slipped down from the rooftop of the nice house and landed on the ground in the shadows of an alley. Before, all of the houses in this district would have been nice enough to entice James, but none of them could distract him from his goal tonight.

James hadn't had time to prepare for the heist like he normally would have, but he was being as careful as possible. He was currently wearing a dark brown cape along with his black outfit. Put together, they should camouflage him with the ground almost perfectly.

Before he could change his mind, James laid down on the ground, covered himself with his cape and began to crawl an agonizingly slow crawl towards the wall. Sudden movements would draw their eyes as surely as yelling at them, and there was no window to move through, no way to keep track of their eyes. Only a slow and steady crawl would not draw their attention... he hoped.

His skin itched to jump up and sprint towards the wall. For all he knew, he had already been spotted. No, he couldn't let himself think like that. "Be logical," he whispered to himself as he crawled. "They would have thrown some sort of alarm if they had seen me, or maybe even shot me with an arrow." He smiled to himself as he kept his head down and limbs moving. Yes, he would know when they saw him.

Marie would not have thought that was funny. That thought wiped away his smile. He had to get back to her alive or she would be furious. It was a testament to James' discipline that he had no idea how close he was to the wall until he bumped into it with his hand as he tried to continue crawling.

James continued to keep his head down as he began to bring his feet in and stand as slowly as he possibly could. A sudden movement now would draw their attention just as surely as a movement in the street. His heart raced as he began to stand against the wall and he sweated profusely as he waited for some sort of reaction. He let out a deep breath that he hadn't realized he was holding when there was no alarm given. The easy part was done, now for the rest of it.

With the same care that he took with his crawling, James began to climb the wall. His hands were wet with sweat as he climbed, but his grip was surer than ever before. He wanted to look at the guards as badly as ever, but he wouldn't let himself look. People knew when they were being watched; he couldn't risk drawing their attention. As long as it felt like it took to climb, he had reached the top of the wall in less than a minute and allowed himself a look at the guards.

Neither of the guards seemed to be looking in his direction, but they looked bored enough to have wandering eyes regardless. He had chosen a spot roughly halfway in between two of the guards, but they were still only about fifty yards away from him on either side.

Knocking any of them out was not an option. Any conflict would definitely alert the other sentries and the guards that lined the actual castle walls. He had no choice but to continue his slow crawl over the top of the wall and down the other side of the outer gate.

Into the darkest part of the night, James continued his slow crawl across the yard. A hundred yards of bare land might have been enough to give him away, but luck seemed to be with him. The guards never gave an alarm and never seemed to notice the slight bump on the ground that crept forward through the night.

James knew that he would not be able to scale the wall undetected, though. There wasn't enough room in between the guards to approach the wall. This would be the risky part.

James lifted his head extremely slowly and noted the guard that was directly in front of him. He would have to knock the guard out before he alerted anyone else, and then climb the wall before he woke up. With as slow as he had to move, it might be the hardest task to accomplish yet. The guard was wearing full armor and stood with his sword at his waist. The soldier stood at attention, but it was clear to James that he was as bored as he possibly could be.

James continued to crawl slowly toward the guard, but at some point the guard would notice the moving bump right in front of him and alert the other guards. James would have to move before that point, but be close enough to reach the man before he would cry out anyway. Yes, definitely a risky move.

Still about ten yards away, James couldn't hold back anymore. In one fluid motion, James hopped into a crouch and sprinted towards the half-asleep guard. For James, time seemed to slow. He could see the surprise appear on the man's face and the words that began to appear on his lips, but James was on top of him before either could resolve. James had no weapon, but that didn't hinder him at all. James jumped and kicked down on the hilt of the sword that the man was beginning to draw at the same time he jabbed the man with his fist.

James was afraid that he had made too much noise, but he couldn't worry about that anymore. The punch had stopped the man's yell in its tracks, but there was nothing stopping him from trying again if James didn't press his advantage. As the guard stumbled backward into the wall from the punch, James ran forward and threw all of his weight into another punch at the man's face.

The guard crumpled against the wall, but James couldn't savor the moment very long. He had definitely made too much noise and he had very little time to climb six stories. Throwing caution to the wind, James began to scramble up the wall in haste. He didn't allow himself to look down, but he was only two stories high when he heard the alarm raised for an intruder.

James pushed himself even harder after the yells started and was almost running up the wall by the time the first arrows flew by his face. He was going to have to change his plans a little bit.

James climbed right past the balcony on the sixth floor and kept running up the wall until he made it to the railing on the tenth. He deftly grabbed the ledge of the balcony on the tenth floor and lifted himself over into safety. The arrows became more and more inaccurate as he had moved higher on the wall and he had surely confused them by going higher than they expected. He only hoped that he had bought enough time to escape once he found what he needed.

James rolled on the ground as soon as he lifted himself onto the balcony and ran into the room connected to it. Inside was the largest bedroom that he had ever seen. The room was covered in furniture and little trinkets. He had only just laid eyes on the canvas with a painting on it when a guard moved out of the shadows to face him.

James had thought that room was empty. How had a guard gotten here so quickly? And why was he the only one here? The guard was not fully armored but wore common garb instead.

Fear began leaking from James' pores, or at least that was how it felt. James automatically started taking deep breaths to calm himself.

James told himself that he shouldn't have been afraid of the man, but the man held a sword that glinted as if baring its teeth and the man held himself with a confidence that would have given any man pause.

James noted that the man hadn't grabbed any armor on his way there, just his sword. Both men locked eyes then, both assessing one another, and James also noticed that the man was older than James would have thought and had a full head of hair despite custom. Who was this guy?

Whoever he was, he almost certainly knew how to use that sword. Maybe James should have tried to escape, but he couldn't give up. James rushed at the man and jumped to the side at the last second. He had hoped to throw the man off balance and then jump to the side to escape out the door, but the man didn't move at all when James charged.

James was still rolling on the floor from his jump when the guard moved forward and swung the sword with the flat part of the blade at James' head. The sword seemed to come impossibly fast, but then the blade seemed to slow at the last second just enough for James to move his head out of the way.

For the first time, the guard showed emotion on his face, and it was pure bewilderment. There was no doubt in the guard's mind that he would have won the battle in that one stroke, but James was still standing and frankly just as startled as the guard.

The swordsman took a ready stance and focused his eyes on James as the moment of confusion passed. He would not be treating him lightly any further. James' heart sank. If the man hadn't been trying before, James surely wouldn't win when the man was trying. Being underrated might have been the only thing that had saved him up to this point.

Both James and the guard squared up to fight once more, but neither moved towards the other. Instead, they began circling each other, both willing the other to strike first. The odd thing was that the guard had dropped his confident gaze and replaced it with a look of confusion. It was almost like the man was warring with himself about what to do. James thought about pressing the advantage of the other man's indecision when the room suddenly burst open to five more guards fully dressed in armor and wielding blades.

Running was his only option at this point; there was no point in dying for a medicine he would never reach. James turned and sprinted towards the balcony faster than he had ever run in his life. Both James and the first guard were equal distances from the balcony, but the other man never moved to intercept him. The man just watched as James ran from the other pursuing guards and jumped out of the window.

James was confused, but he didn't question it. James dropped himself down the wall a few meters at a time. His hands were aching and bleeding, but that would be the least of his problems if he was caught. In his haste, James almost lost his grip on the wall several times, but he eventually made it down.

As soon as James' feet touched the ground, James took off at the outer wall and scaled it as fast as possible. James could hear men following close behind, but he was over the wall before any of them reached him.

The entire way out he felt little pin-pricks on his back as if his body was telling him where he was about to get hit, but it never happened. He had expected an arrow in his back at any second, but there was no one on the wall and no arrow.

James dropped to the other side of the wall and sprinted into the city. They were sure to come after him this time; he would have to be very careful. James rushed down the first road and turned the first set of buildings to put him out of sight as fast as possible. As long as he was still in their line of sight, he could still get hit with an arrow.

James alternated turning left and right every time he reached a turn. He knew the city well enough to not get himself completely lost, but by the time he was pretty sure that he had outrun the sound of pursuing soldiers, he was on the complete opposite side of the city than he had intended.

James' lungs were aching and he was starting to get dizzy, but he wouldn't allow himself to stop running. He had run half the night, and the soldiers had been persistent, but everyone had a limit.

James had almost been caught several times, but he had been able to blend in with the road every time they got close. It had been several hours until they had apparently decided that they had finally lost him.

He had lived through the night, but he had nothing to show for it. Despair threatened to overpower him, but he forced it away with thoughts about the future. Surely there was some other way to survive, he just had to figure it out. He may have to break his promise to Marie after all.

Slowly, James eventually made it to his mud hut and crept inside without a noise. Marie had fallen asleep in her chair once again, but there was no way that he was going to wake her up this time. If she got the chance to ask where he had been, he wouldn't be able to bring himself to lie to her. Better to deal with it in the morning.

Climbing into his bed, James' body let out a sigh of relief, but his mind was still sprinting. Possibilities ran through his head unendingly, but none of them stuck. Only one possibility made its way into his head over and over again, but he dismissed it just as often.

The only way for people like him to make enough money for Marie was to work on the ships. With all of the land dead, all of the work had moved to the seas instead. No one knew why, but pretty much all life on land had died years ago.

The plants withered, trees were used up im- mediately, crops died and never returned, most animals died shortly after, and the humans were looking likely to go next. But they always found a way to survive, turning to the seas to sustain them. The Ocean was where the work was and where the food came from. Anyone that hadn't lived near the coast had long since moved or died.

James had often considered working on the ships; they were one of the only jobs that he might have been allowed to work. But there was no way that he could work on the ships because that would also mean leaving Marie behind for long stints of time.

Marie was going shorter and shorter amounts of time between doses now. James wasn't sure how long she would be able to hold out in between doses in the future. If history was any indication, any lapse in taking her medicine and the Sickness would start to overtake her again and her blackouts would become even more violent. No one lasted long past that stage.

The Sickness always claimed its victims, even Nobles could only keep it at bay for so long. The slums were littered with victims of the disease that they all called the Sickness. The disease had run rampant in the city for the last few years and there looked to be no end in sight.

Still, if he could make enough money to buy large amounts of medicine at a time, maybe she would be able to last long enough to make it in between visits. That could work possibly. James had always dreamed of traveling overseas and making an honest living. Maybe Marie could even go with him. He would never ask that of her, but she might offer herself.

The possibilities were still turning over in his head when he finally drifted into a deep sleep.

James

— —~*~— —

James stood alone in the middle of a dark room. He couldn't see much of anything, but he had the feeling like he'd been here before. Without moving his feet, he searched for something familiar in the room, but he found nothing.

Strangely, he seemed detached from himself for some reason. He tried to put his finger on the reason, but he couldn't quite figure it out. He wasn't sure that he had experienced any other feeling like this before.

Dismissing the line of thought, James focused on his surroundings once more. He thought that he might be able to make out some forms from the corners of his eyes, but whenever he tried to focus on anything they would disappear again.

James eventually tried to move his feet from where they were planted, but he couldn't bring himself to move. It was almost as if his body refused to cooperate with his mind. Was he dreaming? Could he even ask himself that without waking up from a dream? Asleep or not, this definitely didn't feel like a dream.

James tried moving his arms and found that they moved well enough though they were possibly a little more sluggish in their movement than normal. He was just about to pinch himself to test his dream theory when a scene seemed to form around him in the room.

The room was smaller than he expected, but more than that was the overwhelming feeling of familiarity. With a start, he knew where he was. In a matter of seconds, he found himself standing in his old home. He had not set foot in his old home in ten years, but this was exactly how he left it. The room was small, cozy, and on fire.

The fire held his attention only for a second before James realized that standing right in front of him was his younger self. He had been eight-years-old when his home had burned down. He had watched as his parents' bedroom burned, his mind unable to comprehend that his parents themselves lay dead in the middle of the floor.

James had rushed inside his home once he had seen the front door ajar. He had been playing with some of the neighborhood kids and was messy after having just won a mud ball fight. His mind had frozen once he made it inside of the house, and the next thing he remembered was holding Marie in his arms as he ran outside of his burning home.

That is what James remembered happening, but he was here right now, watching his younger self stare at his parents.

His eight-year-old self couldn't understand what had happened and was staring in shock at his dead parents. His twenty-one-year-old self couldn't move any more than his younger self could. James looked around the room and soaked in all of the details of his past.

His dad laid in front of his mother, presumably trying to protect his wife. The flames licked at both versions of James and his sister who was still crying in her mother's arms. Distantly, he remembered thinking that he should pick Marigold up, but it was a distant thought; one overpowered by shock and forgotten.

Older James stood frozen in place as younger James finally snapped out of it and rushed forward to save his little sister from the flames. As soon as little James moved, the scene froze completely with the exception of twenty-one-year-old James.

At first, James couldn't figure out why everything would have stopped. What exactly was happening here? Gradually, just as the room had come into focus before, a hooded man came into focus directly in front of James in the room. Even more than the flames, the man radiated heat and power. For some reason, James felt drawn towards the man.

As much as James wanted to see the hooded man, he also desired to run as far away as possible. By the time that the man had come completely into focus, James had started sweating profusely. He tried to move his feet once more to run before the man noticed him, but he again found his legs rebelling against him. This was definitely not a normal dream.

The hooded man was facing the ground and hadn't seemed to notice James, but with a suddenness that sent shockwaves down James' spine, the man raised his eyes and stared right at him.

The man was no man at all. He looked as though he might have once been a man, but where skin should have been there was crust instead. It looked as though the man's skin had turned black and dry to the point of cracking all over his face. Where his eyes should have been, there were only black pits that seemed to peer into James' soul. Despite the man's skin, he seemed to pull at James with some sort of invisible magnetism. James almost couldn't help but sympathize with the man. Surely he had not always been this way.

At the exact moment that James thought it, the man's skin changed. The man that was there before was now replaced by a man that almost looked friendly. For some reason, this man made James think of his father. And in a flash, that man was gone and was replaced by the crusty man once more.

"You are weak." The crusty man stared right at James, but he spoke to James as if from memory. "You will not win."

James trembled at the voice of this man. He spoke as if stating a fact; there was no emotion in that voice, there was only truth and non-truth.

"Who are you?" James was surprised that his voice only quivered slightly as he spoke, but the man either did not know he was being addressed or he didn't care.

"You failed your family."

James finally felt an emotion other than fear since the man appeared. A burning hatred bubbled up from his gut at the man's accusation and James almost couldn't contain himself. He was angry at the man for accusing him of failing his family, but deep down he knew that he was even angrier that he agreed with him. He did fail his family, and he had to live with that for the rest of his life, but the man had no right to bring it up.

"How do you.." James was interrupted this time, his eyes bulging at the effort it took not to yell over the man's words.

"I see you, Micael. You will die." The man made no movements towards James, but he felt a very real and tangible wave of hatred seeming to radiate from the man.

James frantically looked for a way out of this. Surely he must be mistaken. His name was not Micael, he couldn't be talking to James. That must be the case; the man had mistaken him for someone called Micael. He knew that this mysterious person couldn't have possibly wanted to kill him.

James knew for a fact that he had never stolen from a man with black crust all over his body, and that was the only possible reason that someone might want him dead so badly. But then why had he shown James his own past?

"I'm not Mica...," but the man was already gone. It seemed that the man had only come to deliver a message, and he had apparently delivered it to the wrong person. Would he have to deliver the same message to Micael? He did not particularly want to pass along what he had been told to anyone.

Just as the scene had come, it also faded away from James' view. The room became less and less clear until he couldn't see his parents anymore. The room had become just as black as before and the details faded from his vision as the room slipped away from him completely.

The words that the man spoke were fresh in his mind when he woke up to a scream.

"You are weak."

"You will not win."

"You failed your family."

"I see you, Micael."

"You will die."

$$——\sim^*\sim——$$

James' first thought was that he was still dreaming, but he wasn't. The thoughts came too quickly and too slowly. His sister had screamed. He was sleeping. No one was sleeping anymore. He scrambled out of bed and was immediately swung at with a knife.

James hadn't even registered that there were attackers in the room, but his instincts guided him just out of range of the knife. As he lunged backward, time seemed to slow and he was able to identify two men in the room. The first was on top of his sister and was dragging her from her bed. He had covered her mouth with his left hand and had a knife at her throat with his right hand as he dragged her out of their home.

The second man is who had attacked him with the knife. The man was still in the motion of swinging at James and was moving slowly. James was still on his way to hitting the ground as he took in the situation. There was a look of shock starting to appear on the man's face as he registered his miss.

Both men were wearing all black and had masks that they must have worn when they broke into their room, but both men's masks had apparently been tossed aside inside of their room and James recognized the classic features of the Pyiasion people.

James could tell that the men were both slightly darker than normal and both had long black hair pulled back into a long braided tail. Not many Pyiasions made their way over here except to seek work from Nobles. At this point, James had an idea of what kind of jobs those were.

James finally landed on the ground from his lunge backward and time seemed to speed back up. He had no idea what happened, but whatever it was it had saved his life. The man hadn't lost his balance from the missed swing, but he had been temporarily stunned from the failure to stab a half-asleep man.

James took the opportunity to get to his feet and face his attacker head-on. There was very little room to maneuver at all in their room, and he had thrown himself as far back as possible with his lunge. The assailant took a ready stance across from James and pulled out another knife from his back to dual wield.

The familiar feeling of panic came and immediately went. James was at an utter disadvantage here, but he could focus on nothing but his sister. His sister was still captive and had just been dragged out of the hut.

James didn't have time to panic; he had to get past this guy as soon as possible. He couldn't let anything happen to Marie or he wouldn't be able to live with himself.

The man closed the space between them faster than he could blink and James barely had time to get his hands up when the man had come with his first knife. Time did not slow this time, in fact, the man seemed to be moving faster than possible.

It was only through instinct that James was able to keep from being skewered the very first time the man had attacked. It was mere luck that the man's swings had not been successful. Well-aimed attacks landed way off the mark and skilled strikes were rendered ineffective by happenstance. The assailant was a hurricane of swings and stabs, and James could do nothing but struggle to survive.

Both men could not hide their amazement at what was occurring, but it could not last forever. The flurry of movement ended abruptly with a knife in James' left rib. James sunk to his knees at the landed hit and looked up to see a relieved look on the man's face as the knife finally found its target.

James' eyes began to slide to the back of his head, but he forced himself to focus on getting to Marie instead. The realization that his sister was already gone injected James with renewed energy. The man was still holding the knife in James' ribs, and he was sure that he didn't have much longer to live if it stayed that way. In an act of desperation, James grabbed the man's arm and tried to yank himself free.

James tried to struggle free of the knife that was lodged in his stomach, but the man wasn't letting go. James could feel himself losing consciousness, but he couldn't give up. With another sudden burst of energy, James was able to force the man backward and watched in disbelief as the man crumpled to the ground.

One second ago he had been too strong for James to handle, and the next he was struggling to breathe. The man looked completely unharmed, but his eyes were terrified as he struggled for breath. James forced himself to his feet and watched as the man finally stopped moving and took his last breath. He had no idea what just happened, but he didn't have time to figure it out, he needed to rescue his sister.

The man's knife was still in his rib and James looked down at the hilt sticking out of his body. He didn't have a choice. He quickly yanked the knife out of his rib and almost passed out immediately, but he couldn't be dead yet; he had to save his sister first.

James slowly and painstakingly got back to his feet and limped to the door of his hut. He leaned against the doorframe and frantically searched the night for his sister.

There was no sign of his sister or the man who had taken her. There weren't even any sounds that might have led him to her. She had disappeared into the night and he had let it happen.

Reality began to set in for James as his world started spinning around him. There was no way for him to get to her. He could hardly even move.

Panic had a much better grip on him now as he fought down despair. It would have been easy to despair at that moment. He had every reason to, but he fought the temptation with everything he had. Despair would not get Marie back, and neither would panic.

James tried to go after them even so, and immediately sunk to his knees. He had to force himself to keep breathing. Who would have done this? Where could she have possibly been taken?

James tried to shake off the dizziness that had set in and focused on trying to search his mind for the answer. There was only one conclusion that he could think of that made any sense. He must have been followed last night from the castle.

If he was right, then he was to blame for her kidnapping. The guards must have followed him to his home and then sent the Pyiasions to kill him.

But why would they have taken Marie instead of killing her? It made no sense, but then nothing did at the moment as his head continued to spin.

He must be right, and there was only one place that she could have been taken if he was right. Painstakingly, James began to crawl through the mud towards the castle that he had just escaped from.

Somewhere in his sanity, he knew that it was a dumb idea. But he couldn't think straight. It would take him some time, but he would get there eventually and save his sister.

James had crawled only a few yards away from his hut before he finally collapsed from loss of blood.

Arianna

— —~*~— —

It was dark out when Ari made her way to Aaron's chambers with his supper. The castle felt eerily quiet as she walked up through the empty corridors. Gratilda had declined to follow her to Aaron's chambers for dinner this night; she would probably be avoiding Ari for a while.

She couldn't help but feel hopeful as she approached her brother's doors. Maybe it was because she was trying something new, or maybe it was because she was by herself this time, but she had a good feeling this time. Mentally, she ran through the list of questions that she wanted to ask him to make sure that she didn't forget any of them.

So used to having a maid wait on her, Ari paused when she arrived at Aaron's chamber doors as if to let someone knock on the door for her. Internally she chastised herself. 'When did you start letting yourself rely on servants?'

Ari lowered her brother's food and wiped her hands on her yellow dress before knocking on the door. She knew that there would be no answer at the first knock, but he would answer the second. She waited only a few seconds before she straightened her dress once more and knocked a second time and picked up Aaron's food.

A few more seconds went by before Ari began to grow concerned. For whatever reason, Aaron had never answered the first knock. Not the first time she brought him food, and not the last. But he had never failed to answer the second knock before. She had always imagined that the entire process was a game to him. That he would wait at the door for the second knock, ready to open it and smile back at his sister when she brought his food.

This time was different. The air was too still. The hall was too quiet. Aaron was not at the door this time, she was certain of it. Knowing that the door would be locked, Ari tried to open it anyway. The door didn't budge, but neither would she.

Ari put the plate of food down and turned back towards the door. Without double-checking the hall, Ari began to change her appearance. It had not been long after she discovered her little power that she had mastered this particular trick. Ari hardly had to concentrate at all as she watched her right index fingernail grow into an abnormally long and thick shape. The result was a fingernail in the shape of a key.

She hadn't memorized the exact shape that she needed, but it wouldn't take her long to discover it. She stuck her long fingernail in the key hole and forced the nail to shape itself to the hole. Seconds after she stuck her nail in the keyhole, she was able to turn the latch with a twist of her finger.

With a bad feeling in her stomach, Ari shoved the door open to search for her brother and hit her head on the door as it stuck only a few inches in. Ari panicked and began furiously shoving at the door to move it. The door was stuck and would not budge, but Ari had worked herself up into a frenzy and felt herself using her power unconsciously.

Slowly, Ari began making progress against the door and opened the gap enough for her to be able to stick her head through it. What she saw sent her head spinning and forced her into an even more forceful fight against the door.

At first, Ari only saw a man with his back turned to her and ran out onto the balcony with impossible speed. The man was large, robed completely in black and didn't look back at all as he swung down from the balcony and out of sight.

It was only at that point that Ari took in the rest of the room. Her brother had a rope around his neck and was hanging from the ceiling. Not even her wildest fears included this possibility, and as Ari broke free from the door, she screamed louder than she had ever dreamed before.

From the deepest part of her soul came the gut-wrenching yell that seemed to part her from her body, and even as she scrambled towards his body her eyes became clouded with a torrent of tears.

Ari tried to support him, to give him slack on his rope so that he could breathe, but he was gone. A part of her knew that he was gone, that he was beyond saving, but she could not stop herself from trying. In a moment of lucidity, she forced herself to focus.

Ari forced herself to close her eyes and began to change her smaller and stronger form that she had unconsciously changed into to force the door open. Slowly she became taller and skinnier, tall enough to cut the noose with her sharp nails and free him from the rope.

Aaron fell to the ground and Ari fell down on top of him in her haste to help. He wasn't breathing; she was too late.

Aaron! Her big brother was gone, but she couldn't bring herself to believe it. "You're supposed to be here to protect me!" She shouted the words at the top of her lungs as they threatened to destroy her.

"You were supposed to watch me grow up! Why couldn't you just stay with me? You can't both leave! You can't!"

Ari broke off her words, sobbing uncontrollably. Her chest eventually felt like it would explode from her sorrow and she threw her head back in a bloodcurdling scream. It was the only way to get the emotion out. She could feel that it was the only way.

Hours later, though it was probably only minutes, Dismus showed up with a couple of other guards and broke down the doors the rest of the way.

Dismus embraced her and tried to comfort her, but she couldn't focus on him. She would not let go of her brother, but at some point she realized that she was crying into Dis' chest rather than her brother's dead body.

She struggled to find Aaron's body again, but she couldn't bring herself to escape Dis' arms. An hour had passed by the time she finally ran out of tears.

Arianna

1 Year Ago

Ari was focusing all of her attention on sitting as still as she possibly could on her stool. Her mother had told her more than once that it wasn't necessary, but Ari was determined all the same. Now and again she would realize that she was sticking her tongue out as she concentrated and pull it back in.

She really hoped her mother hadn't painted her with her tongue out. That would be mortally embarrassing, and painting it was something that her mom just might do.

Ari eyed her mother over the painting easel as she mentally accused her mother of doing just that. The Queen must have seen her expression one or two times before because as she eyed her for the fourth or fifth time, her mother finally put down her brush and turned the painting.

"See?" she said as she showed Ari. "I'm not painting your tongue, nor you scrunched up nose." Ari's hand shot up to feel her nose out of instinct.

"I was scrunching my nose?" She had no idea she did that when she concentrated. She would have been mortified had she known that earlier.

Noticing her mother watching her, Ari forced her hand back down to her knee where she was supposed to be keeping them. Striking a dignified pose as she straightened her back, Ari amended her statement.

"I mean, I was not scrunching my nose, Mother. You must have been mistaken." She was never so formal with her mother except to overcompensate for something. She hoped her mother got the message to move on. It turned out that her mother had seemed to get the message as she turned her easel back around to continue painting.

What Ari had seen of the painting really was beautiful, though she was not surprised. Her mother was a genius painter and the most beautiful woman in Valladar. She was probably the most beautiful woman in the entire world, Ari mused as she consciously refrained from scrunching her nose.

Ari did not have to concentrate much longer before they were interrupted by a knock at their door.

"Come in." This was the Queen's quarters and there were very few people that would come to her here.

Aaron poked his head in the room before following with the rest of him. As soon as he spotted Ari posing on the stool, he began smiling widely. He often smiled, but he was especially appreciative of anything that embarrassed her.

"Not one word, Aaron. I am posing for my royal portrait." Aaron just smirked back at her as he walked over to where his mother had not stopped painting, which made her feel the need to continue explaining.

"It's normal for Princesses to do, okay?" Aaron wasn't even looking at her anymore, but he still had the same smirk on his face. "Whatever, Aaron, just leave me alone." He had gotten under her skin without saying a word. Brothers.

"Father wants a word, Mother." Both Aaron and Ari looked at their mother then, waiting for a response, but there was none. The Queen just continued to paint as if oblivious to the rest of the world. She did tend to get absorbed at times.

"Mother." Aaron had spoken abruptly and it seemed to finally get her attention. The Queen looked up from the easel at Aaron and smiled warmly as if she hadn't truly been aware of his presence until then though she surely had been.

"Hello, Son, what's the matter?" Aaron rolled his eyes at Ari before restating what he said, which earned a smile from Ari and a stern look from their mom.

"Father wants a word with you, Mother." Ari watched as their mom just looked expectantly at Aaron. She was every bit as demanding as their father at times.

Aaron seemed to be searching for what to say next, as their mother obviously expected more information.

"Umm, I think it has something to do with some other King. He seemed distressed, Mother. I think he wanted your advice on something. I'm really not sure on the details." It was surely true, Ari thought. Their father had always been careful with his information, even amongst his own family.

The Queen smiled when he finished stammering. "Thank you, Aaron, I will go to him shortly."

Even as she spoke, she started cleaning her brushes and choosing a dress to change into. Ari took that as her cue to finally stand, and she couldn't help but stretch her legs in a most undignified manner. She didn't care, and neither did their mother.

Aaron did, though, and he shook his head as he turned to report back to the King. Most of his responsibilities as Prince were to run errands for their father, but he didn't seem to mind. He would make a fine King one day, Ari thought as he left the room.

Ari helped her mother put on a formal dress before following Aaron out. As much as she wanted to know what was going on, she knew that she would never be allowed in on their meetings.

Maybe she would finally go to class this week, but then maybe not.

— —~*~— —

It was the next day when her entire world had been ripped apart. Her mother's dead body had been discovered in her chambers by one of her maids.

Ari had been one of the first ones to see the body, but she had gone into shock. She could not think clearly. It was as if she had suddenly been surrounded by a fog that she could not escape.

She had been taking a bath one morning when the fog finally lifted and she had come to terms with what happened. Ari screamed for a long time then.

She had tried to shove her head under water and keep it there, but her maids had rushed to save her from the screams. Every day since then was a struggle. Everyday tasks seemed meaningless, and every little task would be difficult for her, but she did them anyway because they were expected.

Life returned to Ari one day at a time, but it had never been the same. There was always a part of her that would yearn for her mother. But she had learned how to keep the pain at bay. She had learned how to manage.

"I will see you again, Mother. One day." Those were the words that kept her sane every night when she would think of her mother. "One day."

Arianna

————~*~——

The congregation was silent as she moved towards the podium. A funeral was always a solemn affair when a member of the royal family was involved. It didn't matter that most of the people did not know Aaron well, the entire kingdom seemed to occupy the Cathedral as Ari stood at the podium.

She had been volunteered by her father to give the eulogy for her brother. Hardly a day after it had happened and she was supposed to give a speech about it, but she couldn't even think about her brother without breaking into tears. She had no choice, however, but to give the eulogy regardless. Her father had insisted.

Behind her lay her brother's coffin and twelve priests with torches in their hands. The coffin was elaborately decorated and seemed to show off the carpenter's crafts-manship, but it was all to burn as soon as Arianna finished speaking. The Princess' hands were sweating uncontrol-lably and her head seemed to stop working as she took a breath to begin.

"Thank you, Friends, for coming to my brothers' funeral." This was about as far as she had gotten in writing Aaron's eulogy. That was part of why she was so upset really, the fact that she didn't even know what to say.

It shamed her to think it, but she didn't know Aaron when he died. He had become a stranger to her over the past year, and she didn't feel equipped to speak about him in front of basically the entire kingdom.

"He would have appreciated your show of support by coming today." She had no idea if that was true, but it seemed like the right thing to say and the crowd seemed to react positively to the kind words. They probably would have clapped if they had been allowed to do so at a funeral.

"Umm, Aaron was a kind soul." She had finally decided just to describe him from when she used to know him. Ari relaxed slightly and her chest seemed to unwind enough for her to breathe. She even managed a smile before she moved on.

"He truly cared about the people, about you. And he would have done anything for you." Ari paused and took a deep breath as she surveyed the people in the Cathedral.

The high ceiling and the stained glass windows lent to a feeling that there was something more to the world. Manufactured or not, she believed that there really was something more to this life. Some great purpose that everyone else seemed to ignore.

She was in a cathedral with a thousand people hanging on her next words and a thousand more standing outside to hear those same words passed on to them. It seemed to Ari that she should say something important.

"I cared about my brother deeply. More deeply than I realized before." Tears came unbidden to her eyes, but she could not force them down, not anymore. "I promise." Ari was surprised to hear the words echo out of her mouth, but as they left her mouth, she knew that she meant them. "My brother will be avenged."

The words rang through the cathedral and silenced all sound. The people of Valladar sensed the truth in her words and seemed to not move even a muscle until Ari moved away from the podium and kneeled at the foot of Aaron's coffin.

As if waiting for her cue, all twelve Priests of Death lower their torches at the same time and set the coffin on fire. The elaborate coffin went up in flames immediately and engulfed Ari's world as she knelt beside the fire. She barely noticed as her father knelt beside her and embraced her; she never looked away from the flames that consumed her brother.

King Aandal took Ari's face in his hands and aimed it at his own. Ari didn't think that she could handle looking into her father's eyes, but he left her no choice. His face was completely empty of emotion as he looked back into her eyes.

She knew that he was upset, but he wasn't showing any signs of remorse. She supposed that he just didn't have any room for emotion after her mother's death. Her father looked like he was trying to think of something to say, but eventually he seemed to settle on silence.

That was fine with Ari, as far as she was concerned, there was nothing to be said. Awkwardly, her father put his arms around her in what must have been his attempt at comforting her and then made his way back down the aisle. His leaving signaled the closing procession. He was closely followed by the rest of the congregation. It was a slow process, but slowly the room began to empty of all of the people who had come to mourn.

Eventually, the fire died, and Ari was left kneeling in front of a pile of ashes. The priests left long ago, and with them the people of Valladar, but she remained steadfast.

Her knees had gone numb long ago along with the rest of her body, but inside she was restless. She wished that she could remain there until she was able to feel anything again, but she was certain that she couldn't possibly wait long enough for that to happen.

Finally, slowly, Arianna got to her feet and turned around to see Dismus standing behind her. Something about him standing there with her gave her confidence. Whatever she chose to do, she knew that he would be there to help her. Reaching down to straighten her dress, she was acutely aware of Dis' presence. He seemed so confident, it made her want to be strong as well.

Straightening herself, she decided that she could not allow herself to mourn any longer. Neither of them said a word, but as soon as she walked past him, Dis turned to follow on her heels. He knew that she wanted him there, even if neither of them could bring themselves to say it.

With every step that she took, she pushed her sadness further to the side. She had a purpose; she was going to find the person that killed her brother. She had promised that Aaron would be avenged, and nothing was going to stop her from delivering on that promise.

Even as she walked, a plan began to form in her head.

James

— —~*~— —

James woke up with the sun shining on his face and cursed. The memories of what happened the night before came flooding in and he yelled in misery. Everything was his fault and he had failed to fix it.

Planting his hands on the muddy ground, he forced himself to his feet with relative ease. Thinking back on last night, it was a miracle that he was alive, let alone healthy.

He didn't know very much about healing, but he was pretty sure that he should have been dead. He had lost a lot of blood from the large wound in his stomach the night before. James looked down as he made his way through the mud huts and felt the scar with his fingers.

Not only was he alive, but the wound looked like it had been made months ago, not the night before. For some reason, he had been healed almost completely during the night.

Though his wound had been healed, there was still blood on his clothes from the night before. More and more people came out as the morning grew later, and the vast majority stared at him as he went by. James moved with determination through the streets, not caring that people watched him as he went by.

James wracked his brain for any other scenario that made sense, but there was none. He must have been tracked to his home after he fled the castle. It was the only explanation for the timing of the attack. Besides, no one else was likely to hire men to do it. Marie had to be in the castle; it was the only explanation and his only lead. However thin, he couldn't afford to let go of it.

He was in a hurry, but he wouldn't accomplish anything by running through the city while it was full of people. He would only draw unwanted attention to himself that way, and he wouldn't have any energy once he actually made it to the castle itself.

Instead, James formed a plan as he moved through the streets and to the heart of the city. His sister had to be in the castle, that was the only thing that made sense. The question was how to break-in for the second time? And in broad daylight no less.

He knew he couldn't take on the entire castle full of guards, only a crazy person would have tried to take the entire thing through force. James wracked his brain for a better option and decided there was only one option.

It was the middle of the day when he arrived at the outer gates. The sun was out in force and the heat was blazing. James hoped that would make the guards less scrupulous, but it was wishful thinking. James stood in a line with several other people, and they were all trying to get into the castle.

It was a daily occurrence that the King would welcome people into the castle to listen to their petitions, but it had been years since James had been inside, with the exception of last night.

The King only saw a small number of people a day, and the number had dropped considerably in the last year. Eventually, most people had stopped trying, but there were always a few that kept coming back.

James drew his cloak tighter over himself to try and hide the blood stains on his shirt as the guards looked them over. This was by far his best chance to get in the castle itself. After getting in he would just have to figure out his way to the cells. She had to be there, it was his only lead, and he hung on to it like his life depended on it.

One of the guards at the gate stuck his head close to James and locked eyes with him. The guard looked skeptical and was trying to peer into his soul. James wasn't sure that he wasn't succeeding, but eventually the entire line was let through into the castle.

The gate was opened and the line of commoners were rushed through. James let out a sigh of relief as the line was led to the castle and brought inside. He really hadn't expected it to work, but it had gone smoothly so far.

Once inside, James couldn't help but stare. The castle was an entirely different world than the one outside. Everywhere, James was surrounded by extravagant furniture and wooden pieces.

James had almost forgotten how gross the difference was between the Nobles and the rest of the population. He fought between disgust and wonder as they were moved steadily through the castle in the line. Two guards walked beside them and never took their eyes off of them. It was like they were trying to make sure that the commoners didn't touch anything and spread their filth.

James had to admit to himself that he didn't want himself to touch it either. He probably really would have tainted anything he touched, especially after spending the night in the mud. But who was to blame for their filthiness in the first place?

His line had gone up multiple stories before he finally figured out the next step in his plan and saw an opening. For the briefest second, the guard closest to James finally looked away.

James had been waiting for that exact opportunity and immediately jumped behind the guard to steal the sword from his right hand. Judging by the guard's expression, that had never happened to him before.

James acted in the split second that it took the guard to recover and swung the sword with the flat of the blade at the guard's head. The man reacted fast enough to try and duck, but the blade still caught the top of his head.

He hadn't landed the hit with the full intended impact, but it was enough to stun him. And James swung again immediately and knocked him out before the man could regain his bearings.

Now came the hard part. The other guard was already coming at James with his sword, and he looked furious. James had planned to surrender to the other guard, but the fury in the man's eyes made him change his mind at the last second. If he had tried to surrender to this man, he would have lost his head immediately.

James parred the first strike from the other guard and went on the defensive while he tried to come up with another plan. He needed a way to find the holding cells without dying first. The other guard was talented enough to keep James focused on defending himself, but James was ultimately the better swordsman. The other commoners had watched at first, but they had begun to move away from the fight as soon as they realized how furious the guard was.

James didn't blame them for their fear, the guard could just as easily take out his wrath on them as he could on James. They didn't need a reason to punish commoners, they could be killed just for being there. And surely enough, James watched them flee back down the castle stairs and as far away from the fight as they could get. They would probably even tell any other guards they ran into about what happened in hopes of getting in their good graces and avoiding punishment.

James had to hurry this up. The guard had slowed down his attack a little bit, but the swings were still accurate and strong. It seemed that his original fury was abating, which was good and bad.

The guard had settled down and started attacking with precision instead of his earlier reckless swings. It was getting harder and harder for James to defend himself and he was fairly sure that the guard would still kill him if he could.

The fight had only been raging for a few minutes when the guard that James had knocked out started stirring and James did the only thing that made sense; he ran. James ran up the stairs as fast as he could with absolutely no idea where he was going. He had a vague plan of turning himself into any random person that he ran into, but there was no one to run into.

James stayed ahead of the pursuing guard, but only barely. He thought about opening doors as he went by them to search for people, but the guard would have probably caught up to him before he could go in. So James just kept on running, hoping for someone to appear for him to turn himself into. Anyone who wasn't in a blind rage, anyone… except for him.

James was running down yet another hallway and was dying from exhaustion when he finally spotted someone at the end of the hall and promptly turned around to run the other direction.

At the end of the hall was the man that had fought James the last time he had broken into the castle. Only this time, the man was wearing a full suit of armor and somehow looked even more menacing than last time. James had no desire to re-enact that fight right now.

James had already started running back where he came from when the pursuing guard appeared in front of him around a corner, clearly just as winded as James.

The man's eyes were still filled with rage and James had no doubt that he would kill him where he stood if he had the chance. Not believing his luck, James turned back around and ran to the man at the end of the hall.

He felt like an animal that had been trapped and cornered. He had gotten almost exactly what he had intended, but he very much did not like the bitter taste of defeat that was in his mouth at the moment.

The man was wearing armor this time, but there was no mistaking his eerily confident stance and his menacing eyes. He was the scariest man he had ever met, and his only chance of finding his sister.

The man made no movement towards James as James ran towards him. He never moved once, but his eyes followed James like a hawk.

James could hear the other guard chasing him, but at the leisurely pace. He must have had every confidence in this man's ability to stop him. James was not surprised, the man probably was fully capable of stopping him.

Still a few paces away from the man, James stopped running and laid down his sword at the man's feet. There had to be no doubt that James was surrendering for this to work.

"I surrender, please have mercy." James was out of breath, but he was able to squeeze the words out clearly before lowering his head to the ground in submission.

There was silence for some time before someone spoke. "Surely, Captain, you can't have mercy on this boy! He killed Derick." The guard clearly wanted to keep speaking, but silence followed once more.

'Captain?' James tried not to press his luck, but he finally looked up to see what was going on and he made eye contact with the man. 'So this was the Captain of the Guard?'

He looked thoughtful, but James couldn't figure out what he was thinking. He might need to try and fight his way out of this if this went sour. "For the record, Captain, I only knocked Derick out. He is still alive."

James watched for a reaction from the Captain and thought he caught a flicker of amusement on his face.

"Grott, take this boy's sword back." Relief flooded through James, and he was grateful for the next order as well.

"We will bring him to the cells." Those were the magic words that James was hoping to hear.

"Yes, Captain." James could hear the regret in Grott's voice, but James was sure that he would follow orders. That had gone better than he had expected.

Grott grabbed James' wrists from behind while the Captain led the way through the castle. Grott's grip was extra tight and obviously overcompensating for losing him earlier, but the Captain looked completely unconcerned. He could have been on an afternoon stroll instead of leading a prisoner to prison.

After several floors and too many turns to keep track of, their party finally stopped to let the guard unlock the door to the dungeon. Inside the dungeon, there was very little light apart from the torches that lined the walls, but there was enough light for James to see the prisoners in their cells. Or at least, he would have been able to, if there had been any other prisoners.

Grott pushed James past every cell and in every cell, James expected to see his sister curled up in a corner. But there was no one there, just stone walls, and empty spaces. The slow droplets of water falling into puddles in the dungeon only emphasized the emptiness of the cells.

It was only when he was shoved into the last cell in the dungeon that he lost his cool. He had expected to see his sister here nice and safe. He had planned to figure out a way to break out with her. But now he was stuck in a prison cell by himself with no idea where Marie even was. The desperation of his situation finally sunk in and he lost it.

"Where's my sister?" He was yelling at the top of his lungs now, but neither men gave a reaction. The silence of the place was magnified between every scream.

"Where's my sister? Where's my sister? Where's my sister?" Some deranged part of him expected them to answer him if he asked the question enough times. Somewhere in his mind, he just couldn't accept the fact that he had lost her.

Grott walked away from his screaming without a backward glance, but the Captain just stood and watched James from outside of his cell for a long time. He never showed any inclination that he might answer, neither did he show James any emotion at all. He merely watched as James screamed himself hoarse and banged on the cell bars.

Eventually, James went silent and the Captain walked away. James was trapped in a prison cell. He had failed himself, and he had failed Marie, just like he had failed the rest of his family all those years ago.

Dismus

— —~*~— —

The dungeons were dark, dank, and not a place where Dismus usually spent his time. The only light in the cellars came from the torches that lined the walls, but even the light from the torches were non-existent near the actual cells. The darkness of the dungeons tended to break the prisoners faster than any other means. Even with a torch in his hand, the darkness unnerved the Captain as he walked towards the only occupied cell.

If he was honest with himself, it was much more than the darkness in the dungeons that unnerved him. The boy was likely more important than he knew. If Dismus was right about the boy, then things were about to get a lot more complicated than he had anticipated. He needed to make sure that he was right before he made his next move; the boy might have changed everything.

A guard with another torch walked in front of Dismus to show the way to the correct jail cell. Dismus had his most trusted men watching the boy. A guard by the name of Freddy was on duty at the moment and Dismus trusted

Freddy with his life. Freddy carried a wooden chair along with a torch at the request of Dismus.

The guard stopped in front of a cell at the end of the stone walkway and eyed the Captain for confirmation before unlocking the cell door. Dis could tell that Freddy didn't approve of secret conversations with prisoners, but he was a loyal soldier and did as he was told.

Dismus stopped in front of the steel bars and analyzed the man before him as the other guard opened the door and placed the chair next to the captive. Neither the boy nor the guard moved as Dismus walked in the cell. The boy hadn't even looked up once this entire time. Though he was surely awake, he kept his eyes on the stone floor and continued to lay slumped against the back of his cell.

If Dis had ever seen someone defeated, this was it. Dismus moved to stand directly in front of the boy and then waved his hand in a gesture meant to dismiss the other guard, but the other man didn't move. "You are dismissed, Freddy. I will call you when I need you." Dismus never took his eyes off of the boy, but he heard the man close the door behind him and walk back down the stone corridor.

It was several minutes before the boy raised his head and finally made eye contact with Dis. "My name is

Dismus." There was only silence to answer the greeting, but the boy never looked away from Dismus. "You may call me Dis if you like." The boy might not have heard a single word that he said so far.

"The chair is for you." Dis finally saw some sort of recognition in the boy's eyes. "No," Was all the boy said. The refusal did not seem to be an act of defiance, but it was not the start that Dismus had in mind for them. Dismus moved with at a deliberately slow pace and instead, sat down in the seat himself.

"I need to talk with you." The boy's eyes seemed to gleam a little more in the dim light of the torch that Dismus continued to hold, but he otherwise showed no sign of hearing him. "I just have some questions that need to be answered."

The boy sat up from against the wall and finally looked Dismus in the eyes. He looked wary of Dis, but at least the boy had finally showed emotion. "What questions could you possibly have for me?"

The boy's voice sounded weak after such a long stint of near-silence, but the intensity of his stare betrayed a certain amount of strength that remained dormant for the moment. That was good, the boy would need his strength if he was who Dis thought he was.

"Well, the first question is easy." Dismus was pleased to have finally gotten something out of the boy, but he kept his face expressionless. "What is your name?" It was the easiest question possible and hopefully one that he would be willing to answer truthfully.

The boy was slow in answering, but he seemed to come to some sort of conclusion after a few moments. "My name is James." That matched with what Dismus knew, but it didn't prove anything. Still, he was almost sure about this.

"And what were your parents' names?" James again showed no signs of emotion besides the darkening of his eyes. Dis could tell that James was uncomfortable, but he eventually answered.

"My parents died a long time ago. I don't know why that could possibly matter to you." Dis stayed silent, matching James stare for stare until he finally gave in.

"Their names were Ani and Jotham." The news wasn't exactly shocking to Dismus, but he couldn't help but feel saddened anyway. Most low-born people lost their parents at a young age.

"How did they die?" He thought it was a simple enough question, but James hardened his gaze threateningly.

"Fine, next question then. Do you know what Ahren are?" Dismus paused here to give James a chance to respond, but all he got was a blank stare. "I'm not surprised, most people have no idea that they exist, but they do." James looked more confused with every second.

"All humans have Angels that protect them, but most of them live their whole lives without noticing. Those humans who are in touch with their Angels are called Ahren. Or at least they used to be." If at all possible, James looked more skeptical now than he had before. Dis didn't blame him.

"But I am willing to bet that you have noticed. Unexplainable things have happened to you, and around you. Am I right?" James' widened eyes told him that he was.

When James gave no indication of speaking, Dismus continued. "That means that we are powerful, or more specifically that our Ahren are powerful. In fact, only four of us exist. Your Ashmark proves it, I have the same one."

Dismus pushed his hair to the side to make his Mark more visible. James looked surprised, but not necessarily convinced. They really did have the same Ashmark, and Dismus was willing to bet that James had never seen another like it. He was determined to force James to respond this time and waited for him to speak.

"None of that even makes sense. Why are you telling me this?" James was looking Dismus in the eye, but the boy had suddenly looked very uncomfortable. It was a lot to take in, Dis knew this all too well.

"Because." Dismus attempted a smile at James, but he could not force himself to keep it. "I found you, and I am responsible for you." Dismus waited for James to respond again. He was not sure how to proceed at this point, there was too much to cover at one time. "The truth is that I want to help you, James."

Minutes went by before James finally looked up from the floor to make eye contact with Dismus again. "Help me do what?" It was a good question and an important one. Maybe he should have led with it.

Dis stood abruptly, "To help you find your sister." He had gotten the reaction that he expected. James jumped up immediately and looked like he was going to grab Dismus by the collar before he stopped himself.

"You know where my sister is?" Dismiss nodded, but he decided not to elaborate, this was a delicate subject for him. "How do you know where she is? Why isn't she here?" The questions flooded from James' mouth like a torrent that had finally been released.

"I can't answer those questions, but I promise that I do know where she is and I will help you find her." Dismus rose as if to leave and called to Freddy. Both Dis and James waited for the man to come and unlock the door in silence before James asked one last question.

"Why would you help me?" Dismus heard Freddy coming towards them, but they still had some time before he would be in earshot. "Because." Dis had to take a breath before answering. "I'm on your side."

James' face was still frozen in a look of disbelief when Freddy arrived and released Dismus from the cell. He knew that the boy would need some time to digest the information, but he hadn't expected him to go catatonic on him. Maybe he should have waited to tell him, but he had asked.

Dismus' heart was torn as he followed Freddy out of the cellar. He was completely sure now. He didn't like lying to the kid, but he didn't see any other option. As much as he wanted to help him, Dis found himself playing a very dangerous game.

Arianna

— —~*~— —

Ari had to try extra hard to avoid her lessons recently. She would have thought that her teachers would be more lenient with her considering her brother, but it seems that they thought it was important to distract her with meaningless facts even more now than ever.

However, she was fairly certain that no one would find her today. Hardly anyone went down into the dungeons, not if they could help it at least.

She was on her way to talk to the boy thief, James. Dismus had assured her of his innocence, but Ari had to see for herself. It could not be a coincidence that two people would have broken into the castle within two days of each other. Normally she would take Dis' word for it, but this time she had to be sure for herself.

Ari's guide was extremely reluctant to bring her down here, but he eventually gave in. Freddy was his name, and he kept on mumbling to himself about orders. Dismus must have ordered him to keep James isolated, but she was the Princess after all, and the Princess outranked the Captain.

Ari used to come down here to play as ghosts when she was younger and the cells were empty, but she hadn't been down here in years. The dark and wet corridor was even scarier than she remembered if that was possible.

Freddy stopped to open the last cell in the dungeon not a second too soon. She was beginning to hyperventilate in the close confines of the corridor. "You can keep the cell closed, Freddy." It embarrassed her to ask it, but she thought it mere prudence to stay on this side of the bars. A mixture of surprise and satisfaction crossed Freddy's face before he turned the key back in its lock and closed the door again.

The boy never stirred, but he watched Ari with a wariness that put her on edge. His eyes seemed to see straight through her and it made her nervous. All the same, Ari wanted this to be a private conversation.

"A little privacy please." She gave him the most innocent smile that she could manage, but he seemed unfazed. Eventually, Freddy moved back towards the entrance, mumbling unintelligibly the entire way.

Ari turned her smile towards the captive boy, but he didn't react except to make eye contact with her. Once again, she felt like he could see straight through her. Maybe it was best that she just break the silence.

"Dismus says that your name is James." There was no hint of surprise or recognition at the fact that she knew his name. "He also says that you were the one who broke into the castle two days ago." She decided to leave the statement as it was. She could not bring herself to say it outright, that he might have killed her brother.

For a moment, confusion seemed to flicker across his face at the accusation. But surely he knew to what she referred.

"Stand up." She put on the most demanding voice that she could muster, he was a prisoner after all. At first, the boy smiled wryly at her from the ground, but after a few seconds he slowly climbed to his feet in the back of the cell.

Ari ruffled a little bit at the boy's amusement, surely she had every right to order him to stand. Why did he find that amusing? This was not going as she had planned. The boy seemed to tower over her even from a distance. He wore tattered clothes that reeked of dirt and sweat, but even those things he seemed to wear with dignity. At least, he might have, but his eyes told a different story.

Now that he was closer, she could see something in the boy that spoke of despair and brokenness. With his high cheekbones and large eyes, he was what a sad puppy would look like as a grown boy. This was a proud man that had broken, and sadness seemed to cling to him like a drowning man. This man's agony was recently experienced.

Arianna felt herself softening toward him and stopped herself. Inwardly, she chastised herself, 'You do not know this boy, stop being foolish.' She physically shook herself when she realized that she had been staring for several moments without saying a word.

James moved closer to her and placed himself just out of arms reach on the other side of the bars. The closer he got to her, the harder it was for her to pay attention.

"What were you doing three nights ago?" It was best to be direct at this point, she believed. James pursed his lips and it looked like he would not answer her question, but after a few moments he looked away from Ari for the first time and responded.

"My sister was taken from my home and I almost died trying to save her. I wish that I had died… Is that what you were looking for?" James' voice was trembling and Ari found herself believing him, but she knew that there was more to the story.

"I'm sorry about your sister, but I'm talking about before then." Ari didn't want to push the subject, but she had to know. "Did you break into the castle that night?" James shuffled his feet and for the briefest moment he looked uncomfortable, but just as quickly he straightened himself and became defensive.

"Yes, I broke into the castle that night. But then I ran into that Dismus guy and he chased me right back out again. I hardly even made it out alive after being in the castle for two minutes."

Ari let out a breath that she didn't know she was holding. For some reason, Ari no longer wanted to believe that James had anything to do with her brother's death.

"Why are you so interested in three nights ago? If all you care about is that night, then why don't you just let me go?" James looked as if he had been holding his questions in and just couldn't hold them in any longer.

James did not seem angry, okay maybe he seemed a little angry. But he mostly just seemed distressed, and she could understand why. Still, it took her some time before she could respond to his questions calmly.

"Three nights ago, a man broke into the castle and murdered my brother." She had intended to stop there, but she felt compelled to continue speaking under the gaze of the captive. "He tried to make it look like a suicide, but I saw the man leaving the scene out the balcony of my brother's room." Arianna met James' gaze and to her own surprise, continued in a steady voice. "The same way that you broke into my room."

Arianna waited or a response and was rewarded with a nod from the boy. "Well, I've never seen your brother." He continued nodding to himself and then suddenly stepped forward to the bars of the cell. "And I promise you, that I had nothing to do with your brother's death."

Ari could have been mistaken, but it looked as if James' eyes began to water. She was still studying his face when he seemed to think of something. But whatever his thought was, he didn't seem to want to share it with her. His eyes still watering, James stared at the wall behind her, lost in thought as his mind wandered elsewhere.

Tears began bubbling up in her eyes as well, but she was able to force them back down before James could see them. "I believe you." Ari meant it though she was not quite sure why. James focused back on Ari and gave a slight nod in acknowledgment of her words and walked back to the back of his cell and slunk back down on the ground.

She didn't take it as a slight, they were both done with the conversation.

Vaguely aware of what she was doing, she called for Freddy and excused herself from James' presence. She was relieved at the fact that James was not her brother's killer. But her chest started to tighten as she looked on to what she had to do next.

There would be no easy way to do what she had planned. And she was certain that she had to go through with it, now that she knew that her brother's killer was still out there. There was no way around it; there was only one way that she could think of to find her brother's killer. She was going to catch her brother's killer by using herself as bait.

Arianna

— —~*~— —

Ari had been staring at Lady Elizabeth's mouth for several minutes without hearing a word she said. She had never been very good at parties, but she was having a particularly hard time tonight.

This was the first ball to be thrown since her brother's death and she just didn't feel right about moving on without him. Not that either of them attended these often really. But it seemed to her that the party just seemed too normal like no one even remembered what had happened to Aaron.

The room was one of the larger ones in the castle and it was completely packed with Nobles and their servants. No one missed an opportunity to attend a royal ball, if only for the food selections. The entire room was surrounded by tables full of exotic food and intoxicating drinks. It was a welcome change for most of them from the fish and poultry that they were surely used to.

Truthfully, she would rather be anywhere but here right now, but she had to be here. More than fulfilling her duties as Princess, she would fulfill her duties as a sister tonight if everything went well. That was the scary part, everything would have to go well. This is where she would set her trap for the killer, and it was the reason for the copious amounts of sweat currently dripping from her brow.

The King would have never allowed her to do what she was going to do, the only person who knew was Dismus, and even he didn't like the plan. He didn't try to stop her, though, and his help would be essential moving forward. As scared as she was, she also felt alive for the first time since Aaron's death. At least she was doing something about it.

Painstakingly, Ari forced herself to listen to what Lady Elizabeth was saying.

"… so, what have you heard about this boy-thief?" The lady's lips were pursed as if she knew that the Princess wasn't listening, but she would not give up on the Princess that easily. Few were so privileged to talk to her. She rolled her eyes inwardly at the thought, but she pasted a smile on her face and replied in the most ladylike way she could manage.

"What about him?" She would play clueless for as long as possible to avoid talking if she could. It allowed her to stare mindlessly at the ladies who tended to ramble on about rumors about so and so and who and who.

The lady looked at her as if she were holding back on purpose… which she was. "Well haven't you finally caught him? The scoundrel stole my favorite necklace right from my very bedroom two months ago!" The lady looked more impressed than distraught, but she obviously expected some sort of response from her hostess.

"I can't believe it." Ari put on a look of shock on her face, but she knew that it could not have passed for genuine emotion. Luckily, the Lady was satisfied with her display and moved on to bombard her with questions about the man.

This is exactly what she needed, a reason to continue to think about their captive. Yes, he was attractive in a way. Maybe even impressive if he was outside of a cellar and not dwelling in his own soil. It was not his fault, but then it really kind of was.

Ari couldn't stand the tension any longer, she had no desire to stay here. It was as good of a time as any to get on with her plan, no more overthinking it.

"Excuse me, Lady Elizabeth." The woman had rambled on nonstop for the last two minutes and looked flustered at being interrupted during such an interesting piece of gossip. "I must be attending to certain matters." She gave no reason to leave, she didn't need to explain herself to Nobles.

The lady seemed perturbed, but it was her turn to plaster on a smile as she bowed to her Princess. "Of course, my Lady." Ari gave a slight bow back as a courtesy to help smooth things over and promptly moved through the crowd to one of the doors that led out to the hallways of the castle.

The room was stuffed to the brim with Nobles and successful merchants looking for their next thrill. The colors truly were marvelous to behold when she stopped to watch, every single house trying to outdo the others in style and extravagance. Ari couldn't let herself think on it too much, however, or it would make her sick. What are these people really doing with their lives? And she was in the middle of it, that was the worst part.

She managed to avoid too much attention as she left and courteously declined invitations to talk many times before finally reaching the hallway and making her way down the halls. It was time to execute her part of the plan. She chose a servant's room a few halls down from the ballroom and slipped inside.

She was alone on the inside of the room, it was a small room with only the bare essentials. After scanning the room, she closed her eyes to concentrate and almost fell over from fright as the door opened to let in Dismus right in front of her.

"What are you doing in here?" Ari was furious, but she tried to reclaim her cool as she faced down the Captain.

"I am not leaving you alone tonight when you have this planned. You will not leave my sight." He said it in a matter-of-fact way that brooked no argument. He would be immovable in this state and she couldn't say that she blamed him.

"Fine, but can't you just wait in the hallway while I do this?" He seemed surprised that she wasn't arguing with him but pleased all the same. "Fine, but make it quick. I don't want to draw attention to ourselves by hanging out outside of a servant's room. With that, he swung the door back open and stepped out to let her do what she had to do.

Quickly, Ari changed into her brother's clothes that she had borrowed from his room and stored in her purse during the party. She would have to look the part to pull this off. And, for the first time, she tried making herself look exactly like her brother.

The transformation felt the same as it always did but added to it was the sensation of growing several inches in a span of a second. She opened her eyes and looked down at her brother. She was almost the exact twin of her deceased brother, the only difference was that she was skinnier than he was.

She could not transform into something bigger than her, nor could she change into something smaller. Whatever she changed into kept the same amount of body mass. The result was a boy much taller than her, but also much lankier.

It would have to do. She steeled herself for what she had to do and then stepped out of the room. Immediately, Dismus threw a cape around her head to hide who she was and led the way to the ball. He acted as if the Princess transforming into her deceased brother was something that happened every day. He had taken off his own cape to hide her presence as long as possible. This would have to be timed perfectly.

Dismus did not move people out of the way for her, that might have drawn suspicion. Instead, he made his way through the party several paces in front of her that was supposed to help her get through with less distraction. From under the cloak, she could see the eyes that flitted back and forth between her and the other guests, but no one guessed who she was.

It wasn't until Dismus arrived at the King's side at the far end of the room that people seemed to stop what they were doing to watch her approach the King. Nobles approached the King sometimes, but even that was a near-rare occasion. For someone unannounced to approach the King was an intrigue of great proportions in the Nobles' world.

It was now clear to the on-lookers and the King that Dismus had escorted this person through the room. As Ari stood under the cloak and looked at her father, the room had finally reached a point of dead silence. This is what she had been waiting for.

'Now or never,' she thought as she lifted the cloak off of her head and stared her father in his eyes. The King had taken a look of shock upon seeing her face.

She knew that he would never believe that Aaron had come back from the dead, but the Nobles might be just superstitious enough to believe it. She just had to sell the Nobles on it, not her father. So she took the opportunity to make eye contact with the rest of the room before speaking.

"I am Prince Aaron, returned from the dead. My killer must confess within one day's time, or I will kill him myself!" She had not planned to yell her lines, but she was nervous and couldn't think of how else to do it.

The looks on their faces ranged from incredulity to sheer terror as the Nobles apparently attempted to understand what was happening. The silence only lasted a second before the room erupted in noise.

Some of the guests fled the room as if she had announced their immediate doom, other rushed towards her in hopes of getting a better look at the Prince returned. But none moved faster than Dismus as the Captain moved towards her before she had finished talking and swept her away from the crowds.

The King suddenly had a look of suspicion on his face and contented himself to follow Dismus as the entire Royal party left out of the back doors behind the throne. He must have realized that it was her after the initial shock, but he must have believed it if only for a second. She felt horrible that she had to do that to her father, but she had to follow through with it.

Her father and Dismus were not the only people taking her to the King's chambers. There was a good number of guards escorting them as well, which meant that she could not reveal herself to her father yet. Once they made it to his chambers they would have privacy, and she would have plenty of time to explain to her father.

She only hoped that her trick had worked. Enough people saw her that the word had to get out. If this would not draw out her brother's killer, then nothing would. She only had to wait for the assassin to come and kill her.

She had made herself bait, but there was no other choice. She would just have to trust that Dismus could keep her safe, and hope that her father won't kill her first.

James

— —~*~— —

James knew that he reeked even worse than normal, but he couldn't bring himself to care. His nose had
adjusted by the end of the first day in the dungeon. The
only thing he did care about was freeing himself from this
cell, but every way he looked at the problem, he couldn't
find a way out.

There was no weakness in the cell itself. All of the
walls were made of stone and the bars were pure steel.
There was no way to pick the lock and no way to get
through the dungeon door even if he had been freed from
his cell. Outside of all of that, he was also under watch at
all times by guards and he was in the middle of the castle.

James had never been more frustrated in his life.
Not only was he stuck in prison and lost about what to do
next, but he also had so many questions. How did the
Captain know about all of the strange things that had happened to him? How did he know about his sister? Was he
involved in taking her? He had no idea what to think.

James wanted to believe Dismus, but he couldn't
bring himself to do it. He just couldn't bring himself to trust

the man. He would find his own way out of this prison and find his own lead on his sister. His entire family was as good as dead unless he found Marie soon.

James forced himself to his feet and started pacing the prison cell. He couldn't shake off the feeling that he won't ever have the chance to find Marie. But he would never stop trying to find her as long as he still lived.

Eventually, James stopped pacing and slumped against the back of the cell. He hadn't made any progress towards escaping, but the pacing had exhausted him enough to make him tired.

There was no way to tell if it was dark out or the middle of the day, but he didn't care. There was only one escape for James in this place, and it was in his dreams. As he drifted to sleep he kept on repeating the same phrase in his head over and over again.

"Where are you, Marigold? Where are you, Marie?.."

————~*~————

He couldn't remember the dream that he had just been in, but he had a vague sense of comfort left over from it when he realized where he was. Rather, he realized that he didn't know where he was. James started sweating a cold sweat as he searched the darkness for anything familiar.

This was exactly what had happened to him before he woke up to the men in his room. Was this a part of the assassination? Did they just warn you first every time? He was pretty sure that he couldn't fight off both of them at the same time. He had only survived last time because the other one had focused on his sister.

The pit of his stomach dropped as soon as he thought of her, but the sense of loss was overpowered by the sense of dread that had taken ahold of him. He was stuck the same way that he had been before, but the picture seemed to form before him much faster than it had the first time.

The scene unfolded around him, but he did not recognize it this time. He wasn't sure whether that unnerved him more or less, but he tried to keep calm as he continued to scrutinize his surroundings. He was standing on a giant mountaintop by himself, surrounded by snow and wilderness. He had never seen nor dreamt of anything more beautiful in his life. He immediately felt as if he could stay there forever.

James had lost himself in the billions of visible stars when something suddenly shot out of the sky straight towards him. As he watched, the entire sky seemed to be crashing down upon him. Almost half of the stars in the sky were falling towards the earth in a blazing fire. It was as if someone had taken all of the stars in the night sky and set half of them on fire.

James looked directly upwards and watched as a giant form came hurdling at him surrounded by stars that had suddenly lost their light. As they shot closer to him, he could see more clearly that the stars still glowed, but each one was surrounded by an aura of blackness rather than rays of light. They were still beautiful, but to James, they felt wrong somehow.

It wasn't until it had landed in front of him that James realized that it wasn't a star that had been hurtling at him. All of the black stars had shot right past James and onward below the mountain and out of sight. What landed in front of James was much worse.

What had seemed like a giant black star landed directly in front of James, uncurled itself from a ball, and stretched its wings across the sky. A black dragon as large as the sky looked directly into James' eyes.

The dragon's eyes were the same. They were the same as the man with black scales on his face. They were the same, the hooded man and the dragon, one and the same.

The dragon suddenly spoke with a voice that shook the earth. "You will suffer and die just like all of the others." Flames seeped out of his very being and scorched the earth as he spoke. "I will find you, and you will pass. You will be like every other. Death will claim you, as will agony and despair."

James trembled at the dragon's voice as the entire mountain shook. He had not the strength to stand up to the accusations, they were true. He could feel the truth in the words, but just as strongly he knew that the truth was twisted.

Despite knowing that his words were twisted, despair threw him to the ground, or it would have if he could have moved his feet. As it was, his entire being wanted to shrink and disappear under the gaze of the beast. For some reason, he felt compelled to free the beast, but he fought the compulsion. He did not want to free the beast, no matter what he felt.

Just as James was beginning to not be able to bear it any longer, another star seemed to fall from the sky towards them. Only this time, the star did not lose its light as it reached the earth. Instead, the light seemed to grow steadily brighter as it reached the earth and landed in between James and the dragon.

As soon as the star landed, a word came to James as clearly as if it had been spoken to him: Angel. This was an Angel. The being seemed to have no physical form at first, but as James struggled to make out the Angel, it slowly became clear. The Angel had taken the form of a human that was just as big as the dragon. It looked like a giant beacon of light across the earth.

James felt oddly connected to the glowing human. Not sure of what he was doing, James attempted to reach out to the Angel, but his hand fell short. He was just too far away from where his feet were planted. If only he could move his feet.

Another word seemed to materialize in his head: Ahren. He could feel the connection with the Angel. As soon as it had landed, he felt a sense of peace and comfort, but with it a fear that he could not quite understand. A fear of loss maybe?

The Angel paid no apparent attention to James; its attention was completely on the Dragon and at some point a giant sword of light had appeared in its right hand. The dragon did not even put up a fight when the Angel stepped towards the beast as if it knew that resisting would do no good. The Angel continued to hold the sword of light in its hand and casually threw the dragon down through the earth with its left hand.

As the dragon was thrown down, James saw manacles and chains on the limbs of the creature, and just before the dragon disappeared from view, James made eye contact with it and cringed. It was clear to him that this was not over.

As soon as the dragon had been thrown down, the Angel turned towards James and seemed to speak inside his mind. "Do not be afraid." The words were clear in his head, just a clearly as the title Ahren. James attempted to reach out towards the Angel once more and found himself standing alone in his cellar.

What he had seen was real, he was sure of it. In his shock, he didn't realize that he himself was glowing until he spent a full minute pacing his dark cell. He was glowing, and somehow he knew that if the Dismus were here, then he would be glowing too. He was on to something, something the Captain already knew.

James stopped and watched himself as the glow began to fade from his body. He watched intently as it disappeared, but somehow, he knew that it was still there.

He had never been able to see it before, but he had felt it plenty of times. This was the same thing he felt whenever he climbed a building or defended himself. He had always attributed it to adrenaline before, but he knew better now. He was an Ahren.

Suddenly full of energy, James began pacing the cell once again. He could figure out a way free of this cell, and once he did, he could figure out a way though the castle. He had broken in twice already, why not break out as well?

Stopping in front of the jail cell, James reached out towards the bars and concentrated. He had no idea what he was doing, but it seemed instinctive to reach out his hand towards the bars. Not sure what else to do, James formed pictures in his mind of the bars disappearing.

Beads of sweat formed on his forehead as he concentrated on the bars. He pictured the bars melting, bending, folding, fading, and every other thing that he could think of, but nothing happened. James could feel the power around him, but he just couldn't figure out how to use it.

Never giving up, James continued concentrating on breaking out of the cell well into what he assumed was the night. Nothing would stop him from making it to his sister. That hope was the anchor that kept him from slipping into the Ocean of despair that threatened him. It was only a matter of time now.

Dismus

— —~*~— —

Dismus walked down the familiar hallways with a forced air of confidence. In most cases, he really was confident, but, in this case, he was going to have to fake it. He had brought news about the Princess' plan to his crew and now their boss was going to decide what they were going to do about it.

Maybe he shouldn't have told them about it, but he needed to deflect their suspicions as much as possible. Ari was going to get him killed, he could feel it.

Sweating, he turned a corner and slipped into one of the small rooms in the castle that was almost never used. It was a common meeting spot for his crew though they moved around a lot as a precaution.

The rest of his crew was already in the room, and it looked like they had been waiting for him. Gregor and Hector stood together in the back corner and watched him as he walked up. Malanth was facing them with his back turned to Dismus.

Dismus walked up to complete the circle and waited for their meeting to begin. There had been five of them before; Pater was their shifter, but that was before Dismus killed him.

Dismus was technically their leader, but they all knew who they really answered to. They all had a higher master, and that master would be running the meeting today. Malanth reached out his hands as a signal to start the meeting and they all took his hands.

Energy shot up Dis' arms and through his body. A sensation of power flooded through his veins followed by a dulling of his senses. He hated this part, but he shoved down his emotions and entered into the vision willingly. It was easier than trying to fight it, and once he let himself go he felt a sense of calm.

His sight was the first to go, followed by the rest of his senses, and slowly they were replaced with an illusion. Malanth was their messenger and had a direct link with the King himself. The King was their master and the most powerful being on the planet.

As if Dismus was opening his eyes, King Manthar slowly came into vision along with the other men present. It was as if they were all actually here with their master, though they knew that wasn't the case. Still, what they experienced here would affect them just as much as if it was real; in regard to pain at least, Dismus had experienced that the hard way.

The King stood with his hands behind his back and seemed to be inspecting the men before him. Dismus had the distinct sensation that he was reading all of their souls. He would not have been surprised if that were the case. Manthar could do many things that he should not have been able to do.

"I am told that the Princess is trying to draw out Pater's killer." All three of the other men shuffled their feet but otherwise kept silent. They knew to keep quiet until told otherwise.

"I would be inclined to let her do it, I also would very much like to find this killer." His voice was like steel on ice; smooth but grating simultaneously. It put Dis' nerves on edge, but he made sure not to let it show. He couldn't afford to show any signs of weakness to this man, or whatever he really was. He was not truly a man, not anymore at least.

"However," the King continued, "you shall proceed with the previous order. Kill the Princess, make it look like an accident. Do not waste any more of my time with this, we need to proceed quickly with the rest of my plan."

Dismus' heart sank into his stomach. He couldn't stop the frustration from bothering him, but he was practiced in hiding his emotions. Dis steeled himself and nodded his head with the rest of his crew, hopeful that Manthar had not noticed.

"Leave me. All except Dismus."

Dis' heart started beating rapidly, but he still kept hold of himself. Why was he being asked to stay? Did the King know? Surely not or he would be dead already. 'Calm yourself, Dismus,' he thought to himself harshly.

Gregor, Hector, and Malanth all bowed as one and disappeared from the vision like a flame being put out. As unnerving as it was to be in his master's presence, it was much worse to be in his presence by himself. Despite Dis' self-control, he could feel the sweat starting to drip down his face as Manthar turned his eyes upon Dismus.

"So you have captured Micael." It wasn't a question, but a statement. Dismus stared straight ahead with as little emotion as possible. He would be obedient in this, he had to be.

"And the boy's sister is on the way to me already, I presume?" It was the first real question he had asked so far and only a nod of the head was required. Dismus wouldn't say anything if he could get away with it.

The King stepped close to Dismus in a rare display of passion. "Bring him to me." Again, Dismus nodded in assent. He had no plans to defy his master in regard to the boy; he would do as he was told, he had no other choice.

"Hector and Gregor will go with you." Manthar didn't say it, but the intention was clear. They would watch him and make sure he followed orders. Again, Dismus nodded.

Dismus itched to withdraw from the vision, but he forced himself to stay put. He would leave when he was dismissed.

"Leave as soon as you kill the Princess." The words hit him in the gut, but he again forced himself to be expressionless as he bobbed his head. This was something that he couldn't follow orders on, but he was already working on a plan for that. Hopefully, it worked.

"You know what will happen if you don't follow through." It was a threat that had made him a slave in the first place. He could do nothing while his master had control, but he would change that soon if everything went as planned.

"Yes, Master." Manthar waved a hand in dismissal and Dismus promptly found himself back in the room with his crew. They were all staring at him in wait for any other instructions. He might have been technically in charge of them, but the reality was that he was a slave.

Manthar was his master and these were the guard dogs. Well, he had already killed one dog and these won't last much longer either if his plan worked. For now though, he would play along.

Dismus gave the three men instructions for dealing with Ari and James and then dismissed them back to their normal duties. They would act soon, but Dismus' plan would have to move even more quickly.

None of them knew why Manthar wanted the Princess dead, nor did they understand why the Queen had to die, or the brother had to be replaced, but they didn't need to know. Manthar made the orders, and they obeyed them.

The only thing that Dismus had been able to figure out was that the royal family here was somehow a threat to his rule. And even that was mostly just speculation based off of Manthar's actions. He had no clue why Manthar considered them a threat. 'If only I knew,' he thought.

He was going to need to be really careful if he wanted to save the Princess and not get himself killed in the process. It was more than just their lives that he was gambling with, he could deal with that easily enough. It was someone else's life that he was putting in danger with his plan, and that, much more than putting his own life in danger, was what worried him.

Calviro

— —~*~— —

Calviro had half a mind to cut his losses and leave, but that wasn't how he did business. Still, he might have bailed on the assignment if he had been by himself, but he was not. An entire team of people had shown up at the meeting spot, and he was willing to bet his last dollar that they were all in the same business as he was.

He wasn't sure who had hired this team of people, but he had an idea. Whoever had pulled this team together had a high place in the castle; there was no one else with so much money and so many connections. Calviro had made a good living off of his thieving skills and he prided himself in knowing how to avoid attention. But someone had found him and the rest of the group and pulled them together on very short notice. And that someone was not anyone to mess with.

He still wasn't quite sure how he had gotten here. He never could resist large sums of money, but it was more than that. It had been his dream for many years to break into the castle and have his way with its riches, and someone was making it happen. He only had to trust the directions that they had been given.

It was the darkest hour when he arrived, and he had arrived first. He was early as usual, but the rest had showed up quickly after. They had each arrived to find what they had been told they would: a pile of servants' clothes to fit each of them. It was a good start, but he could tell almost every last one of them was as anxious as he was. No one spoke to anyone else, and everyone stood on edge.

They could be walking in on a trap, an elaborate scheme to round up thieves, but that didn't make sense to him. Why wouldn't they have just killed him when they found him? No, he would trust the plan, for now.

Everyone had already changed into their disguises when a figure slid out of the shadows directly in front of Calviro. A man wearing a black cloak stared at each of the people gathered in the alley. How had he missed that? The man had probably been there the entire time, and no one had noticed.

All twelve of the thieves were completely silent as they waited for the hooded figure to speak. He had given no indication that he would speak or act, but it was assumed by the entire crowd that he would be their leader for the night. Was this their patron?

"Not all the summoned have arrived." His voice was a whisper, but he might as well have been yelling. Calviro couldn't help but shiver from the fear that ran down his spine. "It doesn't matter," the man continued, "we have enough."

Calviro was sure that they were all thinking the same thing as him. There was a shuffling of feet from most of the listeners as they waited for the speaker to finally reveal their job.

"We are going to infiltrate the castle and take the Prince for ransom," the speaker spoke flippantly as if what he had just said wasn't insane. "Follow closely and keep your heads down. You are servants, remember that."

Calviro looked around at the rest of the men. Every last one of them suddenly looked wary. He had heard rumors, as they all had heard about the Prince coming back to life, but they had all assumed that they were just that, rumors. And now they were being asked to kidnap him? Stealing goods was one thing; stealing a Prince was another thing entirely.

The man didn't seem to care or notice the hesitancy. Without waiting for a response, he turned to the street behind him and lead the way to the castle. Calviro followed right on his heels along with every last one of the other men. This was not a man to be questioned, and the other thieves apparently agreed.

'No matter,' he thought. If this whole thing went south, he could always outrun the others. That is, after grabbing something on the way out, of course.

Arianna

Ari had just received an extensive lecture from her father, but she was still in one piece. For a while, she had not been sure that she would make it through the night. But she currently laid on a bed in her brother's room and in the form of her brother. She knew that she would have to stay in her brother's form for a long time, but she didn't realize how hard that would be. She itched to change back into herself, but she didn't let herself. She would have to be ready to play the part when the assassin came for her, and she didn't know when that would be.

Dismus was currently hiding on the balcony attached to the room, ready to face the assassin when he came. Ari couldn't see him as he was, but that is how he wanted it. He would remain unseen until it was too late for the killer. Her father had insisted on staying, but Dismus had finally convinced him that he would do no good by staying.

None of them had any clue as to when the assassin would come for her, but Ari was sure that her plan would work. By now, whoever killed her brother would have heard about his revival and would come to finish the job. Only this time Dismus would be here to stop him and get justice for Aaron's death. Now it was just a matter of waiting.

It was near morning by the time that Ari finally gave up on trying to sleep. It could be several weeks before anyone came to kill her, but she couldn't shake the feeling that she was in danger. She guessed she would feel this way for quite some time before it was all over. Still, she couldn't force herself to sleep.

Temporarily abandoning the attempt to sleep, Ari turned back over to her left side and continued watching the door. Hours of waiting had produced absolutely nothing at this point, which made it all the more startling when she noticed the shadow from underneath the door moving.

She might have dismissed the motion altogether if she hadn't heard a soft thump outside of the door at the exact same time. But by the time that she was able to piece it together, the door was already in the middle of being kicked open. Shock shot through her body, and she was temporarily paralyzed in her bed.

At first look, the men looked like servants that worked in the castle, but she didn't recognize these men. Men came flying through the door towards her just as Dismus came flying through the balcony door to meet them. The first few men did not look like they expected resistance and hadn't even drawn their weapons yet before Dismus had slashed them across the chests.

In the blink of an eye, three men had been slain and laid between Dismus and the rest of the men that had begun to spread out to face him. He was sorely outnumbered, and it was only that thought that shook Ari out of her original stupor. She had to help him.

As fast as she could, Ari rolled out of the bed away from the attackers and grabbed her knife from under one of her pillows. That should have been her first move, but there was no point in kicking herself about it now. By the time that she was standing ready with her knife, Dismus had been surrounded by seven men and two more had moved towards her.

Ari readied herself with her knife and assumed the stance of the Snake. Dismus had spent many hours over the past year teaching her how to use her knife effectively, but she had never been in a real fight before. In the back of her head, she told herself that fighting two against one was not the best way to start.

The first man was dressed as a servant and had moved to face her by himself. If the man had been disciplined, he might have lived, but he was hasty and pulled out a knife to match hers. The other man with him was dressed differently than all of the others. He was wearing a black robe and he seemed content to watch as the other man attacked her. With her current form of her brother and the hooded man waiting, they were pretty evenly matched.

Ari stayed in the snake stance and waited for him to make the first move. Her style was all about redirection and speed, not brute force. Out of the corner of her eye, Ari saw Dismus swinging his sword like a whirlwind. The fight had started seconds ago and only half of the men facing him were still standing. All she had to do was survive long enough for him to help her.

As soon as she had the thought, the man rushed her and swung deftly at her heart. It would have been a quick kill if she hadn't reacted just fast enough to redirect the swing past her. The man was slightly off balance for the briefest of moments, just long enough for her to try a leg sweep and send him flying to the ground.

The man died before hitting the ground. Before Ari could react or follow up her leg sweep, the hooded man threw a knife directly into the other man's heart as he had flown through the air.

Still trying to register what had happened, Ari was hardly able to follow as the hooded man swept in behind her. She tried to turn and defend herself, but the man moved much too quickly for her to do anything about. In the middle of her turn, she was struck a huge blow to the back of her head and her eyes went unfocused.

Before she completely lost consciousness, however, she saw Dismus lock eyes with her from across the room. He ran the last man standing through with his sword and started towards her, but she knew that he was too late to catch her.

However, as she lost her sight, there was no doubt in her mind. Dismus would save her. He had never failed her before.

Dismus

— —~*~— —

Dismus currently knelt in front of King Aandal in the empty throne room. The room was built to hold hundreds of people comfortably and it had once been the center of the city. But in the past year, people had all but completely stopped trying to petition the King. Now the room was almost bare of people. Columns lined the center of the hall and tapestries lined every wall. It was an impressive sight, or at least it used to be.

There was no one else, but the two men and there was no sound except that of their breathing. King Aandal sat on the throne in silence and stared down at Dismus over his long nose. Dis couldn't help but wonder at what the hall used to be like before the people stopped coming.

Dismus had been summoned by the King as soon as he had learned of Ari's disappearance. He had been kneeling in front of him for several minutes already, but neither men had said a word so far. He would let the King have that privilege for the moment, he was content to stay in silence.

The King was furious with him. The entire morning had been spent in a search for Princess Arianna, but nothing had been found. There would not be rest for any of the kingdom's guards until she was found, and it was all Dismus' fault. He was supposed to be the one leading the search, but it seemed that the King did not trust him any longer. That was not something that Dismus had planned for.

Truly, the fact that he had been attacked by twelve men without a single warning should have alarmed the King more than his own failure. But someone had to be singled out as responsible, and, in this case, it was Dismus. Still, he was supposed to be searching with his men. Instead, he had been called here to be berated for losing her in the first place.

"Who took her?" The King finally unfolded his hands and signaled Dismus to stand. Dismus slowly got to his feet and felt his joint creaking. He was not as young as he liked to think at times and his aching knees were unhappy reminders of that fact.

Dismus thrust his fist towards his heart as a sign of gravity. "I had nothing to do with her disappearance." Dis knew that he would have been suspected eventually, but as long as there was no proof, he should be safe for now.

"We were attacked by twelve men, I couldn't fend off so many. It is my fault, my King."

"You are responsible for what happened to my daughter, and you are responsible for finding her." Dis straightened in front of the King, ready for the challenge that the King hinted at. "You will find her, or you will answer to me."

Standing back up, Dis locked eyes with his King once more. Dismus was much stronger than the King, which made it that much harder for Dis to follow his orders. But it was necessary for the moment, even though the end was finally in sight. Maybe if the King wasn't so weak, Dismus would have an easier time playing his part in all of this.

"Bring me my daughter, Dismus." The words were a thinly veiled threat, and not an empty one. The King baffled Dismus greatly. He acted as if he actually cared for his daughter, but he had never shown her an ounce of care in the time that Dismus had been here. Ari would be better off without him.

Dismus waited for anything else from the King, but when there were no further words, Dismus bowed once again to the throne and turned to walk out of the large room. He managed to keep his pace leisurely, but he could not stop his heart from racing.

His suspicions were correct. The King didn't trust him, and he more than suspected him in the Princess' disappearance. Well, then that just meant that he would have to move forward with his plan earlier than expected.

He could feel the King's eyes boring into the back of his skull as the doors closed behind him. Tonight. They would have to leave tonight before it was too late to leave at all. The King was going to be a problem. Well, he could deal with that later if he needed to.

James

— —~*~— —

Hope is a funny thing. James had tried to give up hope, but he couldn't quite manage to do it. Every attempt to free himself had turned up empty, but every time he would convince himself that this attempt would be different.

Hope kept him alive, but with hope came restlessness. There was a way out, he just hadn't figured it out yet. And he could not rest until he succeeded. 'That's just how the world works,' he thought. 'You fail until you don't.'

Ever since the dream, James had paced the length of his cell and back constantly. Over and over again he tried to use his power to escape, but nothing worked.

It felt like days that he had been moving and thinking in the darkness. The darkness was the worst part. He never thought that darkness would affect him so much, he always considered the night to be his. But he was slowly going crazy without the sun.

Where exactly was he in the castle? How many guards were there? What time of day was it? The only thing he had to go off of was the meals that a guard would bring him every so often. But even that hardly told him anything. He had no way of knowing which was breakfast, or which was dinner. He had no idea what time of day it was, only that it was time to eat. How was he supposed to sneak around when he knew absolutely nothing?

It seemed that the best and the only option he had was to use his power to force a way out. The problem was that he had no idea how to do that. Dismus had hinted at some sort of power, and James had seen it, but he still had no idea how to use it.

He sure didn't feel powerful, stuck in the cell and helpless. Maybe if he had a giant dragon with him. That was his Angel, right? He let out a sigh and found himself chuckling. A giant dragon would be quite useful right around now.

"Help." The word came out of his mouth like a groan. He had gone his whole life without asking for help, but he needed it now. There was no more room left in him for pride. He could do nothing by himself.

James stopped his pacing, stood directly in front of the bars that held him, and lifted his hand to touch one of the bars. He wasn't sure what he was doing, but it seemed like the right thing to do. Something was guiding him.

He could hardly see the bars themselves, it was much too dark, but he felt the rust that covered the metal bar and the hard cold that made the hair on his skin stand up. "Concentrate," he told himself. "I Just have to concentrate on what I want, and what I want is to break free."

'Be more specific.' The thought came unbidden to his mind, not his own, but familiar all the same. As startling as he was at the thought, it made sense.

He formed the words as clearly as he could manage in his mind and thought them as if in conversation with the other voice in his head. 'I want to break these bars.' He thought the words deliberately and then waited for a response, but there was no response.

James waited for what seemed like several minutes before he began to give up. He was about to resume pacing his cell when a word came to his mind in the other voice once again. 'How?'

Again, James nodded to himself. Of course, he had again not been specific enough. But how did he expect it to happen? James imagined it happening several different ways; in his imagination, a fire consumed the metal bars, lightning struck them open, and hammers crushed them. He even imagined slicing right through the bars with the sword that he saw in his dream, but nothing happened.

There had to be something there, he could feel that he was on the right track. He was just missing something.

James had taken his hand away from the bar briefly, but now he held the bar once again and said the words out loud for good measure. "I want to break these bars with your help." He said it like a question and it sounded absurd to him when he said it out loud, but he closed his eyes at the same time and pictured it happening. He felt like a dummy, but he held his position, eyes shut, hand out-stretched, and as nervous as could be.

It had only been seconds, but it felt like an eternity when the air around him seemed to come alive. James couldn't help but open his eyes and drop his jaw in aston-ishment. He couldn't see anything, but he felt a stream of water appear around him, whipping up what little clothes he had.

Just as suddenly as it appeared, the water stopped swirling around in the air and shot at the metal bars that formed his cage. The water hit the bars with incredible force and bent them, but it was not enough to escape through. Again, James focused and tried telling them to shoot at the bars.

James still had his right hand outstretched, but he was touching the water instead of the bars. And once again, the water shot at the bars and bent them further apart.

James' jaw dropped as he stared at the opening in the metal bars. Vaguely he thought about the fact that the bars had probably caused way too much noise to escape notice.

He would have to move now though he had no idea where he was in the castle or whether it was night or day. He really should have thought about this. Though if he was honest with himself, he really hadn't expected it to work in the first place.

James quickly, once he had gotten over his shock, stepped through the bars that had once held him, and started feeling his way along the stone corridor in the direction that the guards always came from. Even though he could see them fine a few minutes ago, he could see hardly anything as he felt his way along the walls.

Since when had he had such bad night vision? He used to pretty much only go out at night, and he had just spent who knew how many days in the dark. He would have thought that he would be able to see better than this.

He had only made it a few steps before the door at the end of the hallway opened. Ten seconds in and his escape attempt had been foiled by a guard holding a torch. He really needed to work on his stealth.

James froze in the darkness and shut his eyes to focus. The guard might not be able to see him in the darkness of the corridor, but he was in no shape to fight normally. He was weak and sore from the confined space that he had been stuck in.

Frantically, he tried to command the water to attack the guard, but the water was nowhere to be found. Nothing was happening, but he kept on trying to send the water like he did the first time. He could see the guard walking closer, but he was still far enough away to surprise him.

The guard was almost upon him before James finally gave up on using the water and opened his eyes to prepare himself to fight the oncoming guard. To his surprise, the guard was standing right in front of him and it was Dismus. He was currently staring at James in amusement. James tried to move to attack the man, but he found himself completely immobile. What had just happened?

"I see that you've started to discover your potential." Dismus didn't sound surprised, but he had a smirk on his face that burned at James' pride.

"Let me go." James found that he could move only his head, but that meant that he could speak. He was careful not to show any emotion in his voice when he spoke, and he was surprised to find that his voice was strong and steady. "I'm getting out of here."

"And going where?" The guard seemed to be ready for this conversation and in no rush to return James to his cell. Where were the other guards?

"That is none of your business." James could not keep the heat completely out of his voice. What right did the man have to question him? Though James supposed he had every right, he was just caught sneaking out of the cellars after all.

"If I were you," Dismus gave the air of someone who was settling in for a long conversation while James' already weakened muscles were started to spasm already, "I would not have been captured in the first place." The guard gave a look at James as if admonishing him for being caught and then moved on before James had a chance to respond. "But if I had been caught, I would welcome the opportunity to escape and find my sister."

James couldn't respond, he could only bring himself to stare in rage at the man who dared to bring up his sister again. He wasn't sure if his anger was due to the man's flippant way of approaching the topic or due to Marie's disappearance itself, but he felt livid.

Dismus again continued on with his monolog as if he had said nothing out of the ordinary. "And I can help you do that." The man stared pointedly at James, seemingly in wait for a response to the implied offer.

James felt his anger slightly dissipating. "How do I know that you're telling the truth?" There was still heat in his voice, but he was close to gaining control over it again. The man was not trying to throw her death in his face, merely offering to help, possibly.

"You are going to have to trust me." The man suddenly sounded urgent in his offer. "I was coming to free you, only now it seems that you didn't need to be freed from your cell. But you do need me to find your sister, I guarantee you that.

"And you will still need help escaping the castle, and the Kingdom after that." Dismus waited for James' answer with a look of patience, but he was clearly ready to get out of the darkness and on with the escape.

"What if I still don't believe you?" James couldn't quite manage the confident posture that he intended, being frozen and all. But he composed his face in the most haughty way that he could manage while being tied up.

"Then you are a fool, and I should leave you to rot where you stand." The guard looked ready to do just that.

"Ok." James was ready to be let loose, not matter where the man brought him. The truth is that he really didn't know what to do next, only that he really did need to find his sister and had no idea how to do that otherwise. "I'll go with you. But don't expect me to believe that you're doing this just to help me. I know there's something in it for you."

"Hmph." The man nearly smiled when he responded. "I'd be surprised if you would have thought otherwise."

Instantly, the invisible bonds disappeared from around James and he fell to the floor. He was too weak to catch himself when he was released and his muscles still felt like jelly.

"It looks like you need more help than you want to admit." The comment was harmless enough, but James couldn't help but be put off by it. As soon as he was up to his old strength he would leave the man, that was for certain.

James collected his thoughts as he righted himself on his feet. He already knew one thing, and that was that his sister wasn't in Valladar. It was unfortunate news for someone who didn't know anything about the world outside of Valladar, but it was a lead nonetheless.

Dismus threw a ragged pair of pants and a shirt at James to put on and slid out of the cellar with James following closely behind. He found that his vision had returned and relaxed slightly, but he was disconcerted by what happened. There was way too much that he didn't know.

There were two other guards on the other side of the cellar doors and James almost had a moment of panic. James was prepared to turn and run, but neither of the guards reacted to seeing James outside of the cell.

Both the men hardly looked at James, they just seemed to be waiting for Dismus to lead the way. "James, meet your new friends. Hector, Gregor, meet James." Both of the guards nodded and the one named Hector even smiled.

"Hector and Gregor are with me and they were in charge of protecting you until we broke you free. They are good men, James." Dis seemed so sure, but James was

skeptical. He had yet to meet a good man among the Nobles. "I don't trust them either."

James was just being honest, but all three of the
men laughed. Hector was still chuckling when he responded. "I would have been disappointed if you had. A trusting
man is a dead man."

The procession would have looked normal to any
regular passerby, James supposed, but he couldn't help
but feel conspicuous in servant's clothing and surrounded
by three guards. It seemed to be dark out and the hallways
were almost completely empty of people.

What few people they ran into were other servants
who didn't once look at the procession of guards. Either
this was such a regular routine that it was not worth noticing, or the servants were very well trained here.

The thought of such docile servants angered James.
He just couldn't imagine serving anyone that put themselves above himself. But he supposed it was not their
fault that they found a way to survive in this world.

After what seemed like hours later, Dismus led the
three of them out of the castle and across the castle
grounds. James found himself counting the guards along
the walls before stopping himself. He was not here to scout

the castle, he wouldn't come back even if his life depended on it.

The guards never broke their stride as they made their way through the twisted streets and back again. Dismus began the trek towards the poor sector, but as soon as they were out of sight of the castle, he turned them back around the city and to the other side and towards the port.

There were not many people out in the streets, but none dared approach them. They were four strong men, three with swords and dangerous looking. Not many street urchins or thieves would take their chances with a group such as that. The streets seemed so empty to James, everyone who normally would have roamed the streets disappearing well ahead of the group.

It was nearly light out when the group approached the docks. The docks were technically outside of the walls of Valladar, but they were still in a sector of the kingdom not much better than the slums that James used to live in. The land was littered with shacks and tents hastily built and just as hastily destroyed.

The sector wasn't large compared to the rest of the city, but it still stretched out beyond James' range of vision. What made the dock sector unique is the contest between the shacks on shore and the crown jewels that floated in the port itself.

There were countless ships docked and every single one a masterpiece. These were the real homes to people that lived in the sector, and it was their living.

Ships were too important to not take pride in. They were the defense of the city, the livelihood of the people, and the shelter to most of the sector. Were they going to take a royal ship? They were the best of the best, the strongest and fastest by far of the vessels in the water.

Most of the Royal guard lived on these ships for that very reason; ready to defend against thieves and invasions at the same time. James couldn't believe that he would get to use one, and he was right.

Dismus led them along the docks, but he kept them well away from the royal ships at port. Instead, James followed him to a small ship towards the end of the port.

The ship was smaller than the royal vessels docked down the way, but it was still a fairly large ship. Two large white sails were currently reeled in and tied up, but they would surely have the ship moving quickly when unfurled.

It looked to James that there was probably enough room on the ship for a hundred men, but he had very little experience with such things.

As he surveyed all of the ships next to one another, he wondered how many things there would be to steal on each one. He could probably amass a lot of medicine on the Black Market for the things he could find here.

The sun was still making its way over the distant Ocean when they climbed aboard and came face to face with a man with a huge white beard and a scar along the left side of his face.

There were other men aboard the ship, but they went about their business with no notice for the guests. The man before them seemed to be the Captain and paid no attention to the three behind Dismus.

James opened his mouth as if to speak, but Dis shot him a look that could have frozen a river. The look said that he would deal with this, not James. That was fine with him, he was only going to try and break the tension anyways.

"Gruffold." With a nod of Dis' head, he took out a large bag of coins and dropped it in the waiting hand of the presumed Captain. "Your payment, as agreed. We set sail now."

The Captain felt the pouch thoroughly but seemed to trust Dismus well enough, as he didn't open the pouch before putting it in his pocket. "We set sail now," He repeated back himself to the group with a smile behind his large white whiskers. The Captain looked like a large whale of a man, but he moved with surprising grace as he turned towards his crew and gave the announcement.

"We set sail, Maties!" There was no change in the posture or work of the men on board, and no sign that they had heard at all. The announcement seemed pointless. James thought that they must have already assumed what the orders would be.

The large man turned back to the group of four men and took them all in for the first time with his gaze. The man had a surprising amount of grace as he swept another bow as far as his girth would allow.

"I am Captain Gruffold." The Captain smiled easily at his guests, but the other four men stared back without emotion as the Captain continued. "And welcome to Waveskimmer."

The Captain turned without another word and led them to the trap door. The Captain climbed down the ladder first and James followed right behind. The Captain pointed to their rooms as he passed them and each man turned off into their respective rooms once it was pointed out.

Each room was right next to the other and James was put in the middle, but he didn't mind. For the first time, he had his own room. He felt guilty about it, but he couldn't help but feel excited. He had spent his entire life dreaming about sailing away from Valladar on a ship, but he had assumed that Marie would be there with him.

James curled up on the floor next to his bed and let his mind drift aimlessly as he closed his eyes. It was easier to sleep on the cold steel floor than on the bed after sleeping so long in his cell.

Dragging his blankets over himself, James sighed comfortably for the first time in weeks. Free from prison at last, he was beginning to feel like he was doing something to save his sister. He was finally on his way.

'I'm coming, Marie. I'm coming.'

Part 2

James

— —~*~— —

James was kicked awake with a hard boot. After many sleepless nights in the cellar, he had slept like a baby on the hard metal floor of his cabin.

"Get up, Kid." It took James a few seconds to realize where he was. The only thing he saw when he opened his eyes were a pair of boots and an otherwise empty room. He shoved his moment of panic down and scrambled to his feet.

"What was that for?" Dismus stood next to where James had slept and waited several moments while James composed himself before replying.

"It's time," he said simply, "to begin your training."

James furrowed his eyebrows and fought the urge to spit at his ex-captor. "What training? I didn't agree to any training!"

"If you want to find your sister," Dismus turned towards the door as he spoke, "follow me." And without waiting, he walked out of the room. James threw the rest of his clothes on and rushed out the door to follow him.

As soon as James ran out of the door, he almost crashed into a waiting Dismus in the hall. The man did not look surprised at all. Hector and Gregor, however, were lounging behind Dismus and openly laughing at James.

"You can start with this hall." Dismus gestured behind him and one of the guards stepped around Dismus and handed James a sponge and a bucket of soap and water.

"What is this?" He had come to save his sister. Somehow he hadn't realized that saving Marie would involve cleaning a ship.

"You will begin your training," Dismus' voice brooked no argument, "by cleaning this hall, and then making your way across the rest of the ship. Don't worry about the lower hull, you can save that for tomorrow."

James was only vaguely aware of his wide-open jaw hanging from his face, he could not believe what was happening. As if he knew exactly what James was thinking, Dismus continued to explain the injustice.

"Yes, this will help with your training. Besides, the crew believes that you are my servant. We really should do all that we can to sell the lie." Dismus smiled maliciously at the comment. James' vision was starting to turn red. He supposed that he could see the logic in at least the second point, but he still wasn't sure what he even needed training for. Still, he saw his opportunity for a bargaining chip.

"I will refuse," James held the sponge as if to throw it on the ground, "unless you tell me where my sister is."

Dismus' face was impassive, but James could tell that Dismus was barely restraining himself. "And what good would that do?"

"I'm here." James was not going to give up. "I'm on the ship. We are at Sea, and I can't escape. You have no reason to lie to me now." James took a breath and rolled up his sleeves to show that he would do what he was asked. "Did you really bring me here to help me find my sister?"

Dismus widened his eyes slightly in surprise, but otherwise merely looked thoughtful. "I did not lie to you." Dismus let out a sigh and put his hand on James' shoulder. James had to fight an impulse to shake it off.

"I promise that I will help you find your sister," Dismus stepped back to join Hector and Gregor.

"Marigold is on a royal vessel three days ahead of us. There is no catching that ship, but both ships are going to the same place; Pyiasior. We will find her there, in the castle." Dismus looked at James expectantly as Hector and Gregor blatantly avoided making eye contact with James.

"How do you know that? Why would anyone take her so far away? What's the point?" James felt more confused now than he had before.

"You never mind how." Dismus was all business once more and he began walking down the hall before he even finished speaking. "As to why: let's just say that the King there is very interested in you, James."

James let out a deep sigh as the men turned the corner and out of sight. Still confused, James used his time cleaning to process what Dismus had said. He had no choice but to trust the man, and despite himself, he felt a certain respect for him. A Noble or not, Dismus really did seem like he was telling the truth. They were on his sister's trail, that was good enough for the moment.

With a deep frown and a forced determination, James dipped his sponge in the bucket of water and began the arduous task scrubbing the entire metal ship.

"Why in the world do I even need training?" By the end of the task, there was more sweat in his cleaning bucket than there was water.

— —~*~— —

Hours had gone by before James had finally been relieved of his duty. He had scrubbed the entire ship with the exception of the living quarters and the lowest level of the ship, and he was exhausted. His back ached worse than he could ever remember before, and his hands were badly cramped.

James felt like an old man by the time that Dismus released him for a lunch break. As hard as the work was, James couldn't help but be a little proud of the accomplishment. As he ate the fresh fish, James realized that for the first time, he had done an honest day's work.

He ate his fish on the floor of his cabin and was savoring his time off when Dismus strode into his room once again. James' stomach was suddenly in knots, but what could he possibly be put to that was as hard as cleaning the entire ship?

"The afternoons," Dismus announced, "will be used for instruction, just as the mornings will be used for work." Dismus looked like he was waiting for a response from James, but James stayed silent and continued to sit on the floor.

For the first time, Dismus looked uncertain and maybe even timid as he took a spot across from James and sat down to match him. The two of them looked as if they were settling in for a staring match.

"Judging on our previous encounters, I am going to assume that you know nothing about who you are." James couldn't stop his heart from racing. He was as tense as he could possibly be while sitting down.

"I mentioned before about Seraphim. There are three of them, technically. One of them has not been found for quite some time, and the other two are sitting in this room." Dismus paused, seemingly to let what he said sink in, but James just nodded and waited for him to continue.

"I know very little, but I know that in the beginning, four Seraphim were given power over the world. The first was given dominion over the air and the creatures of the air. The second was given dominion over water and the creatures in the water. The third was given dominion over the earth and the creatures of the earth."

Dismus looked to be in pain, but he pushed on with the story before James could interrupt. "Which leaves the fourth Seraphim. He was the strongest of them and the most beautiful by far until he became corrupted and fell."

James' vision of the falling stars suddenly came to mind. Somehow, he knew what he had seen. He had seen the fallen Seraphim crashing down to earth.

"His name was Helel. He was given dominion over the people of this world, but when he turned evil, his responsibility was taken from him. Now he has taken over the King of Pyiasior. That is who ordered the kidnapping of your sister, King Manthar of Pyiasior."

The silence that followed lasted for what seemed like an eternity. Both James and Dismus sat on the metal ground and stared at each other until James finally spoke.

"What could Manthar possibly want with my sister?" This was the question that had been burning in his brain since Marie was taken. Why her, what could anybody possibly want with a sick girl?

"King Manthar is being controlled by the Fallen, Manthar. At this point, Manthar had been controlled for so long, that there is no difference between the two anymore. Manthar is Manthar, and Manthar is evil." Dismus seemed

content to the leave the statement there as if that explained everything, but then he continued.

"By that, I don't mean that he does evil things. What I
mean is that Manthar is actually made of evil. He wants
nothing less than total domination, utter destruction, and
endless suffering."

James was not sure what he expected when he
imagined tracking down his sister's kidnapper, but he was
definitely not ready for the truth.

Eventually, Dismus leaned in towards James and
looked towards the door before going on. "I'm not sure
what to explain, nor do I truly know how to. Manthar's intention is to destroy us, but he doesn't live only to destroy
us. In some cases, he lives to control us."

The truth was starting to sink in for James. Marie
wasn't taken because she was important. She was taken
because James was important. Was she taken to hold as
leverage over James?

"Your Angel is the Seraphim over water and all of its
creatures: Micael. He was given the power to wipe away
the fires of Helel. Micael is the greatest threat to his power,
and therefore so are you.

"You are one of the most powerful Ahren in the world and he will do everything in his power to control you if possible, or destroy you if not."

Nothing made sense, but James knew that this was the truth. It explained the death of his parents and the burning of his home. Everything fit but James just didn't want to believe.

"You've got it all wrong." James stood back up and began to walk out of the room. He had no idea where he was going, but he suddenly couldn't sit any longer.

"He is the man responsible for your sister." Dismus remained sitting and talked as if James was not leaving the room. "You cannot run from him, Boy; trust me on that." There was bitterness in his voice that startled James.

James stopped in the doorway before walking out. He looked back over his shoulder at the man sitting on the ground, but Dismus was staring at the ground, lost in thought.

"I'm not running." They locked eyes and Dismus finally nodded.

"Good. Because you will need real training if you expect to have any chance at saving your sister. She will have been long kept a prisoner in Manthar's castle by the time we make it there. She will be heavily guarded and in the middle of the enemy's kingdom.

We will have to sneak our way in, not fight our way in. If it comes to fighting, we will be found, and If we are found by Manthar, we will lose. This will be no easy task, Boy."

The man had delivered the entire speech without breath and with a ferocity that shook James down to his toes.

"Why are you helping me, Dismus?" If all of this really was as dangerous as he said, it didn't make sense to James that he would risk helping him.

Dismus seemed to consider before finally answering. "You are not the only one that he has tried to control, Son."

Arianna

— —~*~— —

A rocking motion was the first thing that she became aware of. Everything was dark. She tried blinking several times just to make sure that she was actually opening her eyes. She tried to stand, but her head erupted into a splitting headache and she eventually had to give up.

It had only been a few seconds before panic began to set in. She had been kidnaped. She almost wished her memories hadn't just come flooding back to her. Where was she? She felt like her world was spinning. Ari used all of her willpower to force herself to sit up and think.

Everything was dark around her, but she was beginning to be able to make out a few things. Namely, she realized that she was currently stuck in a metal crate. There seemed to be holes here and there to allow her to breathe, otherwise, there was nothing to see.

Now she could see that even if she had managed to stand, she would have hit her head on the top of the crate and made her condition even worse. They must be smuggling her out of the kingdom on a ship, and it seemed like they succeeded. Why take her away from the kingdom? What good was she anywhere else?

In another wave of panic, she realized that she looked like herself again. She would have changed back immediately after being knocked unconscious. Why would they still have taken her if they knew that she wasn't her brother? Would they even keep her alive now that they knew?

She used her hands to check the rest of crate, but she didn't find anything except for a plate of food in the corner. She vaguely thought about the fact that she should be grateful for the food, but she couldn't bring herself to care. Her stomach was much too preoccupied with the whole freaking out thing to be hungry. It was right then that her stomach disagreed with a loud involuntary growl.

So many questions, but she couldn't force herself to focus. She was trapped in a steel box with no way out and no ideas. She had gotten herself captured and would probably die just like her brother. Would they make hers look like a suicide as well?

Sound. For the first time, she heard something from the room that she was in. She wasn't sure why, but she instinctively tried to make herself as quiet as possible. She steadied her breathing, but her heart was beating so loudly that she was sure that she would be found.

The sound was clearly the clunking of footsteps against the floor, and they seemed to be getting closer to Ari. It must have been a pretty big room based on how long she heard the steps. The sound seemed to come closer and closer to her before, she imagined, finally stopping right next to her.

"Ari." It sounded as if a man were attempting to wake her. If he knew that she was in here, then there really was no point in pretending that she wasn't.

"What?" She tried to sound in-charge and unintimidated, but the word still escaped her mouth as more of a squeak. 'Great,' she thought. 'My first word in what was probably days, and I sounded like I just got stepped on.'

"Watch yourself in there, I'm going to break you out." The voice sounded familiar to Ari, but she was still having a hard time thinking clearly. She couldn't think of a strong response, so she said nothing. Suddenly, air came streaming through the holes in the box and blasted Ari in the face.

Ari's instinct told her that the man had probably been sent to attack her, but she told herself that the notion was ridiculous. They might very well kill her, but they very likely would have found a way to do it outside of a metal crate. She braced herself to fight back when the box suddenly exploded from the inside out. The steel box had been ripped apart, and Ari was completely untouched. Her hair was a disaster, but that couldn't be helped really.

Arianna tried to jump to her feet and run as soon as the box had exploded, but she fell back down almost immediately from the pain in her head. She might have hurt herself even further, but she never hit the ground.

Someone caught her before she hit the ground. She could feel herself losing consciousness once again. Before her vision blackened, she looked into the face of the man that had caught her, and she could almost place him but not quite.

A second face appeared next to the other man's. She would never be able to mistake this face. Dismus was looking down on her with concern and was reaching down towards her face when she lost focus once more.

As Ari lost consciousness, a great weight was lifted from her. She had been saved by Dismus once again. He had probably caught her brother's killer as well. All would be right with the world once more. She wanted to thank Dismus, but she would have to take a quick nap first.

————~*~——

Arianna woke up in a room full of people. Dismus sat with his legs crossed next to her and the other men were on the opposite side of the room, each standing on either side of the door. She recognized them this time, royal guards from her palace. 'What were Hector and Gregor doing here?'

She had only just finished thinking the question when a much more important one entered her mind. 'Where was she?' She had gained her bearing much more easily this time, but it was still taking her some time. Why wasn't she back home yet?

Dismus smiled down at her, but he waited for her to gain her bearing before saying anything. It had been some very long minutes before she finally broke the awkward silence that had taken hold of the room.

"Thank you, Dis." Ari managed a smile, but even that still pained her. Dismus' smile slipped for some reason. "There is no 'thank you' required, Ari."

"How long was I out?" She felt like that was the most important question, but then she realized that there was something else just as pressing. "And where are we?"

Dismus looked nervous, but he remained calm and moved to sit next to her. "That... is complicated," he finished delicately. "But I will do my best to answer all of your questions in time.

"You have been unconscious for about a day. But that was the second time you passed out. The first time you passed out, you were out for two days." Ari laid her head back down on the blanket that lined the steel floor below her. "And we are on a ship called the Waveskimmer if that means anything to you. We are a couple days out from Valhalla."

Ari continued to rest her head down on the blanket, but she turned her face to look at Dismus as he spoke. This didn't sound good. Dismus waved his hand towards the door and the guards stepped out of the room, she assumed to give them privacy. But they stepped back in seconds later and gave Dismus a nod. They must have been checking for privacy then.

Dismus looked more uncomfortable than she had ever seen him before. "Princess." He began timidly, but he was obviously determined to tell her the news. "Your father is dead."

Ari's world began to spin. She was vaguely aware of the fact that she had tried to stand, but Dismus held her still on the ground. She wanted to ask how, when, and why, but she couldn't make herself stop sobbing enough to ask.

Her entire body was wracked with sobs and her head began to explode with pain once more. Dismus must have known that she would want to know, for he began to answer her unasked questions.

"He was killed by the same assassin that took your brother's life, and he would have killed you as well if you had been there." Dismus' face was not without compassion, but he had to press on. In her head, she knew that what he said made sense. But all she could think was that she should have been there with him.

"That is why we are on a ship. We were able to escape in time and smuggle you out on the ship. You can't go back, I'm so sorry."

Ari's mouth was moving, but she couldn't bring herself to actually form any words.

The pain that had taken over Ari doubled as she laid on the ground and cried uncontrollably. She hated to break down in front of Dismus, but her world was shattering all around her. Dismus tried to reach out to comfort her, but she just rolled to the other side and curled up into a ball.

Somewhere in the recesses of her mind, she was aware of the men leaving her room, but she didn't fully realize that she was alone until some time later. Her world had just been flipped upside down and her stomach was flipping with it.

Ari lied in a ball on her bed for hours, she was sure. She would only move periodically to throw up and then climb right back into a ball. The same thoughts kept on swirling in her head like they were stuck in a sick cycle.

She would never see her home again, she would never again be held in her father's arms. And more than she had ever felt before, she felt alone.

She imagined what he had been like before her mother died. Her father, the King, kind and strong. He had loved his family so much, and then he had lost everyone, everyone except her.

She was still lying frozen on her bed when she found herself starting to doze off. Maybe she could have moved, but it was like she had lost the will to move.

She thought about possibly trying to move her arm to see if it could move, but could not focus hard enough to try.

Ari didn't sleep that night; as much as she wished she could, she couldn't. She stared at her ceiling, unseeing and dead to the world. She imagined her family, whole and happy again. It was the way it was before her mother died before her entire family had died. Why couldn't they have just killed her as well?

Right now, she wasn't sure whether or not she was thankful for that fact. She felt guilty somehow like she could have changed something had she known. She would have just died, likely, but she could have tried to save them somehow. And they were like her, the ones that did it. It was unnatural, what they did, and she was fairly certain before the end of the night.

"I'll come back to check on you after you've had some time." The voice seemed to come out of nowhere.

Ari started and lifted her head in the first movement that didn't involve food leaving her body in hours. James was standing in the doorway and had apparently just put down a tray of food on her floor.

He looked like he was expecting a response, but Ari couldn't bring herself to respond. She must have been imagining it, but it looked like James was on the verge of tears as well. "I am truly sorry," and then he bowed as he shut the door behind him.

The brief distraction had temporarily stopped the tears, but they threatened to come back in full force once James had left. Silently promising herself, Ari stared straight up at her ceiling and forced the tears to cease.

She would be okay. She knew it deep down though it was impossible to feel it at the moment, she knew. This was not the end of the world, no matter what it felt like.

Taking deep breaths as she lay on her back, Ari began to run through a list in her head.

'I am thankful for the time that I had with my family. I am thankful for the food that I eat. I am thankful for my life. For a bed to sleep on, for warm blankets, for my health, my working body, my intellect, and my power.'

She forced herself to say everything that she could think of, even though she didn't feel particularly grateful. 'This is the worst time to do this,' she thought wryly.

As she lay in her bed, Ari could not help but to wonder at the questions that had been eating at her. What would happen to her now that her family was dead? What would happen to Valladar? Would she be Queen? Was it safe for her to return as Queen? Where were they going now?

Her entire life had just been flipped inside out. Part of her knew that she was just focusing on the questions to distract herself from the pain, but ultimately she didn't care. The questions lingered until she finally fell asleep in a puddle of her own tears.

Dismus

— —~*~— —

Dismus was slammed against the back of his chamber wall and the entire room seemed to vibrate. Shockwaves flared across his back initially, but the pain receded almost immediately; one of the benefits of being healed by the air around him.

Gregor's face was inches from Dis', it would have been closer than that if Dis hadn't been so much taller than the other man. Hector stood a few feet away and watched impassively, but Dis knew that it was a show. Both men were ready to pounce on him. They probably would have too if they had been truly confident that he couldn't take them.

"What do ya think you're doing?" Gregor's eyes were wide in an attempt to intimidate him, but Dis was ready for this. He knew that he would be confronted about this when they found out.

"I am removing the Princess from the picture, just like I was asked to do." Gregor's grip tightened on Dis' neck and he could feel the oxygen starting to cut off from his brain. Panic threatened to grip him, but he forced it down. He was safe, he knew that.

"You know this is not what the orders meant, you were supposed to kill her, not bring her along!." Hector moved in right next to Gregor and looked Dis in the eyes. "You disobeyed the master, Dis. You know he won't be happy to know that you were behind her disappearance."

Both of these men had always been eager to look for a way to get rid of him, but they had never found a reason until now. Still, they wouldn't be allowed to harm him, not seriously at least. Dismus was too important to the plan for that, he hoped.

"I would be surprised," Dismus forced through what little room he still had in his throat, "if the master doesn't already know." Both men stared him down then and Dis did his best to do the same, but it's a hard thing to stare down two men at the same time.

Finally, Gregor let go of his throat and he slid down to the floor. Dis' neck throbbed, but again the pain went away quickly. Relief took him, but he shoved it down and forced himself to remain expressionless. He could not show them how worried he had been that they might try to harm him anyway.

"We should just kill her now." Gregor looked to Hector for a response but didn't get one. Irritation flashed across his face, but otherwise Gregor held his tongue. Hector was the highest ranked among them on the ship though Dismus really wasn't a part of the rankings in the first place.

"If we kill her," Dismus explained patiently, "we become untrustworthy in the boy's eyes. If we can't control him long enough to get him to the master, then we have failed. The Princess is secondary to this task. Besides, now that she thinks her father is dead, she won't be in any rush to get back."

Gregor hissed at Dis' reasoning but never took his eyes off of Hector. Sweat started to roll down his temple, but Dismus used a breeze to wipe his face without the two men noticing. He could have just taken care of these two so easily at that moment when they weren't expecting it, but there would be no explaining that to Manthar.

"Can't you just bind him and bring him to the master yourself?" Hector put on a mocking smile as he posed the question. He must have thought that Dismus would not admit to weakness, but he was wrong.

"No. Sooner or later he would break free and escape. This is his terrain after all. Besides, that was not the order that we were given."

Dismus was not too certain that he was right about James being able to break free, but the other two wouldn't know that. Either way, Dismus was fairly certain that they would go along with it, mostly because no one risked angering Manthar if they could help it. No one except for him, apparently.

Both men frowned at his answer, but he could tell that they were convinced. For now, at least.

"Fine," Hector crossed his arms in resignation and Gregor groaned in frustration. "The Princess will be left untouched until we reach the master. But afterward, she will have wished that you had killed her when you had the chance."

Dismus' stomach churned at the statement, but he showed no signs of it. Plastering a smile on his face, Dis bowed to Hector and walked out of the room without a second glance.

He could not help but feel guilty as he walked back to his room. He had tried to save her, just like her mother. But he hadn't succeeded; Ari would die at the hands of his partners, just like her mother, and there was nothing more that he could do about it.

James

A full week at Sea and James still had trouble keeping his food down. He couldn't imagine how people stayed at Sea for so long; he would be miserable if he had gotten a job on a ship. Well, he supposed that's exactly what happened, but this was temporary... he thought.

James sat with his legs folded under him in the middle of his cabin with Dismus facing him in the exact same position. He was exhausted after a full morning of manual labor, but there was something rewarding about a full day's work.

After a full week of cleaning and menial tasks, his muscles had begun to stop their continual aching and the tasks were becoming noticeably easier. He might have taken pride in his manual labor, but he was more focused on his lack of progress in using his power. 'My Angel's power, rather,' he amended mentally.

Dismus seemed to do whatever he wanted with the air around him, and James had yet to move a cup of water more than a foot. His escape from jail looked to be an anomaly, he wasn't sure that he would ever be able to replicate what he had done at this point.

The two men were alone on the steel floor. Hector and Gregor stood guard outside of the room to make sure that none of the ships crew saw, and Princess Arianna remained in her room down the hall. It would be time for dinner before long, and James would have to resume chores afterward, but for now, he remained on the floor, staring at a cup of water.

"Concentrate." Dismus arched an eye at James but otherwise showed no emotion. "You can do nothing with a wandering mind." James must have looked as tired as he felt. It was nearly impossible for him to concentrate when all he wanted to do was sleep, but he did his best to refocus.

The metal cup had been placed on the floor in between James and Dismus, and it was taunting James as it remained unmoved in that spot. Again, James focused his mind and stared at the cup. 'Raise out of the cup,' he thought, 'and splash Dismus in the face.'

James spared a look at Dismus to see if he would react to the thought. He would not have been surprised to learn that Dismus could read his mind, just one more impossible thing in a sea of impossible things. Luckily, Dismus showed no signs of knowing what James had been thinking.

Suddenly, the water lifted in the air and splashed James in the face. James sputtered and jumped to his feet, unsure about how to react. He was now soaking wet and freezing, but he hardly cared. "I did it!"

"Ha!" Dismus began laughing uncontrollably and rolling around on the ground. It was the most emotion that James had ever seen from his teacher. "You didn't do that." He was able to force out the words in between laughs and then started in on another fit of laughter as James frowned.

"What do you mean? I told the water to rise and splash you in the face and it did! Granted, it hit my face instead, but you've got to admit that it was close!" James continued standing and waited for Dis to stop rolling around and regain control over himself.

"Well, that was even more entertaining than I thought it would be." Dismus retook his sitting position and James did the same, still soaking wet from the water that was no longer in the cup. "I used the air around the water to hit you with it. It wasn't you though it looks like we both had similar ideas."

James' frown deepened. "What was that for then? Are you just looking for ways to humiliate me or something?"

"No." Dismus had regained his stoic poise and seemed unconcerned about James' outburst. "Besides the fact that it was fun to do and watch... I thought that it might serve as a motivator. You were not focused and unmotivated, now you are alert and motivated."

James forced himself to stay sitting. The unfairness of the situation was only amplified by Dis' calm manner.

"Now," Dis ordered. "Dry yourself by putting all of the water on you back in the cup."

As much as James didn't like the method, he had to admit that he felt much more alert now than he had a minute ago. More out of spite than anything else, James turned his attention to the water covering him.

Mentally, James reached out towards the water and felt a presence there. What was he doing wrong? Still concentrating on the wetness of his clothes, James was suddenly hit with a realization.

He was not the one with the power, not really. It was not his command, but his Angel's command that directed the water. Suddenly he knew what to do.

James could feel the difference as soon as he reached to the water. And just as quickly as James gave the command, the water obeyed him.

The water that had soaked him only moments ago now floated like a mist in between the two men, and with a mere flick of his wrist, James flung the water at Dismus.

James watched the water fly towards Dismus for only a brief second before James suddenly lost his vision. His blindness only lasted for a second, but it was long enough that he actually missed his target.

Dismus should have been sitting on the floor soaked, instead he sat on the floor completely dry. He seemed unsurprised and maybe even proud of his pupil as he sat with water dripping down the wall behind him.

Dismus summoned the air in the room and lifted himself to his feet and the air dried the wall in seconds. James couldn't believe how easy it had seemed once he had focused on what he wanted. Still, he had missed his target.

"It should get easier as you practice concentrating." Dis still had a proud look on his face, but he wasn't wasting any time on congratulations. "It's always easier when you feel the thing that you want to manipulate, it gives you a greater awareness and it's easier to concentrate."

Dismus pushed the bottle with more water in it towards him. "Try again, this time while actually aiming the water." Shame crept its way into James' cheeks. He couldn't figure out what was worse; letting Dismus believe that he had no control over the water or telling him about the blindness that had overtaken him.

"Unless you have some other excuse for missing me," Dismus spoke as if suggesting that James was hiding something. Maybe the blindness was normal then. Should he tell him?

"You went blind, didn't you?" James hesitated, but eventually nodded his head. How did he know?

"You are going to have to learn how to control that, Kid. You didn't miss me, I redirected your shot. But you would have known that if you had been able to see properly."

"But why did I lose my sight? Does that happen to everyone?" James did not like the idea of losing his vision every time he tried using his power. How was that supposed to help?

"Seraphim are powerful, just like I told you before, Boy. What they allow us to do is more than just some trick; it's an entirely new set of senses. Using your new set of senses will overcome your other ones if you're not careful."

"Well, what if I am careful?" James knew that learning how to use his powers wouldn't be easy, but he had still assumed that it would come naturally to him.

"Then you will still lose your other senses." Dismus smiled at this as if it wasn't terrifying. "What you must do is control what senses to compromise for it. For instance, I often shut down my sense of smell, especially when I'm around you."

Was that a joke? This really was a side of Dismus that James hadn't seen before.

"The lack of smell leaves room for my Angel's power to take hold without impairing the rest of my senses. If I push myself harder, I might need to direct the power towards my sense of taste, or touch, or hearing, or even sight. If you can't control it, you will likely lose your sight first, and then pass out."

"Well, that sounds cheery." Just when he finally thought he was getting the hang of this, he learned that he had no idea what he was doing. How was he supposed to be ready to fight the most powerful being on the planet?

"You will get the hang of it." Dismus stood up and started to walk out of the room. "Keep moving the water around, and this time look out for that sensory deprivation. When you feel it tugging at your sight or anything else, try to force it into a different sense. I'll be back later to make sure that you haven't knocked yourself out."

And with that, Dismus left James by himself to lift water out of the cup over and over again until it became second nature.

As Dismus left, James caught himself wondering at the fact that he was beginning to like the guy. How ridiculous was that?

Arianna

— —~*~— —

Four days had passed since she learned about her father. It had taken her a while, but she eventually started eating regularly that next day. James seemed to be the designated food server and brought in a plate of food every meal time. That first day, James tried to make conversation when he came in her room, but Ari hadn't responded once.

James had taken the hint and performed his duties in silence after that with the exception of answering her questions. Dismus had not shown himself since that first day, but Ari had asked James what he knew and he had been surprisingly forthcoming.

She still had no idea what she would do about her Kingdom. She felt responsible for them. 'Well,' she thought with a humorless chuckle, 'I am responsible for them.'

She had, however, learned that she was on a voyage with James to save his sister. Apparently, Dismus located Marigold on a ship headed towards Pyiasior.

Ari wasn't sure what she thought about breaking James out of his cell to save her, but she did like the boy and she had decided to do what she could to help save his sister. After that, she would find a way to take her Kingdom back. She would just have to find a way to deal with the assassins before she returned. Who would want her out of the way?

Someone knocked on her door and she took her time getting out of her bed to get the door. For the third time today, she opened the door to see James smiling back at her with food in his hands.

"I've brought your dinner. It's fish, again." He had developed a habit of not waiting for a response between statements anymore. Before he had tried to wait for a response, but it inevitably resulted in awkward silence.

With practiced movements, James walked past her and set down her plate next to her bed.

"I've learned another trick to show you if you don't mind watching." James did leave a pause here, but he knew full well that she wouldn't respond either way.

"I'll take that as a 'yes, please.'" Ari couldn't help but smile back at him. James immediately reached back and picked up her glass of water. So far, he had succeeded in moving the water about two inches outside of the cup. Impressive, really, but she wasn't sure what else he could possibly do.

"Okay, watch closely." The excitement was very evident in James' eyes. Ari knew that she should try and share his enthusiasm, but she wasn't sure that she would be excited about anything anymore. Still, she leaned closer to the cup of water to watch as James set the cup on the ground and raised his hand over it.

She was in the middle of really hoping that he wasn't going to put his finger in her water when her water suddenly exploded out of the cup and covered her shocked face.

"Get out!" They were the first audible words out of her mouth in days and she was livid.

"Out, now!" She hopped to her feet immediately and pointed towards the door in expectation. James looked confused as to why she was furious, which made her even angrier than she was before. What made him think that this was a good idea?

"I'm sorry!" James immediately started backpedaling when she had started yelling and he had his hands up as if denying that he did it. "I didn't mean to, I promise." At this point, she didn't care what he did or didn't mean to do.

"What were you thinking?" She wasn't actually looking for an answer, she just wanted him to leave. But now that the words were flowing, she couldn't stop them from coming out.

"Just wait one second." James was already in the doorway, but he didn't move to leave. Instead, he closed his eyes and looked downwards like he was trying to ignore her. Ari was about to start yelling again when she noticed water droplets lifting off of her face and drifting away from her.

Ari noticed that James had his eyes open at this point and they both watched as the water all collected itself into her cup. She was still mad, but she was also impressed. She wouldn't be letting him know that anytime soon, though.

"Get out." She didn't quite yell the words, but James jumped out of her room as quickly as she had ever seen him move. Ari closed the door behind him and immediately slunk down to the ground and leaned against her door.

True, she had been yelling. But she had finally felt something besides pain. It started with an involuntary chuckle, but it escalated quickly and for the first time in a while, Ari found herself laughing.

James

— —~*~— —

James was smiling to himself as he made his way back to his room. Sure, Ari had yelled at him, but he was sure that she had been holding back a smile as he left. That was all he wanted to do, just make her smile.

He was almost to his room when he spotted movement at the end of the hall. His first instinct was to blame his overactive imagination, but his years of thievery had instilled in him strong survival instincts. Best that he check it out just in case.

James slowly moved towards the other end of the hall. It was dim and he couldn't make out anything there, but there could easily be someone hiding in the shadows or around the corner.

He put one foot in front of the other, very deliberately feeling the floor beneath him and checking for creaks or groans. This was a relatively new ship and most of the ground was metal and solid, but it was a habit of sneaking that he dared not break.

There was still no sign of anyone as he approached the bend of the hall and pressed himself against the wall. He had seen and heard nothing, but he felt something that put him on edge.

Before he moved any further, James reached down and pulled out a small knife that he kept at his waist. He had never owned a weapon before though he used to play with his father's practice sword before everything burned.

The knife was small but well-balanced. Dismus had given it to him on the second day at Sea. James had hardly trained with it, but he felt more confident with it in his hand. He had promised himself that he would not be taken by surprise again, and he planned to keep that promise.

Taking a slow breath, James sprung out from around the corner with his knife in his hand. Only by reflex did James manage to bring his knife up in time to deflect the blade that had come within inches of a fatal swing.

The blade of the sword nearly knocked the knife from his hands, but he managed to keep his grip. However, his entire arm was shaking from the impact of the blow.

A man dressed in all black was already following his attack up with another before James had managed to reset his feet. The hall was dead silent with the exception of the ringing of the blades as James was put completely on the defensive.

The man was skilled with the blade and moved extremely quickly. James was wielding a blade less than one-third the length of the sword's and was not even well trained. All James could hope for was to survive as he was slowly being forced back down the hall.

Ari had just finished her plate of food when she heard the clear sound of swords clashing against one another in quick succession. Her first thought was that someone was sparring, but she instantly dismissed it. No one would be sparring down here, it was too dangerous.

Fear seized her as she realized what was happening. Someone had boarded their ship, and she had a pretty good idea of who they were after.

Slowly, Ari opened the door to her room and peeked out into the hallway. It was dark in the hall, but she could just make out two men fighting about ten paces away.

Just as slowly, she pulled her head back inside of her room and whispered to herself, "I'm not going to just hide while someone else fights my battle."

Taking a deep breath, Ari poked her head out of the door once more and followed with the rest of her. Neither men noticed her as she crept out of her room and towards the fight. Even as she moved closer to the fighting up ahead, Ari couldn't help but check over her soldier for any other intruders. It was very unlikely that only one assassin would have been sent after her.

She was only a few feet away from the back of the stranger when he suddenly stopped fighting and turned towards her instead. She was sure that she hadn't made a sound, but something had obviously tipped him off.

The assassin was wearing all black and was holding a large sword with one hand as he turned his gaze on her. Ari froze in place as their eyes locked and she felt her heart stop. Time seemed to stop for only a second before the man lunged towards her with incredible speed.

Ari stumbled backward as quickly as she could manage as the assassin's blade approached her neck, but she didn't stand a chance. She threw her hands towards the floor to catch her fall as the man followed on top of her.

As she fell, she knew that she should have tried to slow the man's blade, but she had tried to break her fall instead through instinct. Her eyes followed the blade as he fell towards her and watched as the blade dropped from his hand and hit the ground next to her.

Ari merely stared at the dropped sword next to her as she lay pinned to the ground by the dead assassin's body. She was still trying to process what had happened when James' smiling face poked out from behind the body.

Without saying a word, James came around and shoved the body off of her with apparent ease before pulling his large knife free from the man's back.

"You distracted him pretty good," James said as he pulled Ari up from the ground. He was still smiling as if neither of them had almost just died.

Ari tried and failed to mimic his good nature. "Well I'm glad that I didn't risk my life for no reason," she said as she wiped off her clothes.

"Me too," James said with mock seriousness, or maybe he was actually being serious. She couldn't quite tell with him yet.

"Do you know who that was?"

James shook his head, "But I have a pretty good guess. I saw him sneaking up on your room, Ari. Maybe that was just coincidence, but I wouldn't bet on it."

Ari nodded her head and frowned at the darkness. "Whoever he was, he probably wasn't the only one."

James walked past her towards the corner of the hall and waved for her to follow. "Stay close," he said as he started to creep along the wall in front of her.

She wasn't sure whether she was flattered or annoyed that he just took charge like that, but she was willing to let it happen, seeing as their lives were in danger at the moment.

James led the way with sure feet. The hall was pitch black, but he seemed to know his way around the ship as he led her around. There didn't seem to be much need for sneaking, however. There was no movement anywhere on the ship.

The longer she followed James, the more concerned she became. Where was the crew? Surely at least a few of the men would be roaming around here and there, even this late at night. Once or twice she thought she heard movement inside some of the rooms they passed, but they never checked inside. Wherever James was taking her, he didn't seem concerned about random noises in rooms.

After what seemed like forever, James brought them to a ramp that led to a trap door in the ceiling.

"This leads to the deck." He was still whispering, but she wasn't sure what the point was anymore. "Stay close to me." He didn't wait for a response before lifting the stone tile and sliding it out of the way on the deck. And just like that, he crawled out onto the deck.

"As if I wasn't doing that already," she said under her breath. As soon as James crawled out, Ari poked her head out of the open trap and climbed out after him.

Compared to the pitch black of the hull, the stars in the sky should have seemed bright. But instead there was a dense fog that had filled the entire ship. She knew that James should have been right in front of her, but she couldn't see even him.

Her heart started to beat like crazy and she fought the instinct to immediately hide. As soon as she climbed out of the hole, she threw herself on the ground and started to crawl across the deck.

Luckily, she was wearing loose pants and a warm jacket that protected her against the freezing winds. She continued to scan the deck as she crawled forward, but she couldn't see anything.

"James," she tried calling his name, but she was too scared to say it too loud. "James," she said a little louder, but there was no response.

All Ari could do was continue searching as she crawled and listen for movement. She could hear the muffled sounds of fighting, but it seemed so far away. Ari was still crawling randomly around the deck when James nearly fell over her as he fought yet another man.

Both passed right in front of her and disappeared almost as quickly as they continued, but not before Ari managed to catch the heel of the attacker.

She was only able to keep her hold on his foot for a second, but she hoped it had thrown him off enough to help James. Unfortunately, there was no real way to know. She could still hear the clanging of swords as they moved further away from her along with other voices from where Dismus and the guards must have been fighting.

Ari began to crawl on the deck once more, but then she got an idea. She wasn't going to be any use to James or Dis crawling around on the deck, especially if she was found.

Still lying on the metal deck, Ari closed her eyes and concentrated as hard as she could on the flying creatures that used to terrify her. When she opened them again and was completely blind, she knew that she had succeeded.

Ari spread her wings and flew up into the air as a giant hideous bat dressed in her clothes. She couldn't see anything, but she could sense everything. She automatically released vibrations and read the results like a map. She counted nine men on the deck of their ship and almost all of them were fighting. She couldn't tell any of them apart, but she could guess well enough.

One body was wandering aimlessly on the other side of the ship and she was pretty sure that would be James. From what Ari could tell, the other eight bodies were in one big blind brawl. It looked like five of the men were grouped together, for the most part, but they were being picked off one at a time. The other three men seemed to be circling the other five and attacking one at a time.

The fog seemed to shift out of the way whenever one of the three men tried, but it would come right back to hide them once they landed their hit.

It was interesting to her what she could determine through the vibrations that she was sending out. She couldn't quite see the fog, but she knew it for what it was.

In fact, she couldn't quite see anything, but her mind created the scene before her as if she were watching it.

As Ari watched, kind of, she saw three of the five men drop. Even as she marveled, the last two men split up in the fog and were dropped individually almost immediately. And as fast as it had come, the fog dissipated into the night.

As soon as she was sure that there were no more assassins, she swept down behind one of the boxes and transformed back into herself. Slowly, she poked her head out from behind the boxes to see the main deck and found herself staring directly into the eyes of Dismus.

"What are you doing out here?" He was as mad as Ari had ever seen, but he was also clearly relieved at the fact that she was unharmed. Dismus stood facing her with his guards on either side of him and he seemed to be waiting for a response.

"Since when," Ari blurted, "are you, my father?" She just couldn't handle this right now. He was acting like he was her father. Dis looked hurt, but Ari turned to face away from him before he had a chance to actually respond. She felt bad for the comment but he didn't have the right to tell her what to do, he just didn't.

Silence followed and Ari didn't turn back around until she heard Dis yelling. Ari was startled and relieved to see James slowly walking towards them with ripped clothing and blood all over him. He was clearly exhausted, but he smiled at her when she saw him.

"What do you think you're doing?" Dismus was definitely yelling now. Apparently he hadn't realized that James was out here with them. James exhaled and stopped next to Ari. "Sneaking."

The incredulous look on Dis' face almost made Ari laugh. With visible effort, Dis composed himself. "Well, you obviously weren't doing a very good job. You almost got yourself killed."

"I was just trying to help." James looked over at Ari and she smiled at him in encouragement. He wasn't the only one who could smile at ridiculous times.

Dis shook his head but seemed to take it for what it was as he turned toward Hector and Gregor. "We need to deal with the bodies and gather ourselves below deck."

They didn't look happy about it, but Hector and Gregor immediately went about dragging the bodies into a pile as Dismus led the way below deck.

"We need to talk about what to do about our unwelcome visitors, and it has to be now." Silence followed and she could almost feel the tension in Dismus.

"I'll be in James' room, we can meet there." She wasn't sure that she had that authority, but it felt good to act like the Princess again. It slightly made up for the fact that she had just avoided the entire fight by flying around as a bat.

James

— —~*~— —

"Let me see what you can do." Dismus stared at James in expectation. "Hurry, Boy. I'm not playing games." James jumped to do what he was told; he was not going to miss out on the chance to join Dismus on his mission.

Dismus had followed Ari and James down into the ship and gathered them into his room immediately. He had never performed in front of so many witnesses, but he was determined to not let that affect him.

Still standing, James extended his arms towards the cup on the ground. More than anything, he wanted to close his eyes to focus, but he knew that wouldn't be good enough for Dismus. So with eyes open and the entire room watching, James reached down towards the water and pulled it into the air in front of him.

Even scaling buildings was not as exhilarating as this was. Instinctively, he knew that he had complete control over the water, but more than that, he could feel the water like it was a part of him.

James quickly peeked at Dismus to see his reaction, but there was no emotion on his face whatsoever. However, he was rewarded with a look of approval from Ari. That was good enough for him though he was beginning to think that he shouldn't reveal too much of his control here. She might figure out that he had splashed her on purpose yesterday.

With almost ease, James guided the water back into the cup and turned back towards Dismus, ready for anything else he might throw at him. He hadn't the slightest trouble controlling his senses that time. That wasn't always the case, but he had become much better at controlling it.

James' heart leaped when Dismus gave a slight nod, but he forced himself to play it cool. Any show of emotion and Dismus would probably send him right back to wash the hallway again.

"Mhhm." The Princess looked more than a little confused. "Will someone tell me what's going on here?" She hadn't said anything up to this point, but she seemed completely in control of herself as she posed the question. "What are you going to do?"

Ari's question was obviously meant for Dismus, but she turned towards James as she asked it. He was more

than happy to answer, and he was about to when he realized that he didn't know what the plan was either.

James, Gregor, and Hector turned to Dismus and
waited for him to answer. When he didn't reply, Hector answered for him. "What's going on is that we are being
chased by the people that want to kill you, and Dis and
James over here have decided not to let them."

Dismus matched Arianna stare for stare. "These
people want you dead, Ari. They tried assassinating you
tonight, and they will try boarding the entire ship as soon
as they learn it didn't work. We have to go stop them before they can reach you or the rest of the crew."

"But if there's..." Arianna tried to get her own words
in, but Dismus stepped in and cut her off. "No, but, except
for your butt staying in this room. Hector and Gregor will
stay with you here and protect you while James and I take
care of the other ship." Dismus was giving Ari such a hard
stare as if daring her to address him.

James realized he was staring and quickly looked
anywhere but at the Princess. He was not going to get involved in this one, not if it endangered his chance to join
Dismus on his first real assignment.

A quick nod from Dis signaled their departure, and James quickly found himself following Dismus out the door. A quick look back showed a sour Princess with her arms crossed. He did not want to face her when they got back.

The night was still dark as they climbed out onto the deck and to the bow, but James could make out the other ship through the light of the stars. Their pursuers were definitely gaining on them; James would have been surprised if the lookout on their crew hadn't spotted it by now.

Even as he watched the approaching ship, James noticed the fog rolling towards them at a startling pace. "I have provided us cover." Dismus spoke with urgency, but on the surface he still looked as calm as he could be. "Now I need you to get me to the ship."

A sudden wave of uncertainty hit James as he looked down at the Ocean through the fog. Somehow, he hadn't expected such a big promotion so quickly. A bucket of water maybe, but not an entire Ocean! "How am I supposed to do that, exactly?" James asked with as little of a tremble as he could manage.

"Once we drop in the Ocean," Dismus put on an air of a teacher explaining how to add numbers, "move the water around us towards the other ship. It will not be so hard as it sounds, you will be surrounded by the water down there." James was sure that Dis was trying to be comforting, but his words were having the opposite effect.

James frantically searched for other options, "why can't you just fly us over there?"

Dismus hesitated before he answered, but he seemed to become even more solidified in his response. "No, they will be expecting that. And we need to move quickly, James. The lookouts on our crew will have already seen the approaching ship and it's only a matter of time before we are caught. It's now or never."

"Three," James' eyes bulged as Dismus began counting. "Two," James had just enough time to peer over the side of the boat before Dismus finished. "One," and Dismus grabbed James by the shoulders and jumped over the railing down to the Ocean spray.

There was not much thought going on inside of James' head as he plummeted towards the Ocean. All he could think was, 'I'm going to die. I'm going to die. I'm going to die.' He knew that they weren't the most inspirational last words, but panic had briefly taken over his cognitive skills.

Right before they hit the surface, both James and Dismus were hit with a gust of wind that slowed their descent just enough to keep from dying. As James' head submerged into the Ocean, James was overcome with a mixed sensation of relief and energy. He had never felt so alive as he did at that moment.

James forced his eyes open as he and Dismus drifted underwater and turned to make sure Dis was okay. He found his teacher calmly staring back at him, apparently waiting for James to do something. His arms were even folded across his chest as if he were standing impatiently on the ground. For some reason, that gave James the confidence that he needed.

Without closing his eyes, James stretched out his arms and shot the water away from both himself and Dismus. As easily as breathing, James had just created an air bubble in the Ocean, and it felt good. Dismus had never stopped staring at him and as soon as the air bubble was formed around them, he smiled back at James.

As much as James didn't want to care about Dis' approval, he couldn't help but to admit that he was more proud of getting Dis to smile than anything else that he had done so far.

James began to move the bubble away from their ship and followed the water current that formed in the trail of their ship. More than once he felt his consciousness slipping as he used more and more power, but he was able to force it away each time.

He could tell that his senses were dampened; his sight and hearing were blurry under the water and he couldn't smell or taste anything but he had managed to stay conscious. He was proud of himself.

Eventually, they spotted the foreign vessel coming straight at them and James directed them to the side of the ship.

"Stay here in the bubble and follow along with the ship. You should be able to spot me when I jump over the side into the water to pick me up." Dismus seemed to pick up on James' uneasiness and quickly added, "If all goes well, we shouldn't be in a hurry on our way back."

"What," James gave Dismus a hard look, "if it doesn't go well? Shouldn't I go with you? I can make the bubble again no problem!" Dismus looked like he was beginning to regret bringing James along. "You will do as I say, Boy." James hardly thought that was necessary, but he got the point. "I will do as you say." He practically growled the words, but that seemed to be good enough for Dismus and he immediately shot himself out of the water and out of sight.

Several minutes passed before James couldn't take it anymore. "Who knows how long he might take up there?" James had immediately started talking to himself as soon as Dismus left him alone in the air bubble. "Besides, I'm probably almost out of oxygen in here, I should at least pop my head out to get some air..."

Smiling to himself, James shot himself out of the water just as Dismus had. James emerged out of the water and into a thick fog that covered his vision completely. For the second time tonight, he felt completely blind, but something felt different this time. The fog felt different to him, almost like it was alive.

That's what it was, all around him he could feel the water that was scattered throughout the fog. It almost felt like the Ocean, except emptier, lighter. This time he did close his eyes, there was no point in trying to see anything anyway.

Without moving his arms, James searched the fog with his mind and pushed the water particles out and away from him like he did with the Ocean. He could feel it clearly now, his normal senses of sight and touch had been replaced through the water.

When he opened his eyes, he was surrounded by a thick fog, but he could see several feet in every direction.

"This could be useful." He spoke to nobody in particular, and then reached out to the Ocean once more and began to rise.

The Ocean swelled up under James at his command and pushed him up and into the sky at the same time that the fog dispersed around him. James felt as if he had only just realized that he had wings and had finally stretched them. This was who he was, he understood that better than he had ever understood anything.

As soon as James was sure that he was high enough, James moved forward slightly and found himself plummeting back towards the Ocean waves. This time, his mind was working as he watched the Ocean rise up to meet him. 'Two notes to self,' he thought. 'Work on using water in the air, and keep track of the ship.'

He had forgotten to follow along with the ship as it sailed, and so his attempt to board the ship had resulted in sending himself back towards the water.

It was a testament to how quickly he had progressed that he was able to catch himself with the Ocean spray and send himself through the fog and right back towards the ship. Even if he did almost pass out while doing so.

This time, James landed with a large splash of water on the deck. He felt weak as he landed on the deck and was trying to make himself focus when he noticed what was on the deck. What he saw surprised him more than anything else had that night.

Bodies laid everywhere on the deck, so much so that his splash slammed the closest body against the next. 'Could Dismus really have done this? What could Dismus do with air that could cause this much destruction?'

A quick sweep of the deck let James estimate about twenty stiff bodies, and he didn't see anyone else on board. James reached down to check one of their pulses and jumped back in fear. The man was lying completely stiff on the deck, but his eyes were wide open and staring directly at James.

James instinctively took a fighting stance, but the man made no move except to follow James with his eyes. A quick check confirmed that the same was true for all of the other bodies on deck. It seemed that all of them were alive, but couldn't move.

James shook involuntarily and rushed to find a way down into the ship. He didn't want to spend any more time with the creepy eyes than he had to. As he pushed the fog away from him, James found the trap and hesitated briefly before opening it. On the trap door was the royal crest of Valladar.

What were these assassins doing on a royal ship? Either the assassins were able to commandeer one of the most impressive ships in existence, or these assassins were sent by the King.

With a start, James realized that he had no idea who the King would even be now that Ari's father was dead. Who would have taken the throne now that Ari was the last living member of the royal family?

He didn't have time to question the ship any further. There could have been any number of answers, but he wouldn't discover anything by just standing there. Without a second thought, James dropped into the ship and once again found himself surrounded by bodies.

These were the same as the first and it was almost creepier than the ones on the deck. James had no choice to but to pick his way around the bodies and through the skinny corridor. In a way, he was grateful. There was no chance of getting lost, following a trail of bodies was an easy thing to do, if also incredibly creepy.

James eventually started moving faster as he ran through the hallways. The bodies were becoming more and more spread out and James was beginning to worry that he had missed all of the action. At first he had wanted to help Dismus, but at this point he was just hoping to have something to do once he found him.

And suddenly, there were no more bodies and no hint as to which way Dismus had gone. He couldn't hear anything and he could only see enough to know that there were two options as to which way to turn. 'Should I just stay here and wait? No, what if something happened to him?'

"I'm coming for you," James felt a sudden wave of confidence and chose left. He kept his pace to a slow creep just in case. If there was something that he needed to help Dismus with, he wouldn't do any good if he announced his presence by stampeding through the metal hallways.

It felt like hours later that he first heard sound ahead of him. He had almost turned around several times, but something had pulled him forwards. James slowed and listened as best he could. There were no lights here and he had to resort to feeling along the cold walls. He was going in blind, but he kept on telling himself that surely whoever else was here would be in the same predicament.

He never saw them coming, and he only had just enough time to register that someone or something was coming towards him before several men came out of nowhere and had overtaken him. All this power, but he was rendered defenseless as they knocked him unconscious. He had failed once again, and there would be no help this time, he was sure of it.

James

— —~*~— —

The only light came from the torches that lined the room, each held by one of twelve guards around him. James could still smell the Ocean below them and feel the cold that seemed to be sucking the life out of him. The man that sat across from him looked just like any other man, but James could feel something different about him. James shivered as the man made eye contact with him, and he knew that the cold had nothing to do with it.

"We expected an attack from Dismus, but you were a surprise." The man's eyes gleamed in the night as if made for the darkness. The man must have been middle-aged, but he still held himself with the assurance of a youth.

"I am just a thief." The lie felt hollow in his mouth. "Looking for something to steal on your ship." James had not imagined it the first time. The man's eyes shone in the darkness. James shivered once more at the realization.

"Well, I am the new Captain of the Guard, sent by the King himself to recover his daughter." The man seemed to look right through James. "I didn't come for you,

Boy. I came for the Princess, and for Dismus. Where is he? I know he's aboard the ship."

James could hardly gather his thoughts in the first place, let alone answer a question that he didn't know the answer to. But James was suddenly shocked into alertness as he processed what the Captain said. Was he saying that Ari's father was alive? That couldn't be the case. It was just a hollow lie meant to confuse him, he was sure of it.

"I have no idea what you are talking about." James didn't expect the man to believe him, but instead the man looked thoughtful. Maybe he did believe James.

"I don't believe him." The man directed his words to the guards as a whole. "Torture him until he talks." Two men stepped forward as if they were waiting for those exact orders the entire time. The sudden turn of events sent James into a panic, but as he struggled to stand up on the floor, he was held down by several men that had snuck up behind him.

The man with the creepy eyes never left James as the two men began beating his face. James tried to clear his mind and escape reality, but he was pulled back in with every punch. He could taste the blood flowing down his face and could feel himself starting to drift from consciousness, but he never quite passed out. He wanted relief so badly, but every time he came close, some other men threw a bucket of water on him and kept going.

There was something there. Some way to fight back, but he couldn't quite put his finger on it. And then it hit him, literally, the water hit him in the face and he knew what he had to do.

In between punches, James reached out with his eyes closed and felt for the water in the room. They had to have at least a few buckets left in the room, and there was plenty still on the stone floor around him. With all of the focus that he could manage, he reached out and touched the water.

Suddenly, James could see with his mind. His eyes were still swollen shut, but he could feel the three men holding him down, he could really feel the two men punching him, he could see the seven guards that surrounded him and watched, and could feel the gaze of the man that had interrogated him.

James waited until another bucket of water came rushing at his face and then shot water directly backward at the two men who threw it. James tried to open his eyes to see, but he still couldn't manage to open them completely. Still controlling the water, James dampened the senses of sight and touch. He didn't necessarily need to dampen touch, but it sure did help with the throbbing pain that was still coursing through him.

James then shot the water at the three men holding him and thought that he hit them a little harder than he intended. The three men lost their grip on James and flew backward into the men that lined the back wall. As soon as James was released, he searched with his powers for the door and found five men facing him, including the interrogator.

He knew that he had very little time left; it was time to see what he could really do with a few buckets worth of water. Experimentally, James sent a string of water at one of the guard's ankles and tried to pull him with it. The guard flipped into the air before he realized what was happening and landed on his back with a loud groan.

If James thought that the men would be scared, he was wrong. Surprised maybe, but all of the men were on their feet and seemed to be filled with nothing but hatred for their captive. Maybe he had been too distracted by the one man before, but he hadn't realized just how many men he would have to face.

Thirteen men lunged for James all at the same time and James did the only thing that he could think of. James shot his water to extinguish the guards' torches and ducked towards the ground to begin crawling. Maybe if they had been better disciplined, they would have found him, but the room was utter chaos and James was the only one that could see... kind of.

James had almost made it to the door when he felt a hand pick him up by his soaking wet shirt and opened his eyes just enough to find himself staring into the eyes of the interrogator. Yep, this guy was definitely unnatural. And again, James did the only thing that he could think of. He shot all of the water that he could feel in the room at the man's eyes. Really, it was an easy target.

To the other man's credit, he didn't let go of James when he was hit with the water, but James jabbed both of the man's arms at the exact moment that he was hit with water. James struggled free of the man's clutches as they both flew towards the door and James scrambled out of the door and into the dark corridor.

James still couldn't really see, but he ran as fast as he could down the hall and away from the men that were surely chasing him. His entire face was swollen and he could hardly open his eyes, but he was otherwise un-scathed. Who knows what they had done to Dismus. He needed to find him before it was too late; he only hoped that he was even heading the right direction.

Several turns later, James turned a corner and ran straight into a guard that was twice the size of James. Both of them stumbled, but James recovered first. Maybe it was the fact that James still had his eyes closed, or maybe it was because he would have felt bad for picking on him; either way the guard hesitated long enough for James to slip past the man and keep running down the corridor.

James could tell that the man had turned to chase James, but it turned out that there was nowhere to chase him. James almost ran headlong into the end of the hallway before he stopped himself in time to realize that he was at a dead end.

He came to the realization just in time to defend himself from the sword that came swinging at his head. 'I guess he got over the whole fighting a blind kid thing,' James thought as he set to dodging as best he could. James forced himself to focus once more and he managed to feel the water around him. He could feel the rocking of the boat on the Ocean floor right below them. He could feel the moisture that filled the hallway and the sweat that rolled down both of their skins.

It was the onset of a shiver that gave James the inspiration. Just as the guard swung his sword at him, James reached out to the sweat that covered the guard and the moisture in the air and froze it all in place. It didn't stop the guard completely, but he suddenly found himself struggling to move and push through a mound of ice. At the very least, the man had been utterly astounded long enough for James to figure out what to do next.

There had to be something here for the guard to be guarding, it's what they did. James felt around the wall and found a key hole in the steel and realized that the dead end was not a dead end at all, but a cell. How they captured him in the first place, he had no idea, but Dismus must be in there.

James turned back towards the guard who had almost made it to him already and melted the ice around the guard at the exact same time that James threw all of his weight into a punch at his face. The guard's body dropped and hit the steel floor at the same time as the water.

As quickly as he could, James threw water at the hole with everything he had and formed the water into a key that fit the hole. Exhausted, James finally unlocked the door and threw himself inside. And it was empty.

For some reason, James had pictured his escape as some glorious picture, but instead he had broken himself into an empty jail cell that he now occupied.

James turned frantically at the sound of men running through the ship behind him. The hall was filled with soldiers running towards him and the guard he had knocked out was currently getting to his feet. Using what little energy he had left, James shoved the door closed and locked it right before the men reached the cell.

Panic threatened to overtake him, but he forced it down and concentrated on his situation instead. He might have been able to fight his way free if he was at full energy, but he was about to pass out as it was. If he tried to use his powers anymore, he would almost certainly lose consciousness.

Leaning against the back wall of the cell, James listened to the banging on the door and felt the rocking of the waves on the boat. Where was Dismus? Had he escaped without a problem? James had probably gotten himself in trouble for no reason.

Would Dismus come back to save him? Probably not, he was a Nobleman after all no matter what he claimed. As far as James could tell, he only had one shot at making this work.

Slowly, James reached out to the Ocean and stirred up as many waves as possible. He wasn't sure about how well this would work, but he could feel the waves responding to his touch and so could everyone else. James shut off all senses except for his Ahren's and let the power work.

The ship slowly became more and more unsteady and suddenly James had trouble staying in one place. The ship was rocking violently now. The guards poured through the doors, but they were thrown against the wall just as hard and it was already too late. The ship was sinking, and they would all drown if they did not move quickly.

James could feel the waters rushing through the hallways towards them. The guards were getting to their feet as well, but they were at a disadvantage. The doorway was upwards now and water came pouring through it.

As soon as the water hit the cell, James felt a rush of energy and was suddenly more alive than he had ever been in his life. Without a second thought, James shot up and through the door of the cell and down the hallway. To James' surprise, the interrogator went with him.

The man had a hold on James' ankle and was not letting go as they ascended through the hall. The two of them landed on the side of the hall and ran down the hall-way as best they could, but the man jumped on him before they made it even a few paces.

With blinding pain, James slammed against what was now the floor and attempted to fend off the pummeling of the interrogator. The man was moving faster than James had thought possible, and the only thing that was keeping James from being beaten to death was the rush of water that came straight at them.

The Ocean saved his life. The cascading waters rushed into the hallway and hit them like a ton of bricks. The Ocean spray was washing them straight back down towards the cell. This, James could use to his advantage. James directed the already ferocious waters straight at the man with glowing eyes for the second time this night.

This time, the man let go. Both James and the man were being pushed back towards the cell, but James had finally broken free of his grip.

Struggling to orient himself, James faced away from the cell and shot back upwards against the flow. With amazing speed, he passed by objects and people being swept by the currents, but they shot the other direction just as quickly. James did not stop until he emerged from the hull of the ship and out into the air right before the ship fully submerged.

James flew through the air as he watched the ship break under him and sink into the Sea. He had dampened all of his senses except for sight, and even his vision was blurry as he sailed through the air. In fact, he was pretty sure that he had gone unconscious while he sailed through the air, only to be reawakened as he started to descend back to the Ocean.

The Ocean surface rushing closer to meet him was the only indication that he was falling back towards the water. He tried reaching out towards the water to slow his fall, but he couldn't push himself any harder. Panic started to well up in him and James started frantically searching for a way to save himself.

The water was filled with wreckage as James plummeted towards the surface. James reached out to the Ocean one last time in an attempt to slow his fall but once again nothing happened. He was just about to accept his fate when he suddenly slowed down right before he hit the water.

James hit the water, but he couldn't feel anything. It was pure survival instinct that forced him to search for the surface again and swim to the top. He felt more disoriented than he ever had before in his life, but he was able to make out the sun rising and swim towards the surface.

It wasn't until he finally reached the surface that he realized how he survived the fall. Dismus was sitting on top of the Ocean calmly waiting for James to appear. He knew that he hadn't managed to use the Ocean to slow himself down, it was Dismus that must have used the air.

Now that James was surrounded with the Ocean, he was starting to get feeling back in his body and his senses came back if only to a small degree.

"We can talk about what you were doing back there later. Right now let's just get you back to the ship." Dismus didn't look the least bit concerned. James knew that he should be grateful to him for saving his life, but he couldn't help but feel neglected.

"Aren't you going to ask me if I'm okay?" James couldn't stop the indignation from rising in his voice. He had, after all, just destroyed an entire ship and plummeted to the Ocean from hundreds of feet.

"You're in the Ocean." It was his only response before turning towards their own ship and making his way back. It was a shock to hear it so bluntly, but oddly enough it made sense to James. If he really was connected with a Seraphim of the Ocean, then he would feel at home here. But what if he wasn't in the Ocean? Would he have died from all of his wounds or the exhaustion?

Suddenly wishing he hadn't thought about it, James dove under the Ocean and followed Dismus back to the ship. Dismus created a stream of wind to push the both of them towards their ship with James in the lead.

They did not have very far to go before they reached the ship. Dismus lifted the both of them back onto the ship with seemingly little effort.

James landed hard on the deck and collapsed immediately. Ari was sitting sprawled out on the deck with Hector and Gregor and all three jumped to their feet as soon as they landed.

Any energy that James possessed had been completely depleted as he laid on the deck face up and staring at the slowly clearing sky. Even in the Ocean he had pushed himself a little too hard. He could tell that he would need a very long rest to recover fully from the night's activities.

Hector picked James up by the arms and slung him over his shoulder. Gregor picked up Dis with some difficulty and half carried him behind Hector. James moved his lips in an attempt to thank them, but nothing came out. They went about their duties without question, which is good because James wasn't sure that he had any answers for them.

"What happened to you two?" Arianna looked panicked and it showed in her voice.

"That is a good question." James managed to say before he passed out over Hector's shoulder. "A good question."

Arianna

— —~*~— —

Ari shoved her way into James' room for the third time that day. Hector had tried to keep her out every time, but this time she wouldn't take no for an answer. And when push came to shove, Gregor let her through easily enough. Unfortunately for him, it really had come to shoving this time.

James laid in his bed just as still as he had been hours earlier. Hector had dropped him in his bed the night before and he had been asleep ever since. Ari hadn't left his side for quite some time the night before until Gregor eventually kicked her out.

Ari walked to his bedside and replaced the water by his bed. Every time she came to check on him, she convinced herself that he will have woken up already. And every time so far she had been wrong, but one of these times he would be awake to appreciate the fresh water.

Ari blushed at her own silliness. He wouldn't care about some small glass of water, but it was the best that she could do. Smoothing out her skirt, she sat down on the ground by his bed and resigned herself to a waiting game.

It was an hour later when she stood up and moved further away from his bed. She didn't want to come off as creepy though it might have already been too late for that. Ari sat back down against his wall and continued waiting for James to wake.

Ari shifted positions many times throughout the next few hours and was almost relieved when Gregor came in the room with James' food.

"I'm impressed, Princess." She was startled to be addressed. Partly because she had just gone so long in silence, but mostly because Gregor was a man of so few words.

"Call me Ari, I'm not a Princess anymore." Ari stood up and took the food from Gregor. She would be the one to give him the food, not some guard he hardly knew. She knew that wasn't completely fair or accurate, but she quieted those thoughts fairly easily.

"Yes, Ari, forgive me. I was saying that I'm impressed with your dedication. Most women would not stay so long for a boy." His voice was full of unspoken implications. Ari's cheeks burned at the comment, but she refused to acknowledge them.

She was still looking for a response when Gregor spoke again. "I only mention it to say that it might be time for you to go back to your own room. I will get you when he wakes, I promise." The man had a point, and Ari wasn't sure that she could come up with a way to avoid looking creepy when James finally woke up.

"I will wait a little longer, thank you." As if to emphasize her point, Ari walked over to James and set the food down next to the glass of water.

"I am merely looking out for you, Princess." Ari raised her eyebrow at his comment.

"Ari. I am merely looking out for you, Ari," he amended. "When you are ready, your food is in your room waiting for you." Gregor turned on his heels and marched back out of the room, leaving Ari alone once more with James.

Ari's stomach growled at her as soon as he left. The man had made another good point really. She wasn't sure how to argue with her stomach. She finally made up her mind a few minutes after Gregor left. She really hoped he wasn't out in the hall to gloat when she finally left.

"I will come back for you," Ari whispered to James before she stood to leave.

"That is the sweetest thing anyone has ever said to me." James opened his eyes with her face right next to his. Ari swung at his face immediately and was rewarded with a groan from the now-awake patient.

The first swing was a reflex, but Ari barely resisted the urge to slap him in the face a second time as he looked up at her with that ridiculously large smile on his face.

"I mean it, that was the sweetest thing anyone has ever said to me. I should almost die more often." He had the decency to wipe the smile off of his face, but his eyes were still twinkling with mischief. She hated him, but then she really, really, didn't.

"How long were you awake?" How could she have not noticed? How much did he hear? Did she seem creepy?

"I woke up when Gregor came in, but I didn't feel like listening to him talk my ear off." There was the twinkle in his eyes again and a wry smile that said he was joking.

"Well, then I guess it's time for me to leave." Ari tried rushing towards the door without being obvious, but she couldn't help but try to escape as fast as possible. "Ari, wait," James called out to her before she reached the door.

"Thank you for taking care of me. You are a good friend." Great, a friend, why just a friend? Ari quickly shut herself up to hear the rest of what he was saying.

"I've never had a friend before, but I hope that I can be one to you." His words hit her hard. The truth was that she never really had a friend either. Everyone who spent time with her when she was growing up only did so because she was the Princess. In fact, the only real friend she had ever had was Dismus. And she wasn't sure that he had ever cared about her in the first place.

"I feel the same way." Except for the friend part, but she wasn't about to say that. She immediately shut the door behind her and made her way to her room. She was really looking forward to her food.

Part 3

James

— —~*~— —

James was scrubbing the deck while Dis stood watching over him. A few days had passed since they had sunk the royal vessel and the rest of the crew on the ship had been steering clear of their group even more than usual. Dis claimed that James cleaning the ship around the crew might settle them down a little bit. James wasn't too sure about that, but he was oddly okay with that type of work nowadays.

It didn't take much to figure out that the crew had connected the sunken ship from a few nights ago with the mysterious group that they were giving passage to. James would have thought that they would be grateful, but if anything, they seemed even more afraid of them than before.

Dis had refused to clean the deck himself. He claimed to have had plenty enough experience in that area to last him the rest of his lifetime.

"So," James started after a considerably long time of awkward silence, "that ship that I sunk; any explanation as to why it had a royal seal on it?"

Dis' face never changed, but he shuffled his feet and looked away from James for a few moments. 'Finally,' James thought, 'I'm finally going to get some answers.'

"I didn't plan on telling the Princess for some time, but the people behind the assassinations are now in control of Valladar." Dismus frowned for a moment but apparently decided to continue.

"And I hadn't planned on telling you, but the person behind the assassinations is Manthar."

James stopped scrubbing the deck then and looked Dismus in the eyes as he tried to process what he had just heard.

"How do you know this, Dismus?" James was shooting daggers at Dismus with his eyes, but Dismus seemed unconcerned.

"And don't give me any of that vague nonsense," James insisted, "tell me the truth."

Dismus nodded as if making up his mind and answered once more. "I used to work for him, but now I don't and I will do everything in my power to make sure that he is stopped. That is how I knew to save Ari, and that is how I know where your sister is."

James doubled over with his hands on his knees at the shock of the news as if the betrayal had sucker punched James in the stomach. James told himself that he had expected to be betrayed; that he had never trusted Dismus in the first place, but the truth was that he had. Against his own judgment, he had trusted this man.

But now he realized that he would never be able to trust him. Not because he was a Noble, but because he had lied to James and he had lied to Ari. Somehow, that was the greater sin.

"Fine," he stated finally as Dismus awaited his response, "let's say that I believe you. What now?"

Dismus had the grace to look apologetic, but it did nothing but make James trust him even less.

"We do what we planned to do. We sneak into his castle and we save your sister. There was always a possibility of Manthar finding out about our intentions." James found himself looking away from Dis periodically as he talked. This was too hard to take.

"Besides, they have no idea why we are heading towards Pyiasior. He will assume that we are going to try and kill him, and he won't be afraid of that." His answer was so matter-of-fact that it surprised James.

"Why don't we attack him? We could take him together, I know it. I mean, we just took out an entire ship together. What's one man?"

Dis' reaction was furious. "He is more than just one man." He emphasized the word man and left it hanging in the air. "He is an unstoppable force and cunning beyond any other. There is no defeating him, not now." Dis himself even shook at the description.

"Then we can't let Marie make it to him." James' voice was shaking, but he was never more certain about anything in his life. "We have to save her now. Right now before she gets there, that's her only chance." James threw the broom down on the deck and made off to jump into the water immediately, but Dis grabbed his arm before he could get anywhere.

"She's probably already there by now, James. There is nothing for it but to proceed with the plan." James scrunched his face and nearly spit on Dismus. "You don't care about her. You never did. I will save her myself."

James tried to shake out of Dis' grasp, but Dis was ready for it and was holding on too tightly.

"Even if she wasn't there already, they are too far away for you to make it there before they dock. No, we must wait."

"I'm tired of waiting." James succeeded in shaking free this time. "I can make it there, I am sure of it. Either way, I'm going and you can't stop me." As soon as the words were out of his mouth, James knew that he had said the wrong thing.

Dismus had apparently taken the statement as a challenge and immediately put James into a headlock. "I can't let you go, you will die." James might have replied, but his windpipe was being crushed at the moment. James flailed around, but he couldn't escape the hold. Dis was much too strong for him.

James tried tapping out, but Dismus either didn't know the signal or he didn't trust him. Rightly so because James was planning on bolting off the ship as soon as he could get free. James was starting to lose consciousness when he finally retaliated in the only way he knew how.

James summoned a huge wave of water over the side of the ship and all of the crew members started screaming and running from their posts. James wondered vaguely if they would connect them to this as well.

The wave hit both James and Dis and the two of them went flying across the deck. James had finally gotten free of the grip, but he had only made it two feet before he was bound once more. James dropped face first onto the deck and was stuck there. He could feel the strands of air wrapped around him like invisible chains.

James wasn't done yet though. Careful not to capsize the ship, James summoned several thin streams of water from the puddles around him and used them like six giant arms. Dis re-directed them as best as he could, but the arms kept on reforming and swinging at Dis. James was winning, in spite of the fact that he was tied down on the deck of a ship by air.

The water streams were swinging two at a time from every direction. One hit Dis in the side and sent him sprawling, but he jumped up and kept on fighting back. One after another kept throwing him around the deck. The entire ship was completely clear of crew members at this point, which is good because this would have definitely given them away.

James didn't see a way for this to end well for either of them, but he had to try. He continued to attack with water as he shouted at Dismus. "Unbind me and let me go! I will never give in until I can leave to find my sister!"

James hadn't expected it to work, but right after he shouted he was released from the tendrils of air and hit his head on the ship. As soon as James was released, he sent the water overboard and let it drop into the Ocean. Both men got to their feet and wiped off their clothes as if nothing out of the usual had just occurred.

"You haven't finished your training. You will die before you ever make it to her if you leave this way." Dis was the optimist as ever, but James wouldn't be able to live with himself if he had the chance to save his sister and didn't take it. He had to try, no matter how small the chance.

"I will take that chance." James walked past Dismus and half-expected him to stop him, but Dis didn't move. James walked to the rail and looked out over the Ocean. This was it, there would be no stopping until he caught up to Marie's ship.

"Go North, that's the way to Pyiasior." Dis walked up next to James and was looking out towards the sun that was beginning to set far away.

"I know." It must have sounded like bravado to Dis, but he just nodded as if he had expected as much and James took that as his cue. James took a deep breath and hopped overboard and into the Ocean. The water was cold, but it was life. He had a long way to go to save his sister, but he was on his way.

"I'm coming, Marigold." And James shot northward over the violent Ocean waves.

Dismus

— —~*~— —

Dismus knocked on Ari's door for the first time in days. Even now he was nervous about disturbing her. He knew that he was the last person she wanted to see. Ari answered the door and immediately put on a frown when she saw him.

"What do you want?" She sounded hostile, but she wasn't yelling yet, that was something. However, she looked like she didn't have long before she would erupt again.

"James is gone." He fumbled for the right words, but he couldn't think of any other way to say it. In retrospect, he could have tried harder.

"What?!" Ari looked as if she was about to attack him. Dis quickly tried to explain before she actually did it. Her eyes were already fiery.

"He went ahead of the ship to try and save his sister before she makes it to Pyiasior." Ari didn't look any less mad, but Dis hoped that some of the anger was now directed at James instead. It was a selfish thought, but he couldn't help it.

"Why couldn't he just wait to do it together?" The question didn't look like it was directed at Dis. Ari fumed at the wall to her room as if it were James standing there.

"He's trying to get there before Manthar gets to her, but he will not make it in time." It was a fact and a painful one for Dis, but he couldn't change anything now.

"You shouldn't have let him!" Of course, everything was his fault. "You should have stopped him!" Ari looked like she was on the verge of throwing a huge tantrum like she had so many times in the past year. He knew that things became just too much for her sometimes, but he was not used to being on the receiving end of one of her tantrums.

"I tried, but he forced me to let him go. It was his choice." There was no forgiveness in her eyes, but there was understanding. She knew what it meant to be determined.

"Then we go and save him." Ari looked more determined than angry at this point, but to Dis, that seemed worse.

"I will go and save him, but I cannot risk your life as well. Stay here, where it is safe." Before she could respond, Dismus wrapped a strand of air around her mouth to muffle her speech. The air wouldn't completely muffle her voice, but it would make it a lot more difficult to yell.

Ari looked murderous. He knew that she would understand eventually, but right now she probably would have killed him if she could. Dis felt horrible for using his power on her, but he couldn't think of any other way to make sure that she stayed.

"I'm sorry." Dis began to walk out of her room, but he made the mistake of looking back. He knew that he couldn't look at her and keep his composure, but he did it anyway. Ari looked furious but more than that, she looked scared.

Dismus couldn't help but stop and turn towards her once more. "What would you have me do?" Dismus dismissed the strand of air that had muffled her voice, but he was ready to put it right back on if she tried anything.

"Bring me with you!" The words were out of her mouth before he finished asking. "You are not going to leave me behind. Not this time."

The words hit him hard. He had fully realized what it might mean to leave her behind with Hector and Gregor here. There was a good chance they would risk harming her while he wasn't around. And the truth was that he had no real intention of returning at all.

Suddenly, a whole new plan formed in his mind. The boy was right though he truly didn't know what he was talking about. King Manthar surely knew what Dismus was up to by now. There would be no use in hiding from him at this point.

Really, he should have just turned around and given up on the entire thing, but that just wasn't an option any longer. Dismus had been speaking the truth when he said that they didn't stand a chance against Manthar, at least not without further training on James' end. And now there would be virtually no chance of sneaking in, not unless they got there way before they were scheduled.

"Okay." The word was out of his mouth before he had time to reconsider, but then they didn't have time for that anyway. Ari looked shocked, but she kept her mouth closed, most likely to make sure she didn't say anything to change his mind.

"We will go together, but you have to follow my instructions without question." Dismus looked at her and waited for a response. Ari looked back at him for a second before she finally nodded her head.

"Good, now as soon as I open this door, you need to fly out of the room as fast as possible without looking back."

Ari looked confused, but a stern look had her nodding in agreement once again. Without a second word, Ari transformed in front of him into a sparrow. She was a giant sparrow, but a sparrow nonetheless.

"Fly your way out of the ship and wait for me over the Ocean next to the ship." Ari gave another nod of her beak and flew to the front of the door in wait.

More than a year's time and Dismus was finally going to take down the rest of his crew. He had been held back by fear for so long that he welcomed the rush of adrenaline that began to surge through him as he anticipated the fight.

"I'm coming for you, Grace." And ready for chaos, he opened the door.

Arianna

— —~*~— —

The door flew open and Ari immediately flew through the doorway as a giant sparrow. She barely fit her wings through the opening, but she was out and flying down the hall within seconds. Both Hector and Gregor were standing right outside of her door as she flew past them and she had never seen them more shocked in her life.

Still, Hector moved faster than she thought possible. Two pairs of hands reached for her, but Ari changed form again and again faster than she ever had before. She went from a sparrow to an eel, to a crow, to herself, and back again.

Ari moved on instinct alone as she tried to process why they would be attacking her. It didn't make sense, but she focused on only one thing, and that was escaping. Her transformations should have been enough to shake off anyone, but everything felt like it was moving in slow motion.

Hector succeeded in grabbing hold of her multiple times while Gregor tried calming her down, but Ari was able to ignore Gregor and escape their hold every time.

She moved further down the hall than she thought she would, but she didn't know if she would be able to make it all the way out.

The bird forms were useful to move down the hall, but she couldn't truly escape them. She had only made it this far because of her ability to shock them in her eel form whenever they actually got a hold of her.

Had she a fair playing field, she might have escaped, but they were too fast. No matter how elusive she proved herself to be, Gregor was able to finally hold her with the help of Hector.

The entire thing took place in a matter of seconds and left Ari staring upwards at the two men who suddenly seemed much more vicious than before. Weren't they the good guys? Seconds later, she got her answer.

Dismus, seeming to move very slowly as well, grabbed Hector by his shirt and threw him backward away from Gregor and Ari. As soon as Hector flew across the hall, Dismus seemed to speed up tremendously.

Gregor turned to face Dismus as soon as he realized that Hector wasn't holding onto him anymore and in doing so let go of Ari. Not stopping to watch the fight, Ari immediately turned back into a sparrow and sped down the hallway before anyone had a chance to remember her.

Finally making her way to the trap door, she turned back into her usual self and climbed out the hole as fast as possible.

Ari walked by several crew members, but every single one avoided eye contact. She wasn't used to being ignored and it kind of ruffled her, but she tried not to show it. The Captain at least made eye contact with her, but he didn't say a word.

He nodded back in response to her, but then immediately went back to steering the ship. He wouldn't spare another glance for her, she was willing to bet on it. Ari looked over the railing on the side of the ship and then turned her gaze forward. 'Here goes nothing,' she thought.

With a deep breath, Ari dropped over the side of the ship and would have sworn that she saw some heads turnover amongst the crew on the other side. It didn't matter, though. As soon as she dropped, she changed into a skinny seal and dove into the deep Ocean.

She would wait a while before changing into a bird and flying the rest of the way. She didn't want to draw too much attention to herself by changing into a bird in midair.

There was more of a chance they would notice something like that.

————~*~——

Dismus struggled to draw air to him from around the hallway, but there was precious air here to begin with. Hector now faced him on one end of the hallway while Gregor regained his footing behind him. Truthfully, he was fairly confident that he could take care of one or the other individually with little trouble. But both at the same time was bad news, that was usually why Manthar sent them in teams like this.

With a practiced precision, both of the men moved in to attack. Uncoordinated, it might be possible to win an outmatched fight, but not when they were allowed to work together. Dismus needed to split them up somehow.

Both moved with incredible speed that outmatched even Dismus. That surprised most adversaries, but not Dismus. Hector was a Warper; he could slow down and speed up the things around him. In most cases, that meant slowing down his enemies to embarrassing speeds.

Hector moved in for a jab right at Dis' face just as Gregor threw his entire body at him. Instinctively, Dismus wove air around him to deflect both moves, but it didn't quite work against the body slam.

If he had been able to move at a normal speed, he would have easily evaded such a blunt attack, but not now that he was moving at the speed of a tortoise. The air absorbed most of the impact of the hit, but his body still jolted as he slammed against the floor.

Hector took the opportunity to jump behind Gregor and place a hand on the monstrous man. Dismus groaned involuntarily. He knew what they were doing and it would make it almost impossible to beat them.

Hector was linking up with Gregor and protecting him from the time manipulation around them. Now they would both be moving unhindered while Dismus moved as if underwater.

Gregor was a Brute, which meant that he had enhanced strength and speed. Gregor already had incredible reflexes and amazing strength without his power; adding a severely unfair speed advantage was going to make him nearly unstoppable.

Acting on instinct, Dismus lunged from the ground and grabbed ahold of Hector's leg. Neither man knew what he was doing or they would have tried harder to stop him.

Immediately Dismus felt the effects, or rather the lack of effect on his motions. Before Hector could do anything to stop him, Dismus shot a gust of air and threw them all away from each other. Dismus caught himself in the gust, but it was worth it. He had to keep the other two separated.

All three of the men were on their feet now, but they were on opposite sides of him again. Before they could move in a coordinated attack again, Dismus rushed Hector.

Time slowed considerably as he reached him, but it was not enough to matter; the wind was immune to Hector's Warping. Hector moved in and swung at Dismus in the time that it took for Dismus to get his hand in a fist.

Hector's hit landed square on his face and the pain flared in Dis' head, but the swing had also left Hector open to a full attack with wind. Just as Dismus was feeling the effects of the hit, air hit Hector in the face with the force of a boulder.

The strain of the attack had left Dismus with only his sight intact, but it was all he needed to take care of Gregor by himself. Knocking Hector out had negated the time manipulation and allowed Gregor to rush Dismus all over again.

It turns out Gregor had been trying to run at Dismus that whole time but was stuck in the same time warp as Dismus.

Quickly turning to face Gregor, Dismus again found himself being hit with the big body of someone who could punch through walls. Dismus hit the ground hard though he didn't feel the effects and threw himself backward to roll into a standing position.

They were at even odds this time. Dismus just had to finish this before Hector woke up if Hector woke up at all. Gregor gave up on the body slamming finally and began a flurry of punches instead.

Dismus deflected each blow with careful placement of air flows, but he was quickly losing his sight. He didn't have much time left before he would pass out.

Gregor released a relentless torrent of punches and kicks that would have ended anyone else immediately, but Dismus was not just anyone. Dismus looked for an opportunity as he carefully deflected the attack and found it when Gregor overextended himself in a right hook.

As soon as Gregor swung, Dismus used what air he could to pull him off balance at the full extension of the punch and then landed an uppercut on his jaw.

The punch was not enough to take Gregor out, but it was enough to stun him and let Dismus use what power he had left to bind him where he stood with air.

Swaying on the spot, Dismus sat down in the hallway and bound both of the men around their arms, legs, and mouths. Remaining on the floor, Dismus threw both men into Ari's room and closed the door behind them with the air strands that still existed in the hall.

Dismus had been forced to overextend his power to the oxygen in the hall and was now having a hard time breathing, let alone standing, in the hall.

Slowly, Dismus supported himself against the wall and made his way to the deck where there was fresh air. Finally making it to the deck, Dismus laid on the steel floor for several minutes while he allowed himself to recover with the wind.

When he finally felt up to it, Dis made his way through the ship and walked right up to the Captain of the ship, who for the moment, stood at the helm.

"Captain." Dis had learned over the past few years that it was important to honor the title of a Captain on his own ship.

"Yes, Captain." The Captain of the ship had become as distant and aloof as the rest of the crew in regards to Dis' group. 'He was right to do so,' Dis thought.

"If I am not to be found in the next few days, just stay the course. I will pay generously at our arrival for the trouble we might have caused." Dis needed to be sure that the Captain did not make any rash decisions while he was away.

"Are ya anticpatin' more trouble then?" The older man looked to be close to shaking at the thought of more trouble. Dis understood; this ship was the Captain's livelihood.

"None at all, just a precaution. Oh, and there are two men passed out in a room below deck. You might want to be rid of them quickly."

The Captain looked wary at the news but seemed to accept it fatalistically.

Both men exchanged nods as a formal end to their agreement and Dis proceeded to lower himself into the Ocean on a small paddle boat. The boat was tiny, but it was plenty sturdy with a thick steel frame and a light structure. It was perfect for what he had planned.

Dis rowed away from the giant ship at a painstakingly slow pace. He had never rowed a boat in his life and the result was an awkward pace. He saw several men on the crew watching him from a distance. They likely thought him insane. He was heading in the same direction as the ship, but at a much slower pace.

Eventually, much later than he had hoped, the men stopped watching him and went back to their duties. Dis took his opportunity to search the skies for a giant bird.

He nearly jumped out of the boat in fright when a seal plopped itself on board.

Changing back into herself, Ari looked at Dismus with concern. "I'm fine, Princess." He would be anyways, with time. Ari shot him a look that seemed to say not to lie to her.

"You just might need to take over the steering for a while." Ari nodded in a satisfied manner and turned towards the front of the boat. Before Dismus could object, Ari had turned into a small seal and was pulling the boat forward.

As odd as it seemed, Dismus did not object to the opportunity to rest. They needed to travel fast, but they should be able to make pretty good time with Ari leading the way for the first part.

Ari pulled for a while, but Dismus took over before too long. Ari got in the boat and immediately went to sleep as Dismus summoned a strong gust of wind to push them along.

The boat shot forward like a rocket and kept that pace until the ship was well out of view behind him. He would catch up to James in time or he would die trying.

James

— —~*~— —

James flew across the waves at an incredible speed, but he was not going to be able to keep it up much longer. James could feel the power sucking at his life like a leech attached to his heart. It had taken him nearly two days to feel the effects that the power was having on his body.

James concentrated on his task, but nothing could distract him from what was happening to his body. He could feel the power streaming in and out of his body like some sort of receptacle on the verge of shattering.

It was only an instinct, but he knew that he would not live much longer at this pace. He had been so sure that he would be able to make it in time. He was going to save his sister. He had to save her, it was his responsibility and he had failed again and again to do it. And soon it would be too late for another chance.

James' feet began to drag along the waves instead of over them. He was slowing down against his will, and he couldn't do anything about it. He was still moving at a breakneck speed, but he was gradually declining.

The sun was beginning to set on his second day traveling at this speed and James knew that he would not be able to make it through the night. Either he stopped here and gave up, or he might die tonight. He chose to keep going. If that was what it took to reach her in time, then it was worth it to him.

James knew that it wasn't rational, but he didn't care. With another wave of power, James forced himself to increase his speed for the hundredth time that day. His sister was somewhere ahead. 'Almost there.'

James relied on the Ocean spray to keep him awake, but he felt himself drifting off over and over again, only to snap himself back to attention.

Every time he snapped back, he would increase his speed once more, but even then he was only going half as quickly as he had in the beginning.

Even as he closed his eyes, he refused to admit defeat. He was nothing without his sister. Still, the Ocean called to him one too many times that day.

Somewhere in the drifting thoughts of his mind, he thought about the fact that he might have tried to bring Ari with him. He knew that it would have probably only slowed him down, but he hated the fact that he had left her with Dismus.

Sure, Dismus had just fought an entire ship full of men to protect her, but James reminded himself over and over again that Dismus couldn't be trusted.

Eventually, James drifted into the waves and didn't wake himself up. He was screaming at himself in his mind to keep going, but his body betrayed him. Still fighting it, James drifted into the deepest sleep he had ever known.

James later remembered his dream. He was still chasing after Marie, but she was always just too far away for him to catch. He could see her standing on the deck of the ship on the horizon, alone and crying because he had failed to save her.

Marigold

Two years earlier

— —~*~— —

Marigold was lying on her side on the floor of their mud-hut, fully expecting to die at any time when she felt James kneel at her side. She was facing the back of their hut to avoid filling their doorway with vomit. Luckily, she was in between fits at the moment. She hated when James had to see her sick.

Marigold was careful not to make any sudden movements as she turned herself over to see James. Any little thing could set off a fit for hours if she wasn't careful. How long could she keep living like this? Surely not much longer.

James met her eyes with so much hope when she turned over. It almost broke her heart all over again. He seemed to think that she would pull through this, but she knew better. Thousands of people were sick with the exact same thing in Valladar alone. Not a single one had survived very long.

"Where were you?" She immediately went into a coughing fit once the words were out, but it settled down after a minute or so. Both of them let out a sigh of relief when they saw that she wasn't going to go into another fit.

"I was out... doing important things. You know, like important people do." James had a glint in his eyes that said that he was up to something, but Marigold could not say what that possibly could have been.

"Did someone finally hire you?" Instinctively, Marie had tried to sit up in her excitement, but she had to immediately lie back down again. She supposed she would just have to be excited from the floor.

"Better," James let out his own excitement then, "I have found medicine for you, Marie!" James thrust out his hand then, containing a liquid vial full of a slimy looking substance.

"It's the stuff that rich people use to cure the sickness. Go on, take it!" James was pushing the vile on her hastily to the point that Marie nearly dropped it in the process. She was too weak as it was to be holding fragile containers.

"Where did you get this? You did not just find this! It's worth more than we could make in a lifetime. You tell me right now, James." She had put as much force behind her words as possible, but James looked unabashed.

"I am your older brother. I will do whatever it takes to take care of you. Whatever it takes, Marie." James looked so determined then, she almost gave in.

"I will not have you risking your life for me, James. I don't have a chance." James looked away from her then, obviously in pain.

"Look at me, James." He did, but only after a moment and even then, reluctantly. "I am dead already. This medicine will only work for so long. You will not die for a dead woman, James. Promise me you won't."

"I will find more." Tears were rolling down James' face freely now. "I will find more, and when those are gone, I will find more. And I will keep finding more until we're both dead. Do you hear me, Marigold?" Tears were running down her face as well.

"One day," she forced the words out between hiccups. Hiccups always preceded sobbing for her. "One day, you're going to have to leave me behind." She made herself look him straight in the eyes. What she said was true, she could feel the validity of them as she heard them aloud.

"I will never leave you." James took her in his arms then and held her as they both sobbed. "I will never stop fighting for you." The words came out as a whisper in her ear in between sobs.

"With my life," James said the words over and over again until she finally believed them to be true. "With my life, Marie. With my life." And every time she prayed over and over again that he would not have to.

Marigold

— —~*~— —

Marie had lost count of the days a long time ago. There was no way to keep track of the days when you couldn't see the sky. It felt like years ago that she had been taken from her home. Yet it was her most recent memory.

She had seen nothing since that night except for the inside of her cage. The constant darkness would have driven her insane if her sickness had not already done it. The longer she waited in her cage, the sicker she became.

There was no cure for her illness, there was only delaying it. As far as most people were concerned, if she was sick then she deserved to be sick. The Nobles, of course, seemed to be an exception to that rule. Either way, there was no medicine here, there was no more delaying the inevitable. She would die sooner or later, and having gone for so long without her medicine, it looked like it would be sooner for her.

Marigold currently laid against the back wall of her cell, doubled over with wracking coughs. Blood sprayed out of her mouth violently. She had long since stopped trying to cover up the blood. It had started happening once every other day or so, but her fits had become much more frequent as of late.

She was in excruciating pain, but all she cared about was whether or not James was okay. For all she knew, he had died that night. She almost hoped that was the case. She wouldn't be able to stand the thought of him searching fruitlessly for her in Valladar.

That was the only thing that she had been able to gather; she was on a ship of some kind. And if she was on a ship heading away from Valladar, there was no chance that he would find her. He would drive himself crazy searching for her and there was nothing that he could do about it. No, it was better that he just join their parents after death.

Marie wiped the blood from her lips and closed her eyes though it made no difference to what she could see, and began to sing. It was the only thing that had kept her sane all this time and the only thing that she could remember from her mother.

Their mother had always sung them to sleep with the sweetest lullaby. Marie had used it to put herself to sleep after every third meal they brought her. She had claimed it as nighttime for her purposes.

"Sleep sweet baby and rest in peace, your mother is with you and on her knees. Praying that you may know her love, and see the Angels watching from above." A tear dropped down her cheek. There were other verses that her mother sang, but she never could remember them.

As soon as the song ended, the door to her room opened and let in the first light in a long time. This was the first time that her captors had used a light behind the person so that she could see them enter. That was her first clue that something was different now.

"We have arrived." They were the first words that she had heard in a very long time, and for some reason that she didn't understand, she felt herself stiffen from dread.

Now that she had been told, she could tell that the ship had stopped moving. After so long on the ship, she had gotten used to the rocking motion.

Steeling herself, Marie stood up and waited to be shackled and moved. She would fight for her freedom when the opportunity presented itself but now was not that time. For now, she would play nice.

As she expected, she was immediately blindfolded when her cell was opened. It was probably only precautionary, but Marie found herself grateful for the continued darkness. She might have been blinded badly had she been exposed to sunlight so soon after weeks of darkness.

She stood as still as possible while her ankles and wrists were shackled to each other. She didn't need to give them a reason to treat her roughly.

Eventually, she was led on the long and arduous trek to her next holding place. Despite herself, she couldn't help but still hope to be freed by James. As illogical as it was, and as selfish as it felt, deep down she expected him to save her. She carried that hope all the way to her next prison.

Dismus

——~*~——

It was all Dismus could do to keep himself from passing out from exhaustion. It had been almost two days traveling on the boat since they left, and he had almost collapsed ten different times already. He had only pushed himself this hard once before and this time he knew how dangerous it could be.

Ari had taken over a couple of times, but Dis had refused the last several times that she had offered. They were getting close now; if they didn't find James soon, they wouldn't find him at all.

Ari had finally stopped asking to take over, but she had refused to get any rest herself, the fool girl. She was sitting in front of Dis and watching the waves for any sign of James. If Dis hadn't known any better, he would have thought that she actually cared for the boy.

He had to shake himself several times, but he couldn't help but expect to see James floating on the waves. There was no way that he could have made it this far and stayed conscious. Power like theirs would eventually destroy them from the inside out if they weren't careful and Dis had no delusions about how careful James would be.

Dis himself had completely dampened his senses with the exception of sight and hearing. He would have gotten rid of hearing as well if it were not for Ari joining him.

Now and then he would pull back on his speed a little bit and increase his sense of touch to keep him awake. Every time he did so, exhaustion threatened to overtake him. But at the same time it kept him aware, and he needed to stay aware if he hoped to find James in time.

Still hoping for the best, Dis continued to scan the Ocean as he skimmed the waves on his boat. He might have been able to go faster by himself, but he was just as sure to collapse as James was by the time they would have caught up. No, he would just have to hope that he had moved fast enough to save him.

The sun was almost completely set when Ari snapped Dismus back to attention by speaking.

"Will you repeat that? I didn't hear you the first time." Dis hadn't noticed his sense of hearing dampening, but he had reached dangerous levels of deafness without him realizing.

Ari looked back at him in annoyance but immediately turned her attention back to the waters as if afraid she had missed something.

"I asked if you thought that we might have missed him." There was an obvious worry in her voice though she was trying to hide it from him. She really did care for the boy.

If Dis wasn't already feeling guilty about his plan, then he definitely was now. James was supposed to be a stranger. He was supposed to play his part for Dismus and then fend for himself, but Dis knew what that really meant.

James had a death sentence on him, and Dis was trying to use that to his advantage. The plan had been a lot easier when they were strangers.

"No." Dismus shoved down his own fears on the matter. "I would have known had we been close." Had the boy gone in the wrong direction, though… Dismus chose not to voice that particular possibility.

Ari nodded her head without looking back at him, probably afraid to look away for another second. Dismus understood all too well though the truth of the matter was that they would have plenty of chances to spot him from afar when they came upon him. The problem was that they might never get that close.

When Dismus was sure that Ari wasn't going to say anything else, he dampened his hearing even further and picked up speed once more.

Ari must have noticed as she nodded her head in what seemed like approval. She wouldn't know how hard he was pushing himself, but she must be able to feel his tension.

It was not long after that Dis noticed a glowing in the distance. His sight was at full capacity to the point that he saw the glowing well before the Princess, but he was so exhausted that it took him nearly a full minute to register what the glowing meant.

Hope welled up in Dismus almost as quickly as shame. They had arrived in time, only to send him to his death on Dis' terms. There had to be another way.

Dismus took the opportunity to dampen his sight enough to speed up the boat again. James was alive, but he couldn't have much time left.

Vaguely, he realized that Ari was standing up in the boat now that they had come close enough to see. James was wrapped in a cocoon of energy and floating in the Ocean unconscious.

The ball of energy disappeared when the boat pierced the wall. His Angel had preserved him just long enough, Dismus thought. But now what?

James

— —~*~— —

James opened his eyes to see two familiar faces hovering over him. Ari was as stunning as ever and Dis was just as serious looking as always. At first, their faces were the only thing that his mind could comprehend. It wasn't until he tried sitting up that he remembered what happened to him and flopped back down on the boat in unbearable agony.

"I failed her. I failed. I couldn't make it in time, Marie. Forgive me. Forgive me." James closed his eyes and kept muttering the same thing over and over again. "I'm sorry. I'm sorry. I'm sorry."

"Snap out of it!" James was shocked into silence and opened his eyes to see a very serious Ari staring down at him. "She's not dead yet, James. Unlike my family, she still has a chance. So snap out of it and save her." Tears were running down Ari's cheeks, but she kept a look of pure determination on her face in a challenge.

She was right. Dang it, she was right. James wiped his own tears away and tried to sit up, but he couldn't. All he could do was slightly lift his head to look at the two of them. "You're right, Ari, I'm sorry."

Ari wiped away her tears and replied. "And stop saying you're sorry. You're not sorry, you're strong. So just be strong for us, okay?" She was starting to let go of her forced determination. For the first time in a while, she had been vulnerable with the two of them.

"I will, I promise." James tried smiling, but even that was a struggle. "How did you find me?" He tried to sit up again but finally gave up, he would just have to settle for lying still for a while.

"You were lying face first on the Ocean surface in a giant bubble," Dismus sat next to Ari with a concerned look on his face. "It was pretty noticeable. Your Angel was able to preserve you for who knows how long. The same would have been impossible had you not been in the Ocean. You were lucky, boy." If James hadn't known better, he might have thought that Dismus actually cared about him.

"I thought I could do it." James was beginning to feel ashamed all over again, but a hard look from Ari had him perking right up. "Why wasn't I able to keep going? The Ocean is like the largest source of power possible for me, isn't it?"

Dismus looked to be choosing his words carefully. "Yes, the Ocean is basically a pure source of power for you." The pause after his statement was ominous. "But, you as a human can only handle so much before the power will destroy you." All three of them shifted uncomfortably.

"If you hadn't passed out when you did, you most assuredly would have been ripped apart." James was embarrassed to look either of them in the eyes. "So," Dis continued, "don't do that again."

James made eye contact with Ari and neither of them looked away for some time. It was then that James realized something. He had to do everything he could do to stay alive.

He hadn't exactly decided to die anytime soon, but James had always thought that the only reason for living was to take care of Marie. Maybe that used to be the case, but it wasn't anymore. Ari was his friend, it was clear that she at least cared. If for no other reason, he needed to stay alive for her.

It wasn't until Ari looked away that James realized that he had been staring for way too long. Dang, that was awkward. Why did he always have to ruin everything?

Dis saved him by choosing that moment to move forward. "I have something to tell you both."

James sighed inwardly. That statement never preceded anything positive. "Is it," James interjected, "something that we want to hear?"

"It's something you need to hear." Dis wasn't going to let the subject go. "I know the real reason why Manthar took your sister." James tried once more to sit up and again didn't succeed. Dis was right, he needed to hear this and he wasn't going to like it.

"He wants you, James. He needed to lure you here and ordered us to use any method to bring you to him." James curled his hands into fists and shook from the effort it was taking to not attack Dis immediately.

"You were with him the whole time!" Ari looked ready to attack as well, but it seemed like she was waiting for James' signal.

"I never planned on giving you to him, ever. But I brought you as a decoy while I rushed for the cellars. That was my plan from the beginning, and you probably would have died, though I'm not entirely sure what he had planned for you.

Also," Dismus looked reluctant to continue but he pressed forward, "Ari, you have the right to know that the person behind your family's deaths was Manthar."

Both James and Ari were completely silent at the news. James knew that he should be outraged, but the truth is that he would have been willing to make the same sacrifice if it meant saving Marie. And for once, he was not surprised by the betrayal. He couldn't decide on whether that was a good thing or a bad thing.

"Why would you have done that for Marie? Why me for her? You don't really know either of us." The answer wouldn't make James less angry at Dismus, but he needed to understand. Dis looked unsure of what to say, and his reply was not what James had expected.

"Your sister is not the only one in that cellar."

It was clear that the subject was not one to press on. Still, Dis had been willing to sacrifice him. The tricky part was that James understood completely. If he had to trick someone into helping him save Marie, would he do it?

The answer was yes. There was no fooling himself, he would have done it in a heartbeat.

"That is why neither of you can follow me." So that is why he told them. Inwardly, James rebelled immediately, but he tried not to show any outward response as Dis spoke.

"I will not put either of you in jeopardy by bringing you there. I will save them by myself. I can find another way. Besides, Manthar is expecting us now, it will be better to sneak in myself." It sounded to James that he was trying to convince himself just as much as them.

"Who?" Arianna had her hands in fists and was shaking. There was no need to clarify, they all knew what she was asking.

Dismus stared at the both of them for some time before answering. "I suppose you deserve to know. Her name is Grace… she's my wife."

James could see Ari's fists loosen slightly, but she still looked murderous. Dismus must have seen the same thing and decided to continue.

"Manthar has held her hostage over me for years. If I had not done as he asked, he would have killed her. I need to save her, and this may be my only opportunity to get close enough to do it."

Despite himself, James sympathized with Dismus. He was pretty certain that he would be willing to endanger

Dismus if it meant saving his sister. In fact, that's kind of what he was doing even now.

"I will follow you." James hadn't meant it as a threat, just a promise. "I will follow as soon as I can move." Dis looked sad, but he said nothing in reply.

"If you follow me, you will die," James noted the fact that Dismus did not forbid him from trying. Somehow, that made James respect the man even more.

He didn't like being used the way that Dismus had planned, but he understood. He also believed Dismus. If he tried to save his sister, he would probably die.

"Ari." Dis looked at her until she looked him in the eye. "Keep him safe." Dis stood and looked out as if ready to take off right then.

"I'll keep him safe." Ari sounded vehement. "Safer than you would have him." She had obviously meant it as an accusation, but Dis took it in stride. "Yes," He replied immediately and nodded towards her. "I believe you will."

Without another word, Dis shot away from the boat through the air and out of view. They couldn't have kept up with him even in full health. James gave a deep sigh and stared back at Ari.

"So I can't move." It took her a second to understand what he meant, but with an exasperated look she took up the oars from inside the boat and began rowing towards the city. The rowing was painfully slow, but James couldn't think of any way that he could help.

Besides not being able to move, he couldn't seem to use his power at all either. Every time he tried, he could feel himself about to pass out. His body just needed to re-cover first, he supposed.

It was Ari that realized pretty quickly what to do. Without a word, Ari threw the oars down in the boat and jumped into the Ocean in her clothes. Seconds later, the boat started speeding through the Ocean at a good pace. They were suddenly moving at a much faster pace, and it was probably easier for Ari as well.

James could only imagine that she had changed into some sort of fish. He felt completely helpless as he laid there. He wished that he could help her, but he could only lie still for now. They had a long way to go before they made it to the city, but at least they were on their way.

Arianna

— —~*~— —

They had traveled hours with Ari pulling the boat until James finally felt up to trying to switch with her. Ari was soaking wet after using her dolphin form for so long, but she was not nearly as tired as she thought she would be.

James stuck his hands into the Ocean over the side of the boat and nearly toppled the boat. Ari let out a screech just as James pulled his arms back into the boat to rebalance it. He had the grace to look abashed, but Ari was too busy refusing to admit that she had just screamed like a bat to adequately chastise him.

Before she had the chance to get to the chastise-ment, however, the boat shot forward over the waves. James hadn't tried putting his hands back into the water like before, he had merely folded them in his lap and con-centrated. Now they were shooting across the water faster than she had ever moved before, and it was exhilarating.

It took several minutes for Ari to calm down enough to take a normal breath. She knew that she shouldn't be so concerned about falling out of the boat, she could just change back into a dolphin after all. But she couldn't stop her heart from racing at the thought of James and her flying through the air after a particularly big wave.

Why did he have to look so happy about nearly toppling them into the Ocean?

Luckily, they had mostly avoided the bigger waves and were skimming the water pretty smoothly. Was James doing that, too? Now that she was paying more attention, it seemed as though the waves would move out of their way as they headed towards them. Was that even possible?

More than once, Ari tried to make eye contact with James to start a conversation, but he was too focused. James would make eye contact with her and smile every time, but nothing more. He seemed to be concentrating too hard to hold a conversation.

She was amazed at how quickly he had recovered already. Surely he wasn't completely healed, but he seemed healthy enough to her. If he really could come back from the brink of death like that, how much would it take to kill him?

It must be nearly impossible to kill him in the Ocean, but on land? And that was exactly where they were headed, to face the world's most dangerous being on land. Maybe if Dismus succeeds then they wouldn't need to make it there. Surely he would save both his wife and Marie?

But if he didn't succeed? They would have no choice but to try and save all three of them, and probably from the King himself. That was impossible, according to Dismus. But that was exactly what they were going to try.

What if they made it before Dismus? She had to admit that it was improbable. At this rate, they might be able to make it in the next day. Depending on how fast Dismus flew, they might even pass him. He only really had about an hour on them. James would have to take a break at some point, though, and then it would be slow goings for the two of them.

As she sat there, it had occurred to her that she was probably helping James toward his death and possibly even her own.

She understood the need to save his sister, especially now that she knew that the man that had taken her was the same man that had taken her family from her. But she just wished that there was some other way than heading straight towards the most dangerous man on the planet to save her.

Ari's eyes began to get heavy as she thought about resting. She hadn't really had a decent amount of rest yet. She had been disturbed by James for this ridiculous chase.

"So what's your plan?" She kept on hoping that he would think of something where she hadn't. She wasn't sure that he had heard over the splashing waves, but he eventually answered.

"I'm not sure." James obviously hadn't wanted to admit it, but the admission was oddly comforting to her. "But I promise not to do anything stupid." Ari couldn't help but laugh at that. She didn't think either of them believed that for a second.

"Well as long as you don't do anything stupid," Ari replied while lying down to sleep. James was smiling when she shut her eyes and so was she. But that smile quickly disappeared as she thought about what dangers lie ahead of them.

Surprisingly, she wasn't worried for herself. Okay, maybe she was a little worried for herself. But mostly she worried about James. He had come all of this way to save his sister, but what if he failed? Even if he lived, she didn't think he could go on if he failed to save Marie. Maybe even Dismus and his wife for that matter.

He would try to save every person in the world if he could help it, but she wasn't complaining. As long as he didn't go dying on her to do it.

Dismus

— —~*~— —

Stealth was his only option. If they saw him coming, there would be no chance of Dis escaping. Even if he did make it in, there was almost no chance of escaping with multiple prisoners and staying alive. Dis turned a corner and continued to wind through the streets of Arian. He had arrived in the city only hours before as the sun began to set.

Manthar would be stronger at night, just one more reason not to draw attention to himself. He was no match for Manthar. It was painful to admit it, but it was the truth and he knew it. Avoiding Manthar meant living that much longer.

Dis wore standard street garb that he traded his own clothes for with a street bum. He would blend in until he made it to the castle, but he would have to remain completely unseen at that point. He couldn't risk being recognized by a random guard.

Dismus could see the castle towers looming above him now that he had turned the corner only a few blocks away. He wasn't in much danger until he made it to the outer walls of the castle itself, but it was still necessary to be careful.

The first problem was getting into the castle in the first place. Truthfully, he wouldn't have much problem making it into the castle if he would be able to use his powers, but he was sure to be noticed if he did. The closer to Manthar he was, the more likely that he would be able to sense Dismus using his power.

Even the smallest use of his power would immediately draw his attention. He would have a hard enough time-saving Grace without drawing the attention of the most dangerous being on the planet and a host of evil beings.

He almost regretted not bringing James with him. He had planned so carefully for years and then threw it all out the window when he left without the boy. James really would have been the perfect distraction for Manthar, and Dis had left him behind.

The boy had wanted to come, just like Dis had planned. But he couldn't follow through with it. The boy needed to live. Dis would succeed or fail by himself now. It was the right decision, he kept on telling himself. 'It was the right decision.'

Dismus stopped only a few paces away from the gate and waited to be addressed. This was the only way to break into Manthar's castle. He would walk in plain sight and pray that he went unrecognized long enough to survive.

"What is your business here?" There were two guards in front of Dismus and five more on top of the wall, waiting for any signal to shoot their arrows down on him. There was no room for any false movements here.

"A message for the King." It was the only thing that Dis could think of that would allow him inside of the castle, hopefully. One of the guards stepped forward and inspected Dismus, he was apparently the one in charge. Dis didn't recognize him, but it had been some time since he had been here.

"We will deliver your message, what is it?" The Captain had a look of impatience as he waited for the message, and the others looked downright bored. They couldn't have expected trouble from an older frail looking man. That was pretty much his only advantage right now.

"I must deliver the message myself." Dis wanted to look down on the Captain as he said it, but that would not have made sense coming from a commoner. No common man would have stood up to a Captain of the guard. As it was, his statement sounded more like a plea from Dis' mouth.

"On who's orders?" The Captain looked like he was not going to budge. If anything, Dis' statement had made him more inclined to keep Dis out of the castle. Dis was ready with his answer, though. He had seen enough messengers go through this to know how things went.

"King Aandal's order, Sir." Dis tensed as he waited for a response. He was preparing himself to grovel at the Captain's feet, but he thought that he just might shoot the man straight into the air instead. He still hadn't made up his mind when the Captain finally stepped aside and waved him through the gate.

Dis let out a sigh of relief as he began his way through the gate and almost forgot that he was acting like a commoner. Delayed, Dis went to his knees and thanked the Captain like a commoner might and then continued his entrance into the castle grounds. King Aandal was known to be communicating with the King in recent months and was known to send messengers through. Still, Dis had been far from certain that it would work.

The castle was much taller than it was wide. The entire structure was built as more of a massive tower than a true castle, and Manthar was at the top. That was the easy part, just don't go all the way to the top and he wouldn't run into Manthar.

Dismus was being led into the castle by two guards, one in front and one behind. They always sent at least two guards to guide guests through the castle. That they hadn't sent more to watch him was a signal to Dis that they weren't afraid of him.

Good, they didn't know who he was. Some of them might have recognized him if they had looked closely enough. But they didn't, they saw what they expected to see, and that was a commoner carrying a message.

Inside, the castle looked like a massive cellar. The entire structure was dark and damp. The only light source came from torches that lined every inch of the castle walls. Most people had no idea why that was the case, but Dismus knew. The torches were much more than a fashion statement. They were important, and they required constant upkeep.

Dismus passed several servants relighting the torches as he was led up through the levels of the castle. They still had about thirty more floors to go when they ran into the worst person possible. His name was Officer Houven, and he knew Dismus. Houven often oversaw the tasks of the castle for King Manthar.

"Stop." the Commander was by himself and had appeared right in front of Dismus and the two guards escorting him. "Where are you bringing this man?" The Officer had a perpetually sneering expression and looked down on every man that was not King Manthar. He was also very dangerous.

The guard leading the way spoke first. "This man has a message for the King from King Aandal." Dis winced at the mention of the King of Valladar, he was a connection to Dismus that might trigger the Officer's memory.

"You will go no further, Boy. I will take the message to the King." Dang it, Dis would need to use his powers to fight Houven, and he hadn't prepared an actual message. He had never expected to actually have to deliver it. He had been planning on taking care of the other two guards without his powers, but that was no longer an option.

Dis kept his face lowered and fixed his eyes on his own feet as he thought quickly on what to say. "The message was from King Aandal." Dis knew how messengers normally gave messages and tried to use the same method as he continued to stare at his feet. "He says that Dismus has found the last Seraphim and is bringing him back to the King as ordered."

'Idiot!' Dis had just used himself in the message. If anything would have reminded Houven of the familiarity of the man in front of him, it was saying his own name.

Luckily, the Officer hadn't shown any recognition at the name. In fact, he seemed to be too busy thinking over the message to focus on the messenger himself. The message should work just fine, he thought. His hope was that Manthar had already expected as much from the report that would have come in from the Royal ship that Dis destroyed. Or James destroyed, rather.

He was counting on the fact that Manthar would trust him to follow through on his orders. If that wasn't the case, well he just hoped that he succeeded with this plan before that came to fruition.

"You may go." Dis turned around to start walking back down the floors. This could still work out, he just had to knock out the two guards once they were alone and then head back up to search the rest of the castle. Not too hard. "Not you, fool." Dis turned back around and forgot to look humble in his confusion. The two guards were already making their way back down the hall and had left Dis alone with Officer Houven.

"You will follow me." Houven turned to walk up the castle steps without waiting to see if Dis would follow. Dis watched as Houven called over a page and sent him scrambling up the steps ahead of them.

He didn't dare lift his head up from the ground as he followed the man up the stairs, but he was able to follow close behind Houven by watching his heels.

The Officer had led Dismus up several floors before turning down a random hallway that looked barren. The hallway seemed to stretch out longer than any of the other halls that Dis had seen and seemed to curl around the outer walls of the castle, all lit by hundreds of torches along the walls.

Dis got more and more uncomfortable as they made their way down the torch-lit corridors. There was not a living soul in this place, why would the commander bring a messenger here? And he got his answer as soon as they turned the last corner.

The end of the hallway had one door and two guards currently stood in front of it, both holding swords at a ready position. They must have been able to hear them coming for some time now. This was the cellar, and Dis was now a prisoner. The fact was still sinking in when the Officer grabbed Dis by the neck and proceeded to carry him into the cells with one hand.

The guards let them through without a second glance, this must have been commonplace then. Surprisingly, the doors of the cellar closed behind them as Houven carried Dis down the cellars. Steel bars lined each side of the room and stretched farther than Dismus could tell. The only light came from torches that lined the walkway, there was no light at all in the cells themselves.

Dismus felt powerless. Houven was carrying him like he weighed nothing, and Dis would soon find himself in a cell with no choice but to use his powers to free himself. This was bad.

Dis tried to see into the cells as Houven dragged him by. But he couldn't make anything out in the darkness, not to mention that he couldn't exactly turn his neck at all.

What was that smell? Surely even prisoners wouldn't smell this bad. And as far as Dis could tell, there were no prisoners. They were all the way at the back of the cells when Houven finally threw Dismus down into a cell.

He was surprised that he hadn't landed harder, but that was just because he couldn't see what he had landed on. He had expected to hit a cold stone floor, but what he landed on instead was much worse. He was lying on dead bodies, and it was at that point that he realized he was about to become one of them.

"Now what's your real message, boy?" He was standing over Dismus with one foot on his chest and a blade to his neck. "Tell me before I slice your throat and make this messier than it has to be."

Dismus couldn't move without risking death. Houven was a Brute, just like Gregor. Super reflexes and incredible strength now powered the sword that aimed to take his life.

There would be no rescue without using his power and giving himself away to Manthar, but so be it. Without moving a muscle, Dismus shot stands of air at Houven in an attempt to constrict him, but Houven was ready for them and moved way too quickly to be caught.

Houven was surprised for only a moment before he recovered and attacked Dismus with as much ferocity as he had ever seen. Houven drove Dis farther back into the cell as Dis leaped to his feet and struggled to stay alive.

Dismus tried to weave strands of air to protect himself, but if he used any significant amount of power, there would be no chance of going unnoticed near Manthar. He was using tiny amounts of wind and that much wind could only stop so much power.

The only way to truly protect himself from the attacks was to re-direct them. And there was only so much re-directing that Dis could do in the corner of a cellar. He had to get out of the corner.

Houven was coming at him with a string of attacks that Dis could barely keep track of. The sword seemed to be a part of Houven, one that moved inhumanly fast. Dis waited until Houven was in mid-swing to try it.

Dis jumped as high as he could and then shot himself off of the back of the wall. He used the wind to aid him as he shot over the head of Houven, but he was too fast to avoid completely. Houven came in with a swing upwards as Dis shot over him and cut him right in the abdomen.

Dis felt the cut, but it was not a sharp pain like he expected. It was more like a low throbbing that he barely noticed. Houven was already right in front of Dis and swung before he had finished landing in the walkway between cells. The onslaught was too powerful for Dis to deal with much longer. He needed a plan, and then he found one.

Dis backed up from the attacks as Houven moved forward, but this time it was down the walkway instead of into a cellar. Houven probably thought he was winning, and Dis might have been inclined to agree with him.

"Manthar knew you would be here," Houven spoke without slowing his attack at all. He had probably been holding in these words for some time. "We were waiting for you." Dis didn't feel the need to reply, mostly because he probably would have died if he had tried.

Shock was Dismus' first reaction, but he forced himself to ignore the words. Houven was just trying to throw him off balance. That was it, the words couldn't be true.

The words had worked; a shallow cut on his arm was proof of that. Dismus couldn't let himself be distracted.

"Grace isn't even here. His Reverence has her." Houven's sneer said that he might have been telling the truth, but Dismus shut out the words as he continued to dodge his opponent's sword.

In an act of desperation, Dis ducked to the floor at the exact same time that he pulled all of the wind towards himself and the torch fires with it. Houven might have been able to dodge a well-placed shot, but there would be no avoiding this.

Dismus watched as all of the torch fires in the hall shot Houven in a crossfire. The entire room seemed to go up in flames at the unified attack, and with it, the Officer. The only source of light now came from the man screaming in front of Dismus. Dis could see the hate burning in the man's eyes, and the eyes themselves burning as he became entirely consumed in the flames.

Dis had successfully made it to the cellars, but he had doomed the entire operation in the process. Dis said a prayer over the incinerated man in front of him and collapsed back onto the ground. There was no time to lose if any of them were to survive this.

Dismus

— —~*~— —

As soon as Dis was sure that he had won, he lowered his head onto the ground with the rest of him. He was alive for now, but he could tell that he was bleeding out. He needed to act quickly.

At this point, there was no denying that he had made a scene. There was no way that he was going to go unnoticed any further. With all the remaining strength that he had, Dis summoned the air around him and went about healing himself.

Fresh air would work much better than the stale air that occupied the cellars, but it should still work well enough to stop the bleeding at the very least.

Slowly, Dis got to his feet and began walking back down the cellar. He looked closely at each and every cell as he passed and grew more and more worried with each one. She had to be here, there was nowhere else to keep her, he was sure of it.

With each and every cell that Dis checked, the reality began to sink in. She was not in any of the cells. He had hoped that it had just been too dark to see clearly before, but he had no such hopes anymore. He hadn't found her, and for the first time, he admitted to himself that Houven might have been telling the truth.

Manthar must have the prisoners with him, and if that was the case, then he was ready for Dis. Any hopes of a clean escape had suddenly vanished.

He had given himself away to Manthar. It was of very little consolation that he knew where she was. He was once again, firmly in Manthar's control if he couldn't find her in time. Well, there was one thing left to do. Manthar knew he was here, so there was no more hiding.

Ashamed that he hadn't already, Dis went back and rechecked the cells for any other prisoners. He had come for more than her; he had almost forgotten that. Dis checked and rechecked the cells to make sure, but Marie wasn't anywhere to be found.

As the reality sunk in, Dismus made his decision. There was only one place they could be if they weren't here, and that meant that his plan hadn't worked. Manthar had Grace and Marie with him right now, waiting for Dismus to try and rescue them.

Turning his attention back to the cells, Dismus took stock of the only person in any of the cells. He currently laid in the cell next to Dismus and he was staring straight at Dis in dead silence. He was most likely a man in his mid-forties and he looked frail. Dis came up in front of the man's cell and crouched down to eye level.

Both men stared back at each other without a sound. Dis had expected to find a lifeless body staring back at him, but what he saw was pure ferocity. This man was strong, even by Dis' standards. There was something familiar with the man that made Dis want to help him.

"I'm Dismus. What's your name?" As strong as the man might be, it was likely that he had not used his voice in a long time. However, his voice came loud and clear in the silent cellar.

"My name is Moah." Moah sat with his back against the wall and his legs out in front of him. Based on the relaxed way that he was holding himself, he could have been lounging anywhere except for a prison.

"That is a strong name. Named after the General then? No wonder Manthar threw you in his prison." Moah smiled back at Dis in a knowing way. But it was not until Moah spoke again that Dis realized why.

"Yes, my son always was the rash kind." So he was crazy, maybe that explained why he was so comfortable inside a jail cell. Maybe he should just leave the man in there then. There would be nothing gained from getting involved in the fighting.

"I can see that you don't believe me." Dis wasn't aware of anything that he had done to give that impression, but the man must have seen it in his eyes. "That is usually the case," Moah continued. "And it's why I rarely share it, not that there are many people to share it with in the first place. But I thought that you might believe me, given that you are a Seraphim as well."

Dismus nearly fell over from his crouching position. "I thought that might get your attention." The man that claimed to be Moah got to his feet and walked to the front of the cell.

"My son took my power from me and threw me in this cell. I've been here for fifty years or so since, and with little company. I would offer you a drink or something, but I get very few amenities here."

"That's not possible. You look like a young man. There is no way that you've been here for fifty years." Dis couldn't remember ever being more flustered than he was now. The man who claimed to be Moah, in contrast, was as calm as ever.

Not much was known about the past Seraphim. Few people ever learned of their identities in the first place, and most knowledge about such things were lost to the modern world. But Dismus had heard about the earth Seraphim that was killed by his own son: Manthar.

"We do not age like the rest," Moah said as he searched Dis' eyes, "have you not noticed it yourself?"

In truth, Dis had noticed that before, but he thought that it was his own genes that kept him healthy for so long. Most men his age couldn't move like he could anymore. Whatever he had thought, however, he had not expected to be able to live for so long. He might have been excited about the prospect if he wasn't expecting to die in the next few minutes.

"Manthar killed Moah more than fifty years ago," Dismus was still trying to process when Moah cut him off.

"That may be," Moah said flippantly, "but he didn't do a very good job of it."

Dismus searched for the right words to respond with, but his mind was drawing a blank. The truth was that he believed this man for some reason.

"I can help." That was not what Dis had been expecting. He was supposed to be the one helping, not the prisoner that was still currently behind bars. "The prisoner that you're looking for is with him." The news hit him like a punch to the face.

"Who does he have?" He had to be sure, he had to know.

"A women." Moah looked sad at the mention of his fellow prisoners. "She was pleasant. Her company was a welcome change after such a long period of isolation. She was an older woman. She was in the cells with me for some time now, but how long, who could say."

Dis let out a breath that he didn't know he was holding. They were safe, if at least for now. "I have to find her." Dis began to turn to run out of the cellar, but he was stopped by a noise.

"Mhmm." Moah cleared his throat as if awaiting his turn to speak. Dis turned back to him and waited, embarrassed by getting carried away. "Like I said, I can help. The entire castle guard will have been put on alert at this point. At the very least, I can pull attention away from you."

Moah looked capable enough, but Dis couldn't help thinking that he would be leading this man to his death. He must have seen Dis' skeptical face.

"He has your prisoner with him. It's the only way." That settled it. Dis couldn't turn back, not now that he knew where she was.

Summoning air around his fist, Dis raised his hand and punched the steel bars that held Moah in his cell. The bar bent but not enough to escape through. It wasn't until several more swings were delivered that Moah was able to squeeze through the bent bars.

There was no time to lose. He had used valuable time talking to the ninety-year-old man and now he had a long way to go with probably the entire castle alerted already. He was surprised that he hadn't been barged in on yet.

Moah looked back at his cell briefly, but he seemed to be in just as much of a hurry to leave as Dis was. "If one of us doesn't make it," Moah was facing the door to the castle and looking straight ahead, "it was nice meeting you."

Sure that he was going to his death, Moah opened the door and led the two of them out of the cellar. With what little strength he had left, Dis would do everything in his power to finally save his wife.

James

— —~*~— —

James had no idea what he was doing, but he was doing a pretty good job of pretending like he did. Ari had fallen asleep and stayed that way for the entire ride into the city. It was better that way since he had to redirect himself several times in order to find the city in the first place.

They had originally taken off in the direction that Dismus had flown, but they had quickly found that it was quite difficult to stay on course when they had no real way to determine what the right direction was. Luckily, James' senses were becoming stronger as they sailed, and his senses said that they were heading in the right direction.

He was becoming more and more aware of the reality that he now lived in. Whatever an Angel really was, he definitely had one, and that was definitely the source of his powers.

He was distinctly aware that his powers didn't come straight from him, it was more like he was a channel through which the power was directed. And it seemed that one of those powers was a great sense of direction.

When they came in view of the port, however, James quickly changed course. The port was still some distance away, but it was filled with ships and buildings that lined the coast.

Instead of heading towards the city itself, James now had them sailing towards a rock formation that clearly was not meant for docking. Even James could tell that the area was too dangerous for ships to navigate.

Ari woke up to James guiding the row boat through rocks that jutted out from under the waves. A normal ship didn't stand a chance of making it through the death trap, and even a boat as small as theirs was likely to get destroyed, but James was able to guide the boat with little difficulty.

As exhausted as he was, he could feel the power coursing through him. It was as natural as breathing and as powerful as he wanted. Out on the Ocean, the power was almost unlimited, he was sure of it.

James noticed that Ari very pointedly avoided looking at the water as they flew in between the rocks, but James only smiled. He was in control and quite literally in his own element. 'I could do anything here,' he thought. And it was exactly during that thought when the boat came to a dead stop.

James hadn't noticed the sudden drop in the depth of the water and the boat projected both James and Ari out of the boat as it hit the bottom of the Sea. It was a good thing that he hadn't said anything about his skills out loud.

Ari looked furious, but James acted quickly. Reaching out, James grabbed all of the water that had just soaked her and shot them at himself. It was the second time that he had to dry her that way and he really hoped that it wasn't going to be a regularly occurring thing for them. He did enough things to embarrass himself without accidentally splashing her every day.

At least he had acted quickly this time. In one stroke, he had dried her and soaked himself. He was hoping for a laugh or some sign of appreciation, but he didn't get it. Ari walked the rest of the way out of the water with a 'harumph' and crossed her arms at him. "You are an idiot."

"I'm sorry!" James walked the rest of the way out of the water to join her and then dried both of them the rest of the way by shooting the water back into the Ocean. She didn't like him, he could tell by the way that she looked at him. He was just another peasant to her, he had to remember that.

"This way." James began making his way over the rocky terrain that lay before them. They were just outside of the city and no one else was in sight. Well, technically there were people in sight, but they were far away and busy working on the ports. Now to find a way into the city.

"Do you know where you are going?" Ari seemed unsure but turned to follow James anyway.

"Yes," James lied immediately. Well, he technically did know where, he just didn't know how to get there. "We are going to the castle." He was trying to speak more confidently than he felt. "It's the huge thing right in the middle of the city."

James didn't look back, but he could feel Ari's eyes burning a hole in his back. "And how do you propose that we get inside once we finally get there?" She sounded openly belligerent now.

"Ah, you forget, Little One." James raised a finger and pointed it towards her in a mock of a teacher. "I have experience breaking into castles." She did not look amused. James added on quickly in a more normal voice to try and recover. "Besides, I have a particular set of skills."

"I don't see how that will help us much in the city." Ari seemed genuinely concerned. James understood, but it wouldn't help anything to tell her that he was just as worried as she was. "I'm not sure either, but we can do it, we have to."

Ari nodded though she still looked uncertain. "I trust you."

The words were a shock to James, but not an unpleasant one. He gave her a smile that she returned and then continued to lead them to the outer ring of rocks that faced the city walls.

James peeked over the rock they hid behind and didn't see anyone there. He would have rather checked out the walls more before acting, but they didn't have any time to waste. "Stay close behind me." Ari nodded and waited for James to lead.

James quickly ran to the wall and started climbing. He was halfway up before he realized that Ari probably couldn't climb like he could. James looked down and panicked, she wasn't anywhere in sight. He was about to climb back down and look for her when a large bird flew by him and landed on top of the wall.

Before his eyes, the bird transformed back into Ari, who stared back at him innocently. "Did I know that you could do that?" James finished climbing without much thought to stealth anymore. He was too stunned to worry very much. "For some reason I thought your powers were limited to random water creatures."

"You're not the only one with cool powers. I can change into pretty much anything." Was she flirting with him? No, she was just poking fun at him, no way she was flirting. "Well," He said as he joined her on top of the wall, "that could be useful."

There were no guards anywhere near them. James supposed that there was no need to guard a stretch of wall that bordered a large cluster of rocks. Most ships wouldn't be able to dock there; more proof that James was brilliant. James climbed back down the wall while Ari flew down just as she had before.

"Where do your clothes go when you change shapes?" Okay, maybe it wasn't the best question for him to ask, but he couldn't help himself.

Ari blushed as she changed back into herself. "Shut up." Well, James was on a real roll with embarrassing himself. He supposed that he would never get an answer to his question, either. He guessed that it would have to be one more thing that didn't make sense about his life.

The city was huge, but they ultimately knew where they were going. The castle was visible from practically anywhere, and it was only a matter of time before they found their way there. The thing was, time was something that they might not have if they wanted to help Dismus before it was too late.

James began leading the way through the streets as the sun sank into the horizon. Ari took a stride next to him and was very obviously not looking at him. It might have been romantic if they were not in an enemy city on the way to risk their lives for a man that had intended to betray them.

James looked at Ari and saw that she seemed to be blushing still. Was she that embarrassed about his question? Or was she thinking along the same lines as he was? She really was beautiful…

Well, no time for that thinking. James focused on the streets ahead of them. Why was she here? The thought kept on bugging him. She was risking her life to save his sister. Would she have come all this way with him if she hated him?

A smile crept onto his face and stayed there despite everything. Despite the overwhelming odds of death and the life of his sister on the line, he still had hope. For the first time in a long time, he didn't feel like he was alone on this journey.

They were both on their way to save his sister. He just hoped that they lived to see another sunset after tonight.

Dismus

— —~*~— —

Moah threw open the doors to the cell and immediately jumped back into Dis. The entire hallway was full of guards with their swords pointed at them. Moah looked ready to stand his ground, but there was no way that he could do anything against such overwhelming odds.

Dis took a step forward and put himself between Moah and the guards. "Cover me." The words were barely out of his mouth when Dis rushed toward the first three men.

Dismus threw two of the men aside with a burst of wind and wrapped the third man tight. In a matter of seconds, the first three men had dropped to the ground and were made useless. But that was no deterrent for the other thirty men waiting. All at the exact same moment, the guards rushed Dismus in an attempt to overwhelm them with numbers.

Swords snapped at Dismus like vipers as he attempted to dodge and redirect several blades at a time. Dis gave everything he had to keep his ground, but he knew that he would be driven back toward the cellar at any moment by the overwhelming numbers.

There was only room for three men to face Dismus at a time, and their movements were constricted by the narrow hall, but Dismus couldn't do very much but defend himself without a weapon.

As he deflected two different blades simultaneously, he unwillingly took several steps backward to avoid a third sword that was inches from piercing his chest.

Had he not given ground, he might have died at that very moment. Still, he hated to give ground at all. It was as he was thinking this that he glimpsed the blades that lay on the floor from when he disarmed the first three soldiers.

Mentally kicking himself for not thinking of it earlier, Dismus waited for a clean shot before using a strand of air to fling the sword into his hand.

One moment before, a soldier had seen the opening against Dis and had swung what would have been a death blow. Instead, the soldier had landed a hit on Dis' blade and was completely baffled by the turn of events.

Suddenly, the tables had turned. Dismus' sword moved like a whirlwind through the first line of soldiers and the remaining twenty-something men took involuntary steps backward as they witnessed the ease with which their cohorts had been dispatched.

As Dismus pushed the mass of soldiers backward with his advances, Moah was able to retrieve one of the other blades from the floor behind Dis. Now they were both armed and very dangerous.

Dismus pushed and cut his way through the fray and Moah took care of anyone left standing behind them. They were unstoppable. The resistance was fierce, but they never stood a chance.

Eventually, both men heaved and puffed and leaned on their swords at the end of the hall as they observed the result of their attack. Thirty-something men incapacitated and they had only made it twenty paces down the hall.

They couldn't afford to wait for reinforcements. Without another glance at the wreckage they had caused, Dismus stood straight up, threw his sword to the ground and began moving further into the castle.

He was at a run. He couldn't waste any time acting like he belonged there. Manthar was the only one that he was afraid of, and Dis was willing to bet that he was already waiting for him at the top. No need to hide his powers either.

Dismus cleared the floor of the dungeon and started to make his way up the tower when he heard someone run up behind him.

"I thought I'd be more help coming with you. Just about all of the guards left to distract were down by the cellar." Moah spoke casually, but Dismus knew what he was really saying. He was willing to risk his life to help a man he had just met. Not sure if it was a good idea or not, but Dis just couldn't ignore any help that he could get.

"Sure, just keep up if you can." And the two men bolted up the stairs once more. They were still about twenty floors down, and there were plenty of people around to get in his way. Every floor held more people than the last and every time someone tried to stop him from running further, he threw them down behind him. They were always surprised.

Never had he used his powers with such reckless abandon, and it was strangely exhilarating. Dis could feel his wound healing even faster as he ran up the tower. With no point in holding back any longer and having healed completely, Dis grabbed all of the air around him and began leaping up the flights of stairs in single bounds. Moah would catch up when he could, but Dis couldn't wait.

The people behind him only had time to gape as he shot by them. There was no hiding from them anymore, so his only option was to move quickly. Only a few minutes passed before he arrived at the top level and came face to face with five guards in front of the doors to the royal hall.

They already had their swords leveled at him and seemed ready to fight. There was no doubt that the whole castle knew at this point. Without warning, Dis shot a huge gust of wind at the men and shoved them against the doors that they were guarding.

They must have heard about his powers, but that hadn't made them anymore ready for it. A few of the men tried to roll away from it, but they were shoved backward all the same.

Dismus leaped forward to shove the doors open, but the guards recovered more quickly than he anticipated and the closest two swung their swords down on him just as he realized that the doors were locked. Dis pushed the swords away from him as they sliced downwards and managed to jump backward simultaneously to avoid getting hit.

They really had been ready for him. It still wouldn't help. The other three converged on him from behind as he rolled away from the first two and he dodged them by do-ing a wind-aided handspring off of the floor and over their heads. He was now facing all five of them in front of him just as it was at the beginning. 'Here goes round two,' he thought.

Dis shot a huge gust of wind just like the first and rushed towards the doors once more. This time, three of the two were able to move fast enough to avoid it and were bringing their swords down on him even faster than the first time, but he was ready as well.

As soon as they swung their swords, Dis concentrated on the lock of the door and pushed their swords towards it. Dismus didn't even move as the swords all swung right in front of him and on the lock instead. As soon as the lock sprung free of the door, Dismus shot a wave of air away from him and threw all five guards down the stairs where he had come from.

They would be back soon, he was sure. But they would be uneasy about facing him again, he hoped. Besides, they knew better than most that the King could take care of himself. Moah would be a surprise for them, he hoped.

Just to be careful, Dismus stepped through the doors and wound air around them to keep them shut behind him. They wouldn't hold indefinitely, but they should hold long enough before Moah made it up here.

Dismus turned around once he secured the doors and his heart immediately sank. He had finally made it to Manthar's chambers, but Manthar was not there.

Manthar

— —~*~— —

Hundreds of thousands of soldiers sat at the doorstep of Valladar. The city had not been prepared for them, but how could they have been? They would be crushed by his army regardless of how prepared they might have been.

His men had docked their ships on a coast several days march from here. The city had not been aware of the approaching army until they were nearly on top of it.

His army had stopped to rest before attacking, but that time was over. It was time to move on the city and his soldiers were rife with anxious energy. They had come a long way for a fight and they were finally going to get it.

The only two effective lines of defense that Valladar could have offered against him were the two men that were not here and the Royal family. The plan was costly, but it was necessary. Only King Aandal was left of the Royal family and the Seraphim were on the other side of the world.

Either Dismus or the boy individually could have effectively held off his army from behind their gates had Manthar not been there. And both of them together might have been too much even for him. Better to get them safely out of the way and with no way of protecting their city.

As it was, Manthar's army outnumbered the city's men many times over. He might lose twice as many men as Valladar in the coming battle, but that was negligible next to what was to be gained from taking the city.

Valladar had the finest naval forces on the planet and had never lost a battle on the Seas. For that reason alone, he had planned the attack on land instead. It was also a good reason for him to take this Kingdom first.

The King's mind wandered as he surveyed the tall stone walls and anxious warhorses lining the East side of the city. He recalled a battle fought long ago and a war that ended in victory. This battle should be won much more easily than that day's.

Manthar sat on a black warhorse and had a jewel-encrusted sword hanging from the saddle. It was of little use to him, but he did find that the sheer ostentatious nature of the thing did tend to distract his enemies at times.

Not that he really needed to distract anyone, but it was amusing to see a man dumbfounded as he cut them down. It was the little cruelties in life that made his existence interesting.The large cruelties too, of course, but those were a given.

Manthar was musing on the upcoming slaughter when his vision suddenly shifted. Instead of watching the awaiting city, he was now viewing his own chambers in Pyiasior.

He knew what was happening, but the suddenness of the visions were difficult to get used to.

"Report," he said immediately. He was always the first to speak in these visions if only to maintain the illusion of power.

"My King, a Seraphim has arrived in the castle."

The speaker was his personal Messenger, linked to him in a way that made Manthar uncomfortable, but it had to be done.

"Good, you know what to do." Immediately, the vision vanished and the battlefield was before him once more.

He had been expecting the message any time now. He now had confirmation that Dismus, and, therefore, the boy, were halfway across the world. There would be no interruptions today.

Without warning, Manthar pulled his sword from his scabbard and raised it high in the air. His Field Generals immediately responded in kind and the air suddenly became still. There really was such a thing as the calm before a storm.

Valladar's walls were lined with archers with unstrung bows, waiting for their enemies. Manthar could taste the tension and he reveled in it. Manthar lowered his sword and brought his horse to a slow trot that turned into a full-on charge.

His army followed as the enemy archers released their arrows at the first wave of soldiers. This would be the third kingdom to topple at his command, and it would not be the last.

Arianna

— —~*~— —

James was going to get them killed, and she was listening to him anyway. His plan was crazy, but she couldn't think of anything better. The castle itself was crawling with guards and people that would give them away in a heartbeat. The sun had already set completely, but there were people everywhere all the same. There would be no sneaking into this place.

They were going to have to bust their way in; hence the way-too-dangerous plan. They had checked out every side of the castle. There was one entry point left… the balcony. It was the only way in that was left unguarded and it was at the very highest point of the tower. If Manthar was anywhere, he was there.

James would have to make a run for the wall and scale it without getting shot down by arrows while she flew there. She definitely had the easier job, but she was skeptical all the same. Even if it worked, they would be dropping in on a super powerful being with the power to destroy them easily. She was not eager to face the King in any capacity.

They were counting on Dismus being there to help them take Manthar down, but they had no idea if he was even there. It was too late to turn back now. In the back of her head she thought, 'no it isn't.' But she shoved those thoughts out of her head. She would help James save his sister no matter what, and hopefully get revenge on her family's killer at the same time.

"You ready?" James was all determination; she almost felt like they couldn't lose.

"Yeah, I'm ready." Her voice trembled over the words, but he thankfully pretended not to notice. James peeked over the outer wall of the castle grounds and laid back down next to Ari. They were tucked out of sight behind a small lip that lined the edges of the entire rooftop. They were still about twenty yards from the outer wall and had to cover about a hundred more yards after that to reach the castle itself.

James was going first. He tensed up next to her and then turned his head to speak. "Wait until they notice me." He whispered the instructions and then waited for a nod from her before jumping to his feet and leaping down from the roof.

Ari lifted her head and watched him race to the wall and scale it like it was nothing. There were guards on the ground and on top of the wall. The only reason they hadn't noticed him yet was because he had moved too fast for them to have time to register what was happening. James was already on top of the wall with the guards before they realized he was there.

Ari should have moved at that point, but she didn't care what he said. If he needed help, she was going to come after him. She watched long enough to see that he definitely didn't need help, at least not yet.

There was a guard to each side of him on the wall, and he shot both of them off of the wall with only so much as a flick of his wrist. Both men flew off the wall and landed with loud grunts only a few yards away from her. It was time to go.

Ari concentrated and almost immediately felt herself growing wings. She didn't know how many people knew about the existence of her ability, but based on what she had been told, she was sure that there would be others with the same ability here. Casting her fears aside, Ari stretched her wings and shot off of the rooftop.

Faster than she had ever flown before, Ari soared up the tower as a giant eagle and nearly got her head ripped off. Ari felt a gust of wind and veered to her right just before another bird flew by her with its talons aimed at her head.

Ari whipped around and watched as two dragons spun from their dive to face her. She had heard myths about the creatures as a child. Never in her wildest dreams did she ever think they would exist, and she was now facing two of them. She would definitely have to try that later if she lasted long enough for later.

The dragons wasted no time moving into a circle pattern surrounding her. There was no doubt in her mind, she knew she was about to die.

Ari couldn't think of anything to do, but the eagle instincts seemed to kick in before it was too late and she shot up into the sky to gain a height advantage. It wasn't much against fire breathing, but she hoped that it would be enough to keep her alive.

Both dragons stopped trying to circle her in and shot upwards to chase her farther into the sky. They were much higher than the tower now and Ari lost sight of the land as she flew into the clouds. Even as an eagle, Ari felt sick to her stomach this high up in the air. An eagle with a fear of heights, there were few things more embarrassing.

Both dragons followed her into the clouds and caught up to her within seconds. How were they faster than her? That wasn't fair! The first dragon had dark green scales that looked like muddy emeralds. She noted this as he came right at her and shot a blast of fire right in her face. She couldn't move fast enough, the flames engulfed her face at the exact moment that she felt another blast of fire on her back. She never even saw the other dragon.

She couldn't have chosen a better moment to change. Seconds before she had been attacked, Ari transformed into a dragon herself and emerged from the flames unscathed. If ever dragons could show surprise, it happened then. Ari took a second to see what color she was, but she couldn't tell. Who knew that dragons were color blind? The enemy dragons recovered quickly and came at her with another tactic immediately.

Ari was being circled again, but it didn't look like they were going to try to burn her this time, she was just as immune as they were. She was proud of herself, but her victory was short-lived. There were still two of them against her and both of them were a little bigger than she was. They moved in simultaneously for the kill.

Four sets of claws and two sets of jaws ripped at her neck and face furiously and she couldn't do anything but claw back blindly. One of the dragons latched on with its jaws on her neck and she almost lost consciousness. The other did its best to hover around her and continue clawing at her face. She wasn't going to last much longer if she didn't escape. In desperation, she did the only thing that her slow-reacting mind could think of.

Ari transformed herself into a boa constrictor and latched onto the dragon's neck. The dragon still had a hold on her neck, but the rest of her body immediately had a hold on the dragon's neck as well, and Ari squeezed with everything she had.

She could feel the blood dripping down from her neck from the dragon's hold, but Ari squeezed so tightly and quickly that the dragon lost consciousness and fell from the sky with Ari still on him.

Ari quickly tried to change back to a dragon and succeeded just in time to stop herself from hitting the ground herself. The first dragon was oddly flat as he lay on the ground below. One down and one more to go.

Ari barely had time to throw herself to the side as she flew upwards and out of the way of the other dragon swooping in to burn her alive.

Ari could see the fury in its eyes as she immediately flew back up into the sky. Her neck was still bleeding, but not nearly as much as it was earlier. Still, she needed to end this quickly.

— —~*~— —

James stopped climbing and ducked his head to avoid an arrow for the fifth time in the last minute alone. He wasn't sure how, but he could feel the arrows flying towards him.

Considering the circumstances, he couldn't afford to dampen any of his senses besides taste. And since he wasn't tapping into his Ahren's power, he could actually tell that his other senses were slightly sharper. That was the only way that he could explain the fact that he could tell where the arrows would hit as they flew towards him.

Dodging yet another arrow, James threw himself to the side and caught another handhold directly below the balcony. He was still several stories away, but he was getting close.

James caught himself watching the sky as he climbed. He kept on telling himself that she could handle herself, but he couldn't stop himself from worrying.

He watched her drop towards the earth and nearly jumped down to try and catch her before he saw that she had pulled up in time. He really was an idiot, he couldn't have done anything for her even if she had hit the ground.

Begrudgingly, James turned his focus back to avoiding the arrows that flew towards his head. He was almost to the balcony now and he would have a much better vantage point there anyway.

———~*~———

Ari got the wind knocked out of her as the other dragon threw itself at her. She was injured and the other dragon was still fresh. She wouldn't be able to pull the same move on him this time, and she had to think of a way to end this quickly.

She chanced a look down to see how James was doing and saw that he was almost done climbing the tower. She had to meet him there before they both ran out of time.

She decided to take another chance. Instead of waiting to be attacked, Ari flew at the other dragon this time. Both of them collided in midair and then Ari immediately dug in her claws to make sure that they did not break apart. She could easily die from this, but she would have probably died anyway.

Ari opened her jaws and clamped down on the other dragon's neck as hard as she could and waited for the other dragon to react. 'Come on. Come on you snake.' At first, the other dragon thrashed around to try to escape, but it could not get free. Ari tried turning both of them towards the ground and they both quickly started plummeting towards the earth.

Finally, the other man started transforming. As soon as Ari felt him changing, Ari let go and blew as much fire as she could. As she had hoped, the man had tried to change into a boa constrictor just like she had, but she was ready for it. Before he could finish changing, the snake was burning all over its entire body.

Ari thought that she could tell that he tried changing back into a dragon to survive the fire, but he must have died before he could manage it. She had killed her second dragon for the day and she didn't feel good about it at all. As much as she wanted to pretend like they were just dragons, they were people.

Ari's eyes began watering as she looked down upon the two bodies that reverted back to human form as they died. It wasn't until an arrow nearly shot her in the wing that she snapped out of it and flew back up to the balcony.

There was no more resistance from the air, but she could fall just as easily to arrows.

James was there and completely unscathed. Well, he was covered in dirt and sweat, but otherwise he looked like he always did. He must have obviously thought it was her, but he didn't relax until Ari changed from her dragon form and back into her normal self.

"Well, you are just full of surprises today." He was trying to make light of the situation, and she didn't mind. She didn't want to think about what came next either.

No one came out onto the balcony, it was just the two of them. Still, Ari felt a sense of urgency. Something was going on, but she couldn't tell what. Most likely, she was just scared to take the next step.

James made eye contact with her and gave a nod of his head. He was scared too, but he moved towards the room anyway. Luckily, he hadn't noticed the blood dripping down her shirt. They could deal with that later.

Thick velvet curtains hung in the entrance of the room blocking their view, but it didn't block sound. There was definitely fighting in the next room, and if Ari's nose was still working, smoke as well. They were about to step into a circle of hell.

Ari's heart was beating twice as fast as when she landed. James was about to step into the room before she pulled him back from the curtains.

She wasn't sure what had gotten into her, maybe the fighting had made her bold, but she had no regrets about what she did next. Grabbing the collar of his shirt, Ari pulled James down to her level and kissed him on the lips.

James' eyes opened in surprise and Ari found herself fighting a smile as she kissed him. She felt like she had eels swimming around in her stomach from nerves, but more than that she felt alive. Sadly, the feeling was cut short.

James pulled away from Ari and suddenly looked cold. Regret immediately plagued her. Why did she have to do that? She ruined everything before they had anything. He hated her, she knew it deep down.

"My sister is in there."

It sounded like he said the words regretfully, but she immediately convinced herself that she was hearing things. Though, he had kissed her back at first. Maybe he did care for her.

Either way she had embarrassed herself. What she wouldn't give to have that moment back. James was right, this was no time to dally about. She was here to help him save his sister, not fall in love. If that's what this really was in the first place.

The eels were swimming in her stomach once again for an entirely different reason as she turned back towards the curtain. They couldn't delay any longer.

James was at the curtain now and about to pull it back to enter the room. Briefly, he looked back and smiled at Ari. He must have been just as nervous as she was, or maybe he was trying to make up for her awkwardness.

He really was thoughtful, wasn't he? 'Stop it.' She told herself as she took a deep breath. Hurrying to follow him, she stepped past the curtain behind James. There would be no turning back for her now.

Dismus

— —~*~— —

Manthar's throne room was full of men, but the King was nowhere to be found. Two teams of Manthar's men were in rank and waiting for Dismus when he turned from the door. Houven was right, Manthar had known that he was coming.

The room was an open space with marble columns running along the middle aisle. There was a balcony directly across from Dismus and on the other side of the waiting men.

Dismus braced himself for the attack, but they didn't attack at first. Both teams moved as a unit just like they were taught. They were slowly positioning themselves to surround Dismus and attack simultaneously.

They knew who he was and they would not be taking him lightly. Inwardly, Dismus grunted. Them underestimating him might have been his only chance of surviving this. Separate attacks from these men wouldn't be much of a challenge, but a unified attack of six soldiers against one unarmed man was another story.

Dismus let them form around him as he backed up against the nearest wall. He could at least protect his back that way, but it would be a lot more difficult to retreat if he found himself in a bad spot.

As calmly as he could, Dismus assessed the situation while the men were still forming up. Six men surrounding him, and they seemed to be split into pairs. He would have to rush at one pair at a time and hope that it would be enough to keep them off-balance. Maybe if there was some way to make it to the balcony...

Dismus was still trying to figure out how to do this when he finally caught sight of what he had come for. A woman was laying on the floor in chains all the way to the left of the room. A man stood calmly next to her and watched Dismus intently.

He could not tell who the woman was, but he didn't have a chance to figure it out before he was suddenly attacked by his opponents.

He broke the first rule of a fight; he had allowed himself to be distracted.

Three swords came at Dismus impossibly fast. Two blades nearly went straight through his chest as the other sliced right above his head.

He had thrown up a wind barrier just as he threw himself into a backward summersault that put his back directly against the wall. He now had confirmation about who he was dealing with; the six men were split into three pairs.

Like Hector and Gregor, they seemed to be all Warpers and Brutes linked to one another with chains. Where Hector was forced to keep physical contact with Gregor to keep him unaffected, these pairs accomplished the same thing by connecting themselves to each other with chains.

Each pair gave the illusion that the swordsmen were some sort of chained animals on their master's leash while really the opposite was true. Though they weren't nearly as mobile as they could have been separate, they were ultimately better off pairing with each other.

Dismus could feel the effect of the Warping as he stood up against the wall. All six men immediately moved in against him with incredible speed while he might as well have been trying to move in water.

At the last possible second, Dismus shot himself in the air and pushed off of the wall behind him. The swords had come inches from ending his life, but their speed had not been quite enough.

Shutting off his senses of taste and smell, Dismus was able to move quickly enough to escape the time-bubble if only for a second before they moved against him once more.

He was right back where he started with a wall against his back and six men staring him down, only this time he had the wind to his back.

Not giving the men enough time to coordinate again, Dismus summoned as much wind as possible from the balcony behind him and shot it all at his assailants.

The strength of the men would be too much to manipulate with wind, he was sure, but he could easily keep them off-balance enough to give himself a chance.

As soon as he shot the wind at the soldiers, Dismus charged at the dueling pair all the way to the left. Only taking them one at a time would work in a situation like this.

Just as he hoped, the men were disoriented enough that Dismus was able to get within arm's distance of the pair before the Brute had the wherewithal to swing his sword.

Dis had been aiming for the Warper to see if he could separate the pair, but the man had seen what he was doing and positioned himself behind the Brute as

Dismus had to throw up another wind stream to redirect the swing that had been aimed at his head.

What followed was a desperate wave of defense against the swings that he was not fast enough to track, let alone counter. Most Brutes were not necessarily skilled with a sword of their own merit due to the fact that they didn't need to be.

It was common for both Warpers and Brutes to rely too heavily on their powers, but that was not the case with the man that attacked him now. He knew what he was doing, and Dismus was lucky to have survived this long against these men without a sword.

What saved him was the fact that each pair was affecting the other's Warping. Had they all been linked, they might have been able to all attack at lightning speed at the same time, but as it was, two of the three men attacking Dismus were unaided by their Shifter.

They were all still much faster than they had any right to be, but it was enough to keep Dismus alive. Whenever one of the pairs got close, Dismus would be able to escape with wind-assisted leaps. But he had no idea how long he could keep this up. He briefly considered running but then immediately dismissed the idea.

This would be his only chance to save Grace. He could feel it profoundly. There would be no running.

Dismus was still trying to figure out how to get to the woman safely when he heard a commotion from behind him in the direction of the balcony. Dismus risked a look behind him as he threw up yet another wind stream.

The soldiers let him retreat as he backed up slowly to the opening of the balcony, where James and Arianna had just made their entrance.

"What are you two doing here?" Dismus hissed the words through his teeth without taking his eyes off of the soldiers.

"Saving your life apparently." The comment, for once, didn't bother Dismus so much. The boy had a point.

James

— —~*~— —

James could not count the number of times that he had dreamed of kissing Ari. And yet when against all odds they finally did kiss, it was at the worst possible moment.

He was currently running as fast as he could around the giant man with a sword. It wasn't the smartest move, seeing as the man was much faster than James, but the chains around his waist made for an awkward game of chase.

The truth was it was more of a stalling tactic than anything. James had no idea how he was supposed to beat these guys unarmed, and instead of trying to figure out how to defeat them, he was thinking about Ari's kiss.

Dang it, Ari, if he was killed over this... well, it would probably still have been worth it.

Each of them was locked in a fight with their own pair of soldiers, and none of them looked like they were winning.

Ari had changed back into a dragon and was spewing fire at will, but James could see the blood dripping from her wings where she had been constantly cut. Maybe she was winning, though; it was hard to tell through all of that smoke.

Dismus seemed to be on the defensive, but not any more than James. Both of them hopped around trying to dodge blows and stay alive.

Now and again, the pair of soldiers fighting James would try a swing at Dismus as they passed close by, but he always seemed to see it coming. This was a game of survival right now. James needed to find a water source so he could use his power, but there was nothing here.

The soldier's sword again flashed right in front of James and he dove to the floor in blinding pain. He had been just a little too slow this time. James could feel the blood trickling down his cheek, but he didn't let himself stop moving.

Coming out of his dive, James rolled to his feet and kept on running. The monster of a man was back on top of James before he could take even one step. He had been cornered against the wall. There would be no running anymore.

'If only I had a sword,' was the thought he had as the soldier that had cornered him went for the kill.

Without thinking, James made as if to defend the blow with his own sword. 'Idiot!' he screamed at himself in his mind as he watched the blade make contact with something that had not been there a moment ago.

In his hands was the most beautiful sword he had ever seen in his life. Even as James looked at it, it seemed to flicker between different shapes and sizes as if unable to make up its mind.

Both the blade and the handle were glowing blue and seemed to radiate power. He had needed a sword, and he had been given a sword.

Stunned, the soldier that had attacked him stared at the sword as if mesmerized for only a moment before he continued to rain down blows with his own sword. The brief confusion was the only thing that had saved James' life, as he himself had been staring at his blade as well.

The barrage of swings against James was overwhelming, but somehow he was able to defend against everyone. The sword moved with a mind of its own.

The soldier's attacks moved so quickly that James found that he couldn't even see most of the movements, but James' sword seemed to see the soldier's attacks before they even occurred.

The soldier attacked unceasingly, but James could see the strain in his eyes. He couldn't figure out how James was able to defend himself and he was starting to show fear.

Really, the soldier shouldn't have felt bad. James didn't know how he was doing it either. Still, the man showed no sign of weakening and James began to grow worried himself.

Maybe he could defend himself all day, but the sword showed no signs of trying to attack the man. James even tried to attack the soldier at one point and found that the sword ignored him.

It looked like James had to figure out how to defeat the man without the sword's help.

Forcing himself to focus, James shut off all of his senses except for sight and used his power to search for water. There were small sources far away, but what he noticed immediately was the gigantic source of water that he was holding.

The sword was made of water. Suddenly, James knew exactly what to do. Without trying to stop the sword's movements, James used his power to direct the sword instead.

James shot the blade straight at the soldiers and the sword broke into a million tiny pieces. James had not expected that, but it worked better than he could have imagined.

The pieces of the sword shot straight through the soldier and directly into the man standing behind him. Both men were wide-eyed as they fell to their knees and died on the stone floor, still chained together even in death.

James summoned the sword back to his hand and the tiny pieces flew into his hand in the form of one majestic sword. For one moment, James thought about how powerful he would be with this weapon. And at that moment, the sword vanished into thin air.

James scrambled for a hold on the sword as it vanished, but found that he no longer had control over it. What happened?

James was fruitlessly searching the air above him for signs of his sword when Dismus nearly toppled into him as the man evaded a sword aimed for his head.

Pulling himself together, James searched the room and found Arianna struggling to stay in the air in the far corner. Stopping to pick up one of the dead soldiers' swords, James started to run towards Ari before suddenly stopping in his tracks.

Lying there at the end of the throne room was Marie, chained to the ground and guarded by a man in robes. Shock worked its way through his veins as he stared at his little sister.

After so long without her, he had begun to believe that he might never see her again. As he recognized her lying on the stone floor unconscious, he realized that he had been preparing himself to face the reality of losing her.

Without thinking about it, James had begun to walk towards Marie with his sword raised. But it was the hooded man's calm demeanor that stopped him in his tracks.

Whoever this man was, he had not made a move towards Marie nor himself. In fact, he didn't even seem to be armed, though he very well could be hiding knives in those sleeves of his.

Forcing himself to turn his back on his sister, he began to jog back towards Ari.

Save Ari, then save Marie. Save Ari, then save Marie. He told himself the same thing over and over again as he made his way to help Ari.

He was a fool, he thought, if he thought saying the words would make it actually happen. But he believed them all the same.

Arianna

———~*~——

Her newly found dragon form was all that was keeping Ari alive so far. Her scales were harder than steel, that was obvious, but she bled in a hundred different places all the same.

Primarily she fought one man though another man stayed directly behind him and held onto a chain link tied around the other's waist. The first man held a giant sword and swung it as if it weighed the same as a feather.

She didn't need to see their Ashmarks to know they had special powers just like she did. Both of the men facing her had let their hair out fully, surely to hide the fact that they were special.

She supposed it would help give them the element of surprise in a fight, but truthfully, they didn't need it. Both men moved like a hurricane spiraling around her.

She had been frantic at the start when they began wheeling around her and hacking away at her with that sword, but it didn't take long to settle down.

The sword, no matter how hard the man swung it, would not cut past her scales. However, the man was so strong that he managed to dent her scales so thoroughly that she had trouble breathing due to the amount of scales bashed in around her neck and chest.

She may have a broken rib or two, but she put that out of her mind for now. As long as she could move, she would fight.

Doing her best to protect her face and neck, Ari shot flames from her mouth every time the pair of soldiers got close to her. The flames did seem to affect them, but only enough to keep them at bay for seconds at a time.

However much fire she could produce, she still had to breathe. The pair would move back deftly whenever she threw flames at them, and then would move in a strike in the two second that it took to draw a breath.

At this point, it was a waiting game. They both knew that she could not last like this forever. At one point she had tried to take to the air in an attempt to gain an advantage, but as soon as she had spread her wings, they had cut a large gash in her left wing.

She was not going to make that mistake again, but she was running out of ideas until James came flying from nowhere with a giant sword.

Despite herself, her heart fluttered as he fought off the soldier. 'Pull it together,' she thought to herself impatiently. This was no time to melt.

Steeling herself, Ari moved in to help James. As brave as he was, he was just as much of a fool, if not more. There was no way that he could stand up to a man twice as strong and twice as fast as he was.

Ari put both paws on the ground and moved with surprising agility to position herself behind the soldiers. She kept her wings tight along her back to protect them as best as she could. She was not going to take any chances.

James was swinging his sword with surprising ease, but he was obviously losing the fight. As soon as the soldier had gotten his bearing, James had been completely on the defensive.

The soldier was moving so quickly, that Ari couldn't even see the soldier's sword as he spun and jabbed towards James. The surprising thing was that she couldn't see James' sword either. Was she the only slow-moving one here?

Ari tried a fire blast straight at their backs, but before the flames even reached them, the soldiers had moved clear out of the way while never stopping their attack on James.

She had expected it to happen, but she was frustrated all the same. Again, she ran on all fours to position herself at the back of the duo and looked for an opening.

This time, the soldier in the back holding the chain watched her carefully as she positioned herself behind him. The men were now back to back and the one facing Ari held a chain in one hand and a sword in the other.

He had yet to use the sword though it pained her to admit that he hadn't needed it yet. The man seemed to notice her looking at his sword and he proceeded to smile.

Ari fumed internally, both literally and metaphorically. He did not get to smile at her like that and live, nobody did.

Ari sucked in as if getting ready to vomit fire and ran at the smiling soldier as fast as she could manage. The man stopped smiling, but he didn't look concerned at all.

'Good,' Ari thought as she flung herself in the air at his throat. She had been counting on the man underestimating her. The man could move much faster than she could, but she did not let him have a chance to move at all.

The soldier had his sword raised at her throat. Contempt oozed from him as he stared down at her helpless body. It was not until she was almost on top of him that she shot as much fire as she could manage out of her mouth.

The effect was almost what she had hoped for, except instead of him being roasted on a stick, he escaped unharmed. The victory, however, came in the fact that he had let go of the chain connecting him to the other man.

She did not have to look to know that James suddenly had the upper hand against the other soldier. She would have looked anyway just to see the effect, but she knew that she had no time to lose if she wanted to stay alive.

As soon as she landed in the midst of her own flames, she shot back up in the air with her wings outstretched. She could not fly well, and she was in pain with the big gash in her left wing, but she flew anyway to avoid the counterattack that was sure to come.

Ari spun in midair and immediately shot fire below herself and directly at the chain that still lie on the floor. Maybe she couldn't keep up with the soldier, but if she could only make sure that he didn't pick up the chain again.

Surely enough, instead of attacking Ari, the soldier had gone back for the chain and had to immediately let go of it again. He would not be able to pick it up without burning himself badly.

His eyes showed murder as he looked up at Ari, but she should be safe up here for the moment. Chancing a look at James, Ari watched as he managed to deflect an attack and land a hit of his own on the soldier's left arm.

Even without the other soldier's help, James should not have been able to keep up with the man, but he was winning even still. She briefly considered trying to shoot some flames at the other soldier as well, but she was too worried about possibly hitting James.

Even as she had the thought, the soldier that had previously held the chain was moving towards James to surround him. James probably had no idea that was coming either; this would not be good.

Moving as fast as she could, Ari swept down facing James and shot flames at all three men. If she had waited any longer, James would have had a sword in his back.

All three men jumped out of the way of the flames and continued fighting again as if nothing had happened, but James had noticed the man behind him now and was doing his best to face them both down at the same time.

James had his back against a wall and held off both of the men with surprising effectiveness, but he could not have much longer to live if he kept this up.

Ari considered using her flames again, but this time James had nowhere to go. If she tried burning them again, they would most certainly survive while James would burn.

Ari dropped to the ground on all fours preparing for a the last-ditch effort of stampeding the men when she caught Dismus' eyes from across the room. It turns out that dragons have a surprising amount of peripheral vision.

By the looks of it, Dismus had defeated the soldiers around him and was now running towards James as he signaled Ari. He seemed to be attempting to gesture some message to her, but it was a few moments before she finally understood.

Before Dismus reached James and the other two soldiers, Ari shot flames right in between Dis and the others. She almost second-guessed herself as the fire escaped her mouth, but there was no time to lose.

The flames filled the air in front of Dismus but did not go away. For a few moments, no one else noticed as Dismus began to manipulate the fire, but their attention quickly shifted away from their fight and towards Dis as he shot the fire at the last Evil pair.

Ari could see the horror on the faces of the soldiers until the horror was replaced with fire. Dismus manipulated the fire with ease and almost lazily burned the two soldiers to crisps before letting the fire die. The men had tried to run, and they had run fast, but not fast enough.

For the first time since entering the room, Ari allowed herself to take a deep breath and immediately regretted it. She had definitely broken some ribs.

Slowly and carefully, Ari changed back into her own body as James and Dis walked up to her. She had not known just how hurt she had been.

As soon as she had even changed halfway, she had not been able to support herself. James caught her before she hit the ground and laid her down as she finished changing back.

"I think I broke some ribs." She managed to squeeze out the words, but even talking was painful. She cringed as she looked up at James hovering over her and Dismus just behind him.

"I think you did more than that." James sounded worried, but his voice was playful all the same. He must have finally noticed her neck wounds then. Did he forgive her for kissing him earlier? Why did she care so much if he had? Ari cringed once more, but not because of her injuries.

"I'll carry her," James reached down to do just that. He was careful, but that did not make moving her hurt any less.

As James held her, she realized just how many bruises she had all over her body. More than that, she saw how many cuts James had all over his. How had he held up as long as he had?

It was only once Dis and James had started walking towards the creepy man at the end of the throne room that she remembered that they were not done here yet.

A young woman that could only be Marigold laid unconscious on the floor next to the man in the hood. That man must have seen everything that happened here just now and he looked completely unconcerned as they approached him.

Even as the three of them stopped directly in front of the man, Ari could not see his eyes under the hood. In fact, she could not see anything of the man beside the black hood that he wore and the hands clasped in front of him.

Ari looked up at James again and saw that he could not peel his eyes away from his sister. He looked so pained, but he made no move to put Ari down or approach her.

"James," he seemed startled as he looked towards Ari as if he had forgotten she was lying here in his arms. "You can put me down now." He would not think that she was saying it for him.

Nodding, James put Ari down and moved to Marie's side, though he kept his eyes on the hooded man the entire time.

Ari could not bring herself to sit up at all, but she craned her neck to watch James try and wake Marie while Dismus and the hooded man stared silently at each other.

The man had creeped her out before, but it wasn't until she could see his eyes that she truly felt goosebumps. The hooded man's eyes were completely white and slightly glowing. This could not be good.

"Where is Grace?" The words came out like a growl from Dismus, "Where is my wife?"

Dismus

Three years earlier

— —~*~— —

Dismus had grown up on the outskirts of Pyiasior. His life had been a fairly quiet one up until a week ago when he had started to receive a lot of attention from the King. He had been honored of course; rarely was a farmer given so much attention from his King.

Dismus stared out at the golden fields through the opening in his wooden hut. He was awaiting the arrival of King Manthar for the second time this week. Many would have given much to be sitting in wait for a King, but he would just as soon be out in his field farming as sitting in the cool of his home.

Abruptly, his door flew open and was immediately filled with soldiers filing into his room. Startled, Dismus jumped to his feet but was unable to move any further before the King entered his home while holding Grace by the back of her neck.

Dismus' heart began to race as he swallowed down his response. The King could do whatever he wished to his wife and Dismus could do nothing about it. Best to play along with whatever this was about. If King Manthar had planned on killing her, he would have done so already.

"What seems to be the matter, my King?" Dismus did not have to pretend to be afraid, he had lived under the rule of Nobles since birth and knew the feeling well.

The King merely stared at Dismus for some time before responding. In the previous visits these past weeks, the King had never been warm precisely, but he had been cordial at the very least. Now it seemed as if the King would kill him for no apparent reason.

"You have a gift, my child." The King had always referred to Dis as his child. It was a common enough title for the King to use for his subjects, but it had always rubbed Dismus the wrong way.

"Two gifts, really. You can do… things and you can see certain… people. It is hard to say which will be more valuable to me." Manthar moved close to Dismus and took the seat in which he had been sitting before the King showed up, all the while never letting go of Grace's neck.

Dismus watched his wife anxiously for any sign that she was injured, but she merely stared back at him without so much as a sound. By the looks of her face, you would have never known that she was being held the way that she was.

That had always been the way she was, though, brave until the end and willing her husband to be strong for them both. Anxious to please the King as fast as possible, Dismus went to his knees.

"I will serve in whatever way that I can." The words were out of his mouth as fast as humanly possible and he meant every one of them. He would have said anything at that moment if it meant saving his wife.

Dismus waited for a response but heard none as he kept his head down to the ground. He could see soldiers standing around the edges of the room, all of them radiated a certain scent of danger. These were no ordinary soldiers. Why had Manthar brought so many of his men to his home?

After a long stretch of silence, Dismus chanced a look upward and made eye contact with the King. He was careful not to look Grace in the eyes as he waited for the King to respond, he did not think that he could take that again.

"Oh, I know you will." The King's words were accompanied with a smile that made Dismus shiver. As soon as

Manthar had said them, he threw Grace back towards the line of soldiers and they grabbed her tight as if she had been resisting though she had not been.

"And I will keep your precious wife to make sure of it." Rage filled him then, and fury bubbled over. They could not just take his wife, they would not just take Grace from him.

Dismus lunged for the King and found himself restrained by two soldiers that smelled to him of wind. He knew from past experience that the smell indicated that the men were what the King called "Warpers." They could move much faster than he could. He did not stand a chance.

Still, he could not help but try to struggle and kick his way out of their grasps. He had to save her, he had to.

As if reading his mind, Manthar stood from his chair casually and stepped directly in front of Dismus. Looking back towards Grace, Manthar smiled once more at him as Dismus continued to struggle against the soldiers' restraints.

"You will not save her, not unless you cooperate." Dismus had not seen the punch coming until it was too late to dodge it. That had been the last time that he had been allowed to see Grace.

Dismus

— —~*~— —

The man with glowing eyes pulled back his hood and revealed the Ashmark that indicated what Dismus already knew. This man was a Messenger, and Dismus had a very real guess as to who this messenger was linked to.

James was kneeling next to Ari and the girl, but he had watched as the man pulled his hood back and stood up to join Dismus as the man continued to stare at the both of them.

The Messenger said nothing, nor did he show any emotion, which had probably been tortured out of him long ago if he really was linked to the King. The man merely reached out his hand towards Dismus and waited.

Without saying a word, Dismus ignored the out-stretched hand of the hooded man and reached out his own hand towards James. The boy took his hand without question at the same time that he also took his sister's hand as she continued to lie on the floor.

The man had been left there to connect them with his master. Even if Dismus had been sure that it was a trap, he still would have taken the man's hand. He needed to know what had happened to his wife.

As soon as Dismus was sure they were ready, he turned his attention back to the hooded man. As soon as they took the Messenger's hand, the world faded into darkness.

Dismus had known what to expect; he had met with Manthar through these means many times, but this felt different somehow. Dismus could not see nor feel anything except the hand of the hooded man for nearly a minute before the darkness began to fade. Another world began to reveal itself to him and he fought the urge to throw up.

He had expected an audience with Manthar, not this, never this. The world that he had found himself in was one full of death and carnage. He stood in front of a Sea of dead bodies and even more still in the process of dying.

Dismus looked down and saw that he was stepping on a man's skull, most of the skin had long since been scraped away.

Fighting down panic, he had to leap several times before finding a spot that was not filled with human carcasses. He knew that he was not actually stepping on them, he did not feel the bones crunching beneath him, but it bothered him nonetheless. Even still, finding the untainted spot did not help to dull his horror much, if at all.

He heard wailing and many other sounds of the dying. He knew that it mustn't be true, but it seemed to him that the entire city of Valladar was to die this day.

Dismus forced himself to ignore the death that surrounded him and looked for signs of Manthar or the boy. It turned out that the boy was only a couple of paces behind Dismus and was as pale as could be. Dismus did not doubt that he looked much the same.

James seemed to have found his own unmarked spot and didn't look to be moving from it anytime soon. Dismus did not blame him. Taking another look around, he began to pray that he had been mistaken about the hooded man.

This did not have to be real, it didn't have to be. But Dismus knew it to be true. The man had been a Messenger, and this was the message.

Their home had been broken. Their city had been ravaged, and they were not there to do anything about it.

Dismus allowed himself tears as he looked down the major city street on which they currently stood. No one had been spared along this road. Women and children bled just as men did.

It was looking down the street that Dismus saw what he had expected to see in the first place. King Manthar was walking towards the two of them as he dragged a woman behind.

Dismus did not have to see the woman to know who she was. Manthar was dragging his wife behind him, and there was nothing Dismus could do but watch. This was merely a vision after all, and neither he nor the boy were actually there to save her.

Manthar looked like the evil being that he was. He was covered in blood and ashes as he walked up to Dismus and dropped Grace in front of him.

On instinct, Dismus flung himself down to catch her before she hit the ground, but she fell right through his hands. That did not stop him from tending to her as best he could, however.

His wife laid facing upwards, her eyes open and unseeing. He could not be sure from her wounds, nor could he check her pulse. But he could see the stillness of her chest. His wife was dead.

Dismus ached to take her head and hold her in his lap, but he could not even do that as she laid there dead in front of him. He was cursed to watch in sorrow and do nothing for her but grieve. The worst part was that she would never know how much he had done to save her, how much he had sacrificed to be with her; how much he loved her.

Dismus knelt over the image of his wife and wept openly. He did not care if the King or the boy saw, he cared only for Grace. After a moment, he felt a hand on his shoulder and looked up at James who stood over him.

He should not have been able to feel his hand in the vision; he must have put his hand on his shoulder in real life. In fact, if Dismus concentrated, he could feel the stone beneath his feet in the throne room back in Pyiasior.

He could pull out of the vision at any time, but he could not bring himself to; not when his wife was here. Still, he forced himself to his feet and faced the monster that had done this to her, to him.

"I told you," the words were pure torture to Dismus. "You could not save her," Manthar smirked as he delivered the pointed words. This was punishment for his behavior. This was a display of power meant to destroy him, and he could feel it nearly do that very thing.

"I tell you now." Dismus stood straight up in an attempt to put power behind his words, but he was too broken at the moment to manage it. "There will be no saving yourself."

Dismus looked Manthar straight in the eyes as he said the words and thought he saw insecurity there. Was it possible that there was a way to take him down? As far as Dismus knew, it was impossible to kill Manthar, truly kill him anyway.

Even so, he meant what he said. Whether he expected to succeed or not, he would do everything in his power to see Manthar pay. And from what he saw of James as he stood next to him, James meant to see the exact same thing.

Focusing on the ground beneath his feet, Dismus dragged himself out of the vision and James along with him. The darkness came and went much faster this time as the Throne room came back into view.

The room was exactly as they had left it. Ari laid with her back on the floor and was holding the other girl's unconscious hand for some reason. The hooded Messenger stood with his hands still extended until Dismus and James took their hands away.

As soon as they took their hands back, the Messenger folded his own in front of his stomach and stood with a smirk as if waiting for something.

Dismus could not help it. Anger flared up inside of him and aggression took hold. Before he could take a second thought about what he was doing, Dismus swung his sword at the midsection of Manthar's Messenger.

All of his sorrow for the loss of his wife, all of the anger at Manthar for putting him through this, all of the energy he had spent on trying to save her, all of the frustration at not being able to, everything was put into his swing.

In the half second that it took to swing his blade, he realized that he had made a mistake. This is what the Messenger had been waiting for, and he could see it in the man's still glowing eyes.

As soon as the blade went through the man, the Messenger's eyes stopped glowing and everything was sent into chaos.

All four of them began to glow just as the man's eyes had, and then everything faded back into darkness. The room faded from view as he was ripped from where he stood. The last thing he saw was the still smirking face of the dead Messenger.

James

— —~*~— —

James was beginning to believe that the world would never stop spinning. Images swirled around whenever he opened his eyes though he knew that he himself wasn't moving. His hands were planted firmly on the ground.

James focused on the solid ground beneath him as he waited for the world to stop spinning. Surprisingly, there were green tufts of grass sprouting out beneath his fingers. He could not remember the last time he had seen a plant that was not dead as soon as it sprouted.

Once he got his bearings, he got to his feet and stood up for the first time since waking. As he had feared, he was alone here. And different from the vision he had just been a part of, he could feel this reality.

This was no vision, he had actually been transported somewhere. The question was where, and why was no one else here? Maybe the transportation wasn't precise. Surely they couldn't have been transported far from him. That is if they were transported at all. How did this happen?

'That must be the case,' he decided. They were somewhere here, and he just had to find them. And fast, he suddenly realized as he searched the area around him. Neither Ari nor his sister looked to be in good condition before they were moved. And who knew what damage the transportation might have caused to Ari who was already injured.

Looking around him, James couldn't help but be amazed by the plants that had grown so tall here. The leaves were nearly as tall as he was and blocked his vision for some miles. There wasn't much that he could see really. He would just have to choose a path and search as best he could.

James had taken one step before stopping. He leaped back as fast as he could and reached down to search the grass. He had stepped on something hard and the sun had caught it, reflecting off of it.

Reaching down, James picked up the sword that he had been holding when he was transported. The sword was a large one, heavier than a normal blade, but James handled it easily. It had not been his, but he supposed its previous owner wouldn't have any need of it anymore.

Handling it carefully, James slung the flat part of the blade onto his shoulder and continued his trek. It was bright out here and there was very little to offer shade, but James preferred it that way. There wouldn't be much to hide behind, especially if the people he was looking for weren't trying to hide.

It was not long before panic set in. He had held onto the hope that they were here, but by the time the sun was setting, he had begun to admit to himself what happened.

The sword had come with him because he had been holding it. He had not been touching anything else, not Dismus, not Ari, and not Marie. After all that effort, he had lost her again.

It was dark out when he finally allowed the reality to sink in. He had walked several miles in search of another person, but he had found nothing.

James sunk to his knees when he finally gave in. He plunged the sword deep into the ground in front of him and bowed his head in exhaustion. He was not giving up. No, not giving up. He had to keep telling himself that.

He just needed to clear his head. James stared unseeing at the ground as he allowed all of his thoughts to run through his head.

'I lost Marigold, I am lost myself, I lost my home, and I am being hunted by a demon. But I am also the hunter. I will rebuild my home, and I will find Marigold. I will not go quietly.' Most of his thoughts were a blur. Images flashed through his head, but these words kept recycling themselves through.

Still kneeling on the ground, James picked up his sword and stared at it for some time before bringing it to his head. Carefully, he gathered what hair he could on the left side of his head and chopped it off. It took a while, but eventually James was able to shave the left side of his head as close as possible to his scalp.

The result was identical to the hair styles that he avoided in Valhalla. His Ashmark would be visible to anyone who looked now. There would be no more hiding for him now.

After he was finished, James pushed himself to his feet with the help of his sword. He was no less tired, in fact, he was on the brink of total exhaustion. But he felt a new sense of clarity as he continued his search.

"First," he spoke aloud to the darkness. "I figure out where I am. Then I will find my sister." 'And Ari,' he thought despite himself.

"And then I will see what I can do about everything else." One step at a time, he thought. That was the only way to do this.

"With my life," he almost thought that she could hear him say it. "With my life."

Arianna

— —~*~— —

Ari woke up in an alley though it took her some time to figure that out. Her vision swam every time she made herself open her eyes. She currently laid on her back as she took in her surroundings. Any attempt she made to move from her back ended in excruciating pain, so she eventually gave up.

More distracting than the swimming vision was the excruciating pain in her ribs. She could tell that she was bruised and she felt her body pulsating, but everything else was secondary to the pain in her chest.

The alley was deserted, but there was no telling if it had been that way before. However she had gotten here, she was sure that would have startled anyone that had been lying here.

Eventually, Ari noticed Marie laying next to her in the alley, still in chains but seemingly conscious. Marie just now seemed to be getting her bearings as she began to test the brightness of the sun by opening her eyes.

Ari would have tended to her had she been able to move at all, but the pain was too much. She knew that she should not try moving when her bones were most likely broken or at least fractured, but there was nothing for it.

The girl was still in chains and she was looking more and more terrified as she got her bearings back. Ari needed to help her, regardless of her physical condition.

Ari made eye contact with Marie and spoke her first words in quite some time. "I'm going to try and help you." She had expected some sort of response, but Marie merely stared back at her before suddenly throwing up on the ground between them.

Ari had not realized how sick Marie was. The chains on her wrists and ankles had dominated her attention up until that point. The girl was pale as could be and looked very weak. How much fluid had the girl lost recently? Enough to be dangerous, almost certainly.

Marie had looked back at Arianna after ejecting the last of the contents in her stomach and was making eye contact once more, if a little less focused than before. Taking a deep breath that sent sharp pain through her, Ari focused on her dragon form.

Her body as a dragon was most likely the only form strong enough to move around with so many injuries. Ari focused, and then she focused some more, but as hard as she tried, nothing happened.

She must have been too injured to change forms. She had never had the opportunity to test her limitations before, but it looked like this was one of them. That was not good. How was she supposed to help herself, let alone someone else?

Not even bothering to look Marie in the eyes or give her some sort of explanation, Ari let her head fall back to the earth and closed her eyes.

This was not supposed to happen. They had won! Hadn't they? And yet she found herself alone, practically anyway, and severely injured with no idea where she was. Why couldn't her life just be normal?

Ari was not prone to pouting, it was something she prided herself in. She considered herself a strong woman; a woman fit to lead a Nation, one day at least. And a leader could not afford to pout, no matter much they wanted to.

However, they could cry. And as she laid there in the alley, tears rolled down her cheeks and fell onto the ground beside her. Just one good cry and she would be good to go. Just one.

It had been some time before Ari had finally stopped crying and the sun was beginning to set when she had finished wiping her face clean. She had tried to think of what to do, but she had come up empty. She was injured beyond hope, and if the other girl's complexion was any indicator, Marie was deathly ill.

She was still lying there on the ground, fruitlessly searching for ideas when a shadow fell over her from above. Ari shifted her head just enough to look behind her just as Marie raised hers to look as well.

The shadow belonged to an old man with his hands on his hips and a beard that nearly touched the ground. In fact, if the man had moved about one step closer, his beard would have probably tickled her face.

As soon as the man had spoken, two younger boys moved from behind him and began the process of picking up both Marie and herself from the ground.

"You girls don't look much like the homeless type." The old man had a slight whistle quality to his speech and he didn't seem to be in a hurry or surprised to see them lying there.

When neither of the girls responded, the old man picked up right where he left off without a hint of annoyance.

"Either way, I hate to see ladies beaten as you are. Left to die y'all sure were, but I'll not be havin' any o' that." Both Marie and herself had been lifted from the ground at that point, but Ari nearly passed out from the pain of being moved.

"Hurry yourself, Jotham! Can't you see the lady's in pain? Lay her in the back, gently now."

The back turned out to be the bed of a metal cart that seemed to have been recently used for crops. No sooner had Ari been laid there than Marie had been planted beside her.

Ari breathed a sigh of relief at being put down, which sent even more shockwaves of pain through her.

"I know a place 'round the city where y'all can get the treatment you need. Get those shackles off ya in no time, too. Just hold on tight. If you can." Ari was sure she was not supposed to hear that last part, but she was grateful for the old man.

Wherever they were going, at least they were moving. Now that their immediate predicament was being taken care of, Ari found herself making plans for what to do next.

One thing she knew for sure, she had to protect Marie. She wasn't sure how much she could actually do to keep her from harm, but she was going to try as hard as she possibly could to do it.

James would hate her if he found out that she had let him down. Whether he would have chosen to or not, he was going to have to trust her with his sister. She would show him that he could trust her, somehow she would.

The next step would be to find their way home she supposed. Well, wherever he was, she would find him and she would deliver Marie to him safe and intact.

That is if she ever found that she could move again. How long might it take for a broken rib to heal? A week, a month, a year? James might have found them himself by then.

It was of that very scenario that Ari found herself daydreaming as the cart wheeled down the dry and dusty streets of the barren town. One step at a time.

Buddy

— —~*~— —

"Buddy!" His mother was always yelling at him. What had ever made her think that he was hard of hearing?

"Coming!" He yelled louder than necessary back at his mother as he jumped down from the loft. The loft was where they used to store the hay. That had been back when there were animals to eat the hay. Now the loft was just a metal shelf where Buddy kept his bed.

His mother and he had lived in the barn for as long as he could remember. Their old home and barn had been commandeered by the Nobles in Hishou due to the wood shortage at the time. They had been repaid with a metal barn and they had been living in it ever since.

There was no ladder leading up to the loft. Well, there was, but Buddy kept it behind the barn. It ensured that his mother couldn't climb her way to his bedroom, not unless she put a lot of effort into it.

Buddy had his own way of getting up and down from his bed-shelf. He was still falling down towards the floor when the ground sprung up to catch him before letting him down gently on ground level.

His mom said nothing but she was frowning deeply at him when he landed next to her. The argument played out every other day or so; he just supposed that she was picking her battles. A wise choice really, he would never give up using his powers.

"Wash your hands, Child." His mother was setting the table as she spoke and was focused on the task when Buddy slipped out of the house to clean himself.

The river was not far from their barn. To tell the truth, it had been a lot farther before Buddy moved it; one of the many advantages of what he could do. Everyone else was still baffled about how that happened. Everyone except for his mother of course. She had frowned particularly deeply that day.

Buddy was smirking to himself as he washed his hands at the river when he noticed someone hiking through the foliage upstream. At the second take, he amended himself. The man was a bit older than him but by no means old. And he wasn't hiking through the plants, he was hiking through the river itself. Who was this crazy person?

Buddy finished washing his hands, but he declined to move from the edge of the river. Strangers were interesting enough as they were around these parts, but crazy strangers were just downright irresistible entertainment.

There was no way that he was going pass up seeing this guy closer. Even if he was carrying a large sword on his shoulder. If there was anything that could endanger Buddy, he had not encountered it yet; another advantage of his power.

His mother would do more than frown when he got back late, he thought. 'Worth it,' was the thought that overpowered all else. The man was getting closer now and there was no mistaking the youth of the guy.

There were only hints of a beard growing on the edges of the guy's face. Even Buddy was growing as much already. 'Well, close to it anyway,' he thought as he rubbed the peach fuzz on his chin.

Buddy waited until the stranger was almost on top of him before revealing himself at the edge of the river. If he had expected a surprised response, he didn't get one.

"Hi." The stranger had spoken before Buddy even had the chance to finish his surprise. That put a frown just like his mother's on his face. And he did not like frowning, especially not like her.

"Hello." Buddy plastered a smile back on his face before he began to look too much like his mom. Buddy extended his hand towards the stranger as a sign of peace, but the man just looked at him funny before continuing.

"Can you point me to the nearest city?" The stranger sure seemed to be eager to be moving on. Well, Buddy wasn't going to let this guy off that easily.

"Why are you walking in the river?" The stranger cocked his head, probably out of frustration, but Buddy didn't care. It was a curious thing, what this man was doing, and it would eat at him until he understood it.

"It's easier for me." It was Buddy's turn to cock his head. That didn't make any sense whatsoever.

"How could that possibly be easier? Wouldn't you like to walk on the nice, smooth earth where there is no resistance?" Maybe this guy wasn't crazy, maybe he was just not very bright.

The man smiled then, apparently aware of the frustration he was causing Buddy. Slowly, the stranger moved from the middle of the river and stepped onto the ledge where Buddy was standing before speaking.

"What is your name?"

Buddy kicked himself. He should have asked the stranger his name, first thing. It was the kind of thing that his mother harped on constantly.

"Bud." He liked Bud better than Buddy, but no one around here was willing to call him anything other than Buddy; a perfect opportunity to try out the new name.

"Well, Bud. I happen to like the feel of water. It's refreshing." The stranger looked at Bud then like what he said was supposed to make sense.

"Well, sure I guess. But refreshing doesn't equal easy." Maybe this guy was both dull and crazy. He really shouldn't have to explain something like this to someone older than himself.

"Well, it does for me. I have a gift." That got Bud's attention. He immediately thought about his own gift, but, of course, that wouldn't be what this man meant.

"What kind of gift?" The stranger frowned briefly but apparently decided that it would be okay to share as he raised his hands as if he expected something to happen.

Bud watched the man for a second, unsure of what to expect until he nearly fell over. The water around the man was dancing of its own accord. It was the most beautiful thing he had ever seen; he never wanted it to stop.

Eventually, it did, and the stranger watched Bud for a reaction. What he got was a surprise of his own as Bud raised his own hands and made the dirt around them dance.

Okay, maybe it wasn't nearly as cool or graceful as the water was, but it got the desired reaction. The stranger's eyes popped as the dirt moved about them and Bud smirked once more. Again, his mom would severely disapprove.

"The nearest city is some distance away," Bud finally said once he dropped the dirt around him. "But you are welcome at my home with my mom and me."

The stranger looked thoughtful for a moment before nodding in agreement. Again kicking himself, Bud reached out his hand once more as they began to walk back to his barn.

"What was your name, umm, Sir?" He had finally remembered his manners.

"James." He took Bud's hand this time though he immediately let go again. It was okay, he would get the hang of it eventually.

Bud picked up his pace as he led James to his home, thinking of his mother's impending fury at his tardiness. And again he picked up his pace when it occurred to him that this man probably hadn't eaten dinner yet.

He hoped his mom made enough food for three.

Epilogue

— —~*~— —

King Manthar sat on the throne of Valladar and looked down on his newly made slave. There had not been many left alive in the battle, but there were enough to do the dirty work for his army during their stay here: one of the spoils of war.

The battle for this city had gone smoothly, just as he had planned. But this war was nowhere near done. He had chosen this city as a launching point, and this was just the beginning.

All he needed was time. And with the Seraphim scattered as they were, he should have plenty of it. He could taste the blood on his lips as he smiled down at the terrified former King Aandal. He was one of the last of the Prophet's blood.

After so many years, he was finally almost rid of them completely. But with Dismus gone, he would have to resort to more primitive methods of finding the rest of the Bloodline.

Aandal was shaking on the ground as he bowed to Manthar. It amused Manthar to see someone so dangerous laid bare in front of him. Still, he would have to be rid of his slave soon. There was no sense in putting himself in more danger than was necessary.

"Fetch my Generals, Child. We have matters to attend to." It was time to move on to the next phase of his plans.

Aandal stood from the ground and rushed from his chambers without a single look back. If he had looked back, he would have seen Manthar smiling cruelly.

Manthar wondered how long would it take for the next kingdom to fall. Two weeks probably, maybe three, and he could lose half of his army in every battle and never be outnumbered.

Smiling to himself, Manthar walked out onto the balcony attached to his throne room and looked out over the streets of Valladar. Every street was filled with his soldiers spilling out of the homes nearby.

As if they were waiting for him to appear, they let out a roar of triumph as he enjoyed the view. Yes, victory was near. This was the closest thing he had felt to happiness in a long time.

End of Book 1

The Last Seraphim

Glossary

Ahren: A human being connected to their Guardian Angel

Choirs: Nine orders of Angels indicating hierarchy

Seraphim: Highest Choir of Angels; there were originally four Seraphim until Helel (Dominion over humans) fell and became a Demon (Dominion over fire), the remaining three are Gabriel (Dominion over the Earth and Earth's creatures), Micael (Dominion over water and creatures of the water), and Rapael (Dominion over air and creatures of the air)

Cherubim: or Warpers, can manipulate time around them

Thrones: or Healers, can heal others

Dominions: or Shifters, can transform their bodies

Virtues: or Deceivers, can create illusions around them

Powers: or Brutes, have enhanced reflexes and strength

Archangels: or Trackers, can see and track Angels

Principalities: or Messengers, can send visions to others

Angels: lowest and most common Choir of Angel

Made in the USA
Lexington, KY
01 December 2015